CATHERINE GILLING

FAIR ROBERT

Haunted by a childhood tragedy,
driven by his search for justice

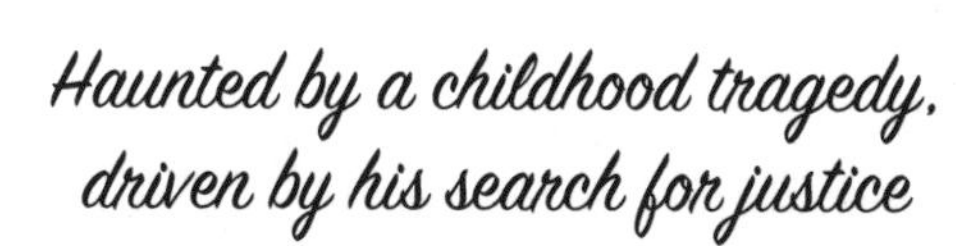

CATHERINE GILLING

Haunted by a childhood tragedy,
driven by his search for justice

MEREO
Cirencester

Mereo Books

1A The Wool Market Dyer Street Cirencester Gloucestershire GL7 2PR
An imprint of Memoirs Publishing www.mereobooks.com

Fair Robert: 978-1-86151-599-5

First published in Great Britain in 2016
by Mereo Books, an imprint of Memoirs Publishing

A CIP catalogue record for this book is available from the British Library.

The address for Memoirs Publishing Group Limited can be found at
www.memoirspublishing.com

The Memoirs Publishing Group Ltd Reg. No. 7834348

The Memoirs Publishing Group supports both The Forest Stewardship Council® (FSC®) and the PEFC® leading international forest-certification organisations. Our books carrying both the FSC label and the PEFC® and are printed on FSC®-certified paper. FSC® is the only forest-certification scheme supported by the leading environmental organisations including Greenpeace. Our paper procurement policy can be found at www.memoirspublishing.com/environment

Typeset in 10/14pt Plantin
by Wiltshire Associates Publisher Services Ltd. Printed and bound in Great Britain
by Printondemand-Worldwide, Peterborough PE2 6XD

Georgian England, 1725. George I and the Prince of Wales, George Augustus, continue to disagree. Banned from the palace and shunned by his father, George and his wife Caroline live quietly at Leicester House and Richmond Lodge, their summer residence.

The ordinary people of England lead uncomplicated lives in comparison to those involved in London society. Their lives rarely cross into one another - except for some who must balance the best and worst of both.

CHAPTER ONE

At Old Hayward Farm, on the fertile slopes of the South Downs in West Sussex, the Hayward family had found their normal routine in some disarray since the startling accident on Fields Hill. Such accidents were unusual in this vicinity. They had taken in the injured stranger, because in contrast to the fine society of Georgian London, these rural communities were in the habit of doing their best to help one another, whoever it was.

Margaret, the elder daughter of the house, paused on the panelled landing, listening intently for any indication that she would be discovered here. Relieved by the silence around her, she waited and listened a little longer, until it seemed she would be safe to venture into the sick room in front of her. So far the strict orders forbidding her or any of the women to go inside had kept them away from the unsuitable task of nursing, and water and cloths were replaced by the male members of the household. But Margaret would not be deterred from her curiosity to see the injured stranger who had been housed there for several days. Convinced that his gruesome injuries had been greatly exaggerated and deliberately ignoring her father's instructions, she gathered her skirts and furtively entered the sick room.

The Haywards were a farming family, well used to the hardships and cruelties nature inflicted on both livestock and people. She wasn't some young silly girl, to be frightened by bloodied bandages or broken bones, she had retorted indignantly in response to her father's orders, a fact she meant to prove by this act of flagrant disobedience.

Despite the warning, Margaret was unprepared for the reality of the awful mangled sight she found. Her involuntary piercing scream was accompanied by the clatter of the chair she had bumped into as she automatically stepped back. That, combined with the sound of the bowl being knocked to the floor, shattered the hushed silenced and echoed throughout the house.

The scream had been loud enough to register in the patient's agonised blackness. Although it was fleeting and soon gone, it was the first thing that had broken that long darkness. How could he know that he had been the cause of that scream?

Confusing sensations battled with his unconsciousness. He could not even open his eyes. He heard nothing except his own laboured breathing. He had lost too much blood and he was too weak to make a sound to the outside world, yet the sudden spikes of pain which shot through him told him he must be alive. He wanted to cry out, to complain. He wanted to stop this burning fire in his head, to tear it out with his bare hands, although he had yet to discover why he could not find his arms to do so. The sensations which identified his limbs remained vague and woolly, without feeling. He did not know if he could move his body or not.

Robert Sutton, for that was his name, had no idea of his grave condition. His head wound was serious. After bathing the matted mess, the local physician had needed to shave off some of his hair before the delicate task of stitching the skin together could start. The dedicated man had attended to him for several hours, having had to stitch the open wound twice with strong gut to stem the bleeding. The deep, ugly gash across the top of his head remained looking little better than it had originally, even when the work had been so carefully completed. His face was already deformed as the patches of raw skin highlighted a black and yellow swelling which began to close one eye in particular to the narrowest of slits.

Robert had obviously been battered and bruised all over, with chunks of bone chipped from other parts of him, his elbow and shoulder in particular. Yet for ages he understood nothing of this, except to wince with every application of the salve to his injuries, despite its rapid coolness soothing the pain. His body did not seem to belong to him. It had now gained a heaviness and every effort of movement brought perspiration to his face.

Gradually, through his blurred vision, he became aware of the figures which came and went, tending to his tortured frame. He had tried to understand their words, but they merely echoed in his head, making little sense, as he battled a spinning sensation and a sickness in his throat.

It had taken time to restore his jumbled mind into any conception of the normal. He had to establish what was real, what was important. What could he remember – anything? His name – yes. His home - yes, just. What else? There were alarming flashes of memory; the thundering, creaking sounds of the wagon hurling down the lane; his horse startled and unseating him, before it took flight. The heavy wagon had bounced him against the wall, the force of the rebound sending him straight back into the path of the rear wheels, where crunching pain was followed by total darkness.

Although still unable to lift his head up or speak, gradually Robert began to recognise his generous host, who visited him every day with a few words of encouragement while his dressings were attended to. He would hear young children creep along the landing outside, to risk taking a sneaking look from the doorway before sharing a whisper and giggle, and then running off as some adult came by. He could hear the sounds of the family about their normal routines which softly drifted from the various rooms throughout the day. They seemed to have the same relaxing, contented, warm atmosphere of his own home, a home he missed and suddenly longed for.

It was a farm with orchards, on the southern slopes of the North Downs, where his uncle and aunt had cared for him and his baby sister ever since the fever had taken their parents and their other sister, over eighteen years ago. The familiar red brick house where they would always be waiting for him, eager for his return and his news. He suddenly felt very melancholy, wishing he could be there with them, to tease his sister, to pat the hounds, to be able to hold them all. He sighed a long deep sigh, letting all his breath out to softly echo around the empty room.

Margaret had been duly scolded, given extra tasks and kept under her mother's scrutiny after her escapade. Then after a few weeks when their injured guest had shown some improvement and the physical nursing duties became less arduous, she had deliberately been given, as a punishment, the tedious task of fetching and carrying various trays and bowls to the young man's room. Not that she minded, because she was curious to see how he fared. He still seemed exhausted and slept a lot, but that was not unexpected after what he had endured.

That evening she waited until her father had left the room before entering to clear the small tray from the table. She paused to study his face once more as she often did. His eyes were half closed as usual, as if he was somewhere else.

"I wish I knew who you were," she whispered quietly, bending down to the tray. Like the rest of the family she had assumed he was one of the many itinerant travellers who had been driven across the country looking for work, but it would be so much more exciting to discover he was something different.

Startled by her words, Robert opened his eyes to look at her. He had become used to the women gliding softly in and out of the room, completing various tasks and leaving him to recover in the peace he obviously needed. He had never expected one of them to speak to him. But he had neither the energy nor the inclination to reply. The effort of conversation was beyond him. He closed his eyes again, shutting it all out. He waited for her to leave. He heard her start towards the door and the swish of her skirts and soft tread across the floorboards, where she paused.

"I hope you recover soon," came her almost too casual comment before the door closed.

Robert felt himself tense up, for poorly as he was, he had the notion that her words meant a little more than they actually said.

As the nightmare of the accident receded, the details of the preceding events began to surface and the whereabouts of his horse Toby and his saddlebags became his main concern. He had been immensely relieved to learn that Toby had been safely retrieved and delivered here after the accident and that his saddlebags were intact and had been lying in his room all the time. At least the confidential papers had been delivered safely some days prior to this accident and his saddlebags contained nothing more now than the unassuming change of clothing he always carried. Even his long dark navy overcoat, the only semblance of a clue to his profession, was not amongst his clothes; it was summer and it had remained at home. So there was nothing he really needed to be worried about, for the moment.

Robert was now sitting up, but all the shock and trauma to his system had left him weak as a kitten. He was still an invalid. He knew he was lucky to be alive with all his limbs intact when he could so easily have broken his neck. He had a great deal to thank this family for.

Mr Hayward, Margaret's father, continued to make his regular evening visits to the check on his progress. Apart from thanking his benefactor on every occasion, Robert was reluctant to encourage his few attempts at further conversation. He knew his silence was the easiest and safest course for the moment; the shock and trauma of his condition made it understandable, but he knew it would not satisfy everyone too much longer.

As Robert waited impatiently for his body to heal, he remembered what had brought him to this part of the county. He had completed his last assignment in Chichester and had been on his way back to London. He also remembered the other people he had been acquainted with and the different aspects of the complicated life he was part of. He shook his head, unwilling to think too much about that for a while. Indeed, he had been lucky to have his long hours and thoughts diverted by the youngest children, two boys, Matthew and Mark, who gradually became regular visitors to his room. It appeared they had adopted him as their friend, whether he wanted it or not, and Robert found himself pleased by their company. He would sit and listen to their infectious chatter, then their stories and the excited games which had them chasing about his bed, pretending to be pirates or soldiers. They were good medicine to his brighten his days, although Mr Hayward often dragged them away, concerned that his two sons would wear him out.

Robert had recovered enough to know he should make an effort to appear more normal. Margaret, during the reduced fetching and carrying, had no hesitation in confronting him about his reluctance to be more sociable.

"You say so little," she commented.

"There is little to say," he murmured.

Margaret did not move. Instead she kept her face turned to his, steadily absorbing every distinctive feature beneath those injuries. She waited for some further response, but none came.

"All we know is your name," she continued. "We assume you travel to find work, because you have said little to contradict that."

"I am not that interesting."

"Mmm. I doubt that."

Robert prepared himself to deflect any searching questions. Yet oddly, she only raised her eyebrows questioningly and then shrugged indifferently before leaving him alone again. He stared after her. For someone so young, she appeared a keen observer and a little too shrewd. He acknowledged that he could not keep completely silent; that would be altogether much too suspicious. He would have to casually, little by little, allow them to know something about himself. He would let the family gather their own conclusions from the highly selective amount of information he provided. Even then he would have to be careful, and his choice of words were important. He must keep his distance, to protect himself.

Thus during the following days, it became his habit to sit chatting to Mr Hayward for a while. The man was easy to talk to, and Robert did not mind mentioning his sister, who was ten years younger with blue eyes, nor his uncle and aunt, who had given them a home after his parents, tenant farmers, had died years ago.

"You travel to support your family?" asked the farmer.

Robert nodded. He was quite willing to reveal some of places he had visited, from Canterbury and Dover to Hove and many of the villages in between, although there was no need to mention his connection to London. He diverted possibly awkward questions with a jolly shrug or laugh and regaled Mr Hayward with amusing incidents from his schooldays or the farm, or his escapades with Becky and Samuel gathering hops.

He also began to entertain the boys with stories of his own childhood. He told them how he had fallen out of a tree, torn his breeches on a fence, chased chickens and climbed ladders, and about the winter custom of wassailing in the apple orchards. A noisy laughter would soon develop in the room, which once more reminded Robert of home. The squeals of laughter and the little humming tunes of contentment of his dear sister were the things he missed.

He desperately needed to get better and be back on his feet, but his legs had no strength. How long would it take? He wished he could heal much more quickly. It was May already and today he had been helped to the window seat briefly, in order to see the head steward, Joseph, parade Robert's precious horse around the courtyard for him. Robert smiled to see how well he looked. No one had made reference to the fine, toned condition of the animal, nor the sturdy quality of the well-used saddle and leatherwork, and Robert was not about to draw their attention to those matters. He had done his best with his simple stories to convince them that he was only an ordinary man, and the family seemed satisfied by what he told them.

He noticed that Martha, the younger daughter, was the only one who kept her distance. A shy girl, so different from her older sister, she always stood meekly out of the way, barely spoke to him at all and only managed the odd gentle smile before she would quickly disappear. In contrast Margaret continued to struggle to stop her curiosity from being voiced. Her mouth would pout thoughtfully and her eyes would narrow and widen as a sign of the many silent questions she had. Margaret was difficult to analyse, and he was aware from past experience that the female of the species could not be underestimated, in any way.

Mr Hayward had never expected his guest to be so well travelled or well educated. Whilst the clothes he had been wearing had been repaired, his other clothes in the saddlebags had been washed and aired. It was these plain older clothes that had given Mr Hayward the closest idea as to Robert's more private past, because they gave the impression of having belonged to a soldier. Maybe a soldier who did not want to be reminded of any battle or the loss of friends; a man, like so many, who had returned and had to find another occupation. Mr Hayward had no intention of being insensitive enough to ask Robert if that was the case. Instead their conversations roamed from one topic to another, for he was eager to hear more about places he had never been to.

Common sense told Robert that he could not linger there forever. All too aware of his own inadequacies, he disliked the unnecessary burden he still imposed on his host, for one thing. He repeatedly expressed his thanks on the matter to his host every time they spoke together; it would be a lack of manners not to.

"Mr Hayward, how can I thank you enough for all you have done?" he said. "Your extreme kindness. I owe you so much. How can I repay you?"

The farmer merely smiled and looked at his guest, his hand waving away such ideas. It was obvious he considered such acts were of little consequence and perfectly natural.

"There is no need. If any of my children were injured somewhere away from home, I would hope that someone else would have the compassion to help them. There was nothing special in my actions," he replied.

Those actions might have seemed of little consequence to Mr Hayward, but Robert knew better. He was acquainted with the make and manners of other less gracious men in this world, although he would not embarrass this man by arguing or insisting otherwise.

"How can I recompense you for what you must have spent out on my behalf?" he asked. "The physician's fees alone must amount to a good sum."

"You must not worry your head about such things, Mr Sutton. We do things a little differently here. The physician was quite willing to take payment in kind. Some eggs one day and meat last week and other produce when he needs it."

That did not seem much of a payment to Robert for all the man's trouble and his great skills. In London the same physician could have earned good coin in his pocket, very good coin.

Mr Hayward interrupted his thoughts. "I only wish I could offer you work here. Our busiest period is harvest time, but that is months away."

"Haven't you already done enough, Mr Hayward?" Robert exclaimed, astonished that the farmer had even contemplated the idea. Although the farm provided adequately for the family and the existing staff and regular labourers, employing unnecessary hands was madness.

"How can I be of use to you?" Mr Hayward continued, regretfully.

Now it was Robert's turn to reassure the man. "Mr Hayward, I appreciate the thought, but please, please do not concern yourself any more about my welfare. I am not completely destitute. At least I have a home to return to, unlike some of the poor wretches scouring the country. As soon as I can, I must make my way home, to see how they are before I do anything else."

The fact that he was not destitute was the only genuine information concerning himself that Robert had divulged to his host. For despite his host's assumption of the opposite, as far as Robert knew, he was still employed. No doubt his masters in London would be wondering about his highly unusual and unexplained disappearance. It was obvious that they would have realised something unforeseen must have happened, but because of the highly cautious nature of their business, he knew any enquiries to discover what had happened to him would be equally discreet.

At least he was on the mend. He had taken his first unsteady steps in his repaired clothes and begun the daily ritual of walking to the stables to visit his horse. Admittedly he had been wobbly and required the support of Joseph while the two boys danced around his feet, but it was progress. The fresh air, the smell of the hay and the way Toby nuzzled and snorted in his face made him feel human again.

Human! He scoffed, looking as he did. Whilst his clothes disguised his battered shell, there was no way to hide the result of his head injury. Although his thick hair had grown back quickly to disguise the scar and dent in his head, the patch of hair around his wound had strangely changed colour. He was marked by a startling grey speckled streak amid his otherwise dark locks. He had long grown used to his changed appearance. The rest of his hair had grown long, and his early stubble had become a beard. He could not go home - for go home he must, and soon - like this.

Accordingly he set about correcting his careless grooming. He trimmed his hair almost to its original length, but left the front longer to hide the hideous scar where it crept slightly forward from his hair line. Then he shaved his face clean to let the natural colour return to his face.

He glanced in the mirror. He did not think he looked too different. Although the streak of grey hair still drew attention to the injury, it did not bother him greatly because he was not the one looking at it every day. He could live with it. He just hoped it would not be too much of a shock for everyone at home.

The weeks were dragging on and Robert was beginning to feel concerned. He could not believe his employers had not made some contact. Had he been that hard to trace? He could not believe the company did not know where he was, for they had known his route and his schedule. When they came, local gossip would soon provide them with his location. The accident had happened in April, yet so far no stranger had ventured near the farm or been seen in the vicinity. How long should he wait? How long could he hold his tongue?

He frowned. It was hard to resist the urge to send someone into town to engage a courier. Although how could he risk sending a message to London without betraying his occupation to these people? He did not want to confuse them. His employment requirements were hard to explain; nothing in his line of work was straightforward, in any case.

If no one arrived soon, Robert decided he would have to no choice except to try to make the first slow stage of the journey home on his own. If he could reach Thomas the blacksmith in Surrey, one of his normal stops, he would be able to send word to those who needed to hear from him. His shoulders slumped at the prospect, knowing he was not fit enough for that journey.

Robert was still pondering his next move when he found his stay about to be abruptly curtailed, before he was ready. The arrival of a letter from a relative provoked an unexpected upheaval of the whole house, reallocation of all the rooms and the news that he was to be housed elsewhere. He watched in amazement as a whirlwind of activity erupted around him, with hasty instructions being added at every hour. It seemed the house would have to be cleaned from top to bottom, beds and rooms aired and extra supplies found.

"She did not even ask if it was convenient," his grim-faced host complained. "She just announced she was arriving, with her maid and secretary. This is just too tiresome and inconsiderate." Indeed this normally close and contented family seemed to actually dread the woman's arrival.

"Who is she?" Robert asked Joseph.

"Mrs Jeskyns. An unpleasant widowed aunt who thinks she can just snap her fingers and everyone will do exactly as she wants."

"Why is she coming to visit?"

"She does not have to have a reason. She flits from one distant relation to another, burdening herself on them whenever it suits her, causing chaos. The old hag married well. She has a perfectly adequate home and the funds to keep it running, but she turns up and always overstays her welcome, relying on the generosity of her host and failing to offer any recompense. She doesn't even bring any gifts for the family, as any normal visitor would."

"Then why do they put up with her?"

Joseph shook his head and shrugged.

"She is one of the matriarchs of the family. I suppose they feel obliged to be polite to her."

Robert felt immensely relieved to discover that he was being rehoused not far away in a cottage belonging to a hurdle maker until he was finally back on his feet again. The man, an old friend of Joseph's, had brought his pony and trap to collect him, and with Robert's horse tied behind with the saddlebags, Robert felt surprisingly sad to leave the warm company of this family. At least his departure would make matters less awkward for them.

"You have a good heart. Thank you for everything, I owe you so much," Robert told the head of the Hayward family as they parted.

The older man patted him on the shoulder and shook his hand. "I'm sorry we could not have kept you. I would rather put her in the cottage, not that I would have wished her on any of my acquaintances."

"I would have to leave some time," Robert comforted him.

The children, with their young, cheerful voices, full of excitement, noisily waved their farewells to their adopted friend, more than once expressing their hopes to visit the cottage where he was going to stay, if only to escape from their dreaded relation. He noted that Margaret remained at the back of the small crowd. He would never know what she thought of him; not that it really mattered.

The woodland cottage was a simple rustic dwelling, surrounded by all the trappings of the man's profession: felled timber, hurdle blocks, tools and a stack of completed woven hurdles. Robert was fascinated by the man's skill and willingly set about moving and stacking the bundles of cut split wood and stakes as required, in an attempt to rebuild his previous fitness. Because his horse demanded attention, he would lead it along the lane and through the woods, once or twice allowing himself into the saddle to walk it back.

The animal having been previously left to its own devices, kicking up his heels and racing around the paddock at the farm, now considered his owner should be on the move and tugged at his sleeve as if to ask when they would be leaving.

"Soon, Toby, soon," Robert told him.

One afternoon when his host had gone to cut more wood,

Robert noticed a man strolling casually along the nearby lane. This was an out-of-the-way spot and he could only assume it was someone looking for the hurdle maker. Yet as the man came closer, Robert heard the gentle whistling of a familiar refrain. It was a tune his colleague Edmund had often played and one he had often whistled to himself out of habit. They had found him. Their employers obviously knew them all too well, he surmised. He slowly made his way to the front gate to wait for the man to finally approach him.

The man in the lane looked at him, first anxiously and then with some relief.

"I apologise for the delay in contacting you. We had assumed you would still be at the farm, only to find you moved to an even more out-of-the-way spot."

"I was getting worried. I almost thought the company had forgotten me."

"As if that would ever be the case. You know how we work, Robert."

"I had no way to communicate," Robert explained.

His contact smiled. He was not here to criticize or find fault.

"The Exchange has been greatly concerned for your safety, Robert. When you had not returned soon after delivering the documents and goods to Chichester, it was obvious that something was wrong. The work you do for them is important."

Robert had known any deviation from the routine would alarm them. He was dependable to a fault, so his prolonged absence would have caused furious activity, plus the hasty need for a replacement. He did not ask how they had found him.

"Within a week we had learnt of the accident and the seriousness of your injuries. You were hardly in any condition to be moved, so it seemed more prudent to let you recover here and avoid the fuss and upset it would have created for your family. Besides the problem of whisking you away even later on, with little or no explanation in itself, could have been awkward for everyone."

"I expect they will be glad to know I'm still in one piece," Robert joked.

"We do prefer our men to be fit and active. You were neither, for quite a while. And I'm still concerned as to your welfare. You certainly don't look as if you could ride anywhere on your own."

Robert was not sure he could, but he wasn't going to admit it.

"Do you want me to arrange someone to ride back with you? I could arrange for Edmund or Henry to change their programme, if necessary?"

Robert had never imagined his employers sanctioning or allowing his fellow colleagues to be diverted from their own important schedules. He shook his head. He could not further inconvenience the company. Besides, after managing to keep a low profile all this time, Robert did not want to attract unnecessary attention by such action.

"They are prepared to make that sacrifice. They dislike the idea of you being incapacitated in this rural backwater and out of touch. You can recuperate for as long as you like at home. They need to know you are safe."

"I can manage, I will be home soon," Robert insisted.

The man still looked concerned, but accepted Robert's further reassurance.

"How is my family?" Robert asked changing the subject.

"They are fine. Luckily your unusual absences and routine do not seem to worry them unnecessarily. Although I think that may change when they see you return this time."

Robert considered his family. They were fairly level headed and had become used to his irregular comings and goings, together with his long absences and travels around the country. They would accept his injuries for what they were, simply caused by an unfortunate accident. There would be no need to pretend otherwise.

Their conversation had been brief and then the man was gone, without anyone else knowing that the meeting had taken place.

Whilst those at home and a few friends knew of his occupation and the sometimes sensitivity and confidentiality of his tasks, Robert never broadcast his office to those who did not need to know. And the Haywards and their neighbours did not need to know. He had already made up his mind; in a few days he would be leaving them, content that they remained in the same blissful ignorance of his true reputation as they had on the day of his arrival there.

It would take several days to reach home, so when Joseph next called in to see him, Robert announced his decision.

"I shall be going home tomorrow. I have rested too long. If I can sit on a horse, I can ride," he said.

A highly sceptical expression met his announcement. "Is that a soldier's philosophy?" asked Joseph.

Robert smiled, not correcting him; he was no soldier. That the change of clothing in the saddle bags could easily been mistaken for the remnants of an old uniform was not surprising. The clothes had been deliberately plain and nondescript, to allow him to mix in easily anywhere. It was convenient to not be too noticeable in some parts of his work. Although he realised that the distinctive mark in his hair might well change that from now on. He could only hope it would eventually blend in more.

Robert mentioned his intention to return to the Haywards' farmhouse to thank them for everything again before leaving. His good manners would not have allowed otherwise, but Joseph advised against it. This time it was Robert who looked surprised. But he was reluctantly informed that apparently the family were not in the best of dispositions themselves. They were still plagued by their awful guest and her demands. Somehow she managed to bring out the worst in all of them, as if deliberately setting out to cause friction and arguments.

"They are far from happy and I know they would hate to appear unappreciative of your visit," the steward explained.

"Are you sure?" Robert queried seriously, greatly disappointed at not being able to bid them farewell or see them once more.

Joseph nodded and suggested an alternative. Robert conceded to his guidance and wrote a letter instead, expressing his deep appreciation for their extraordinary kindness. He handed it to Joseph, who promised to deliver it to Mr Hayward personally on his return to the farm. The letter did not feel the same, however; it lacked the warmth of the smile and the friendship of his parting wave.

Robert knew he could not delay any longer; he had been gone too long from too many other people. Especially home, where his family would be waiting for him. Home, which seemed so far away. Yes, it was difficult at first, just as he had anticipated. He had not ridden for ages and preferred a walking pace while his horse, now once more on the road, instinctively resumed his normal gait. Toby was longing to stretch himself on the long open spaces and Robert was obliged to bounce along uncomfortably, managing to keep his balance until he found his own rhythm again. His muscles ached and he was also soon out of breath. The horse did not understand the frequent halts.

Eventually the time began to pass more easily in the saddle, until one afternoon Robert rode into his own courtyard. It was just like any ordinary day in his life there. He slowed the horse at the usual place, glanced about the brick-walled yard and led his horse into the stables, just as he had always done, to unsaddle him. The sounds and smells were the same, the atmosphere as comforting as it had always been. It was a peaceful, rural place where the gentle air had never been harmed by harsh intrusion. Everything was the same, and he had not realised how much it meant to him. It hit him suddenly, to think what he could have lost. The quiet softness, the affection and love of his family, the kindness of his elders and everything which made this his home. He leant his head against the warm face of his horse and shuddered.

Having got this far, he did not know if he could go any further. Could he bear to see his loved ones flinch, see them frightened for him and crying? He leant against the wall, his trembling frame glad of the privacy to regain control.

Just then John the groom wandered through the doorway of the stables, pushing a barrow. He waved casually at Robert, their usual acknowledgement of each other through the years, and continued his tasks. It was minutes before, startled, he ran back to check this apparition of Robert shifting hay for the horse in the dark cool interior.

"I must tell the mistress you are home!" he gulped, staring at him.

"No. Not yet. I must see my sister first," came Robert's voice, harder than he meant it to be, stopping John in his footsteps.

From the archway he saw his pretty sister Elizabeth sitting in the orchard beyond, the hounds at her feet. She had remained unaffected by the influence of the outside world and was delightfully happy here. He had missed her infectious smile and soft lilting voice, the touch of her hand in his, her head on his shoulder, the smell of her hair and her laughter as she pushed him over in their games.

He continued to walk towards her slowly down the slope, his heart thumping with every step, slightly nervous of her reaction. He paused within touching distance, not knowing what to say, when she turned, sensing someone was there.

Her eyes had barely taken him in before she was on her feet and throwing herself at him, hugging him and saying his name over and over again. The hounds soon followed her example, leaping up, bounding towards him and nudging against his legs, nuzzling for their welcome and demanding to be stroked.

With his hands full, trying to please them all, Robert could not but laugh. A soft, mellow and much-needed laugh which warmed his whole being. The relief was enormous. He felt much better. The worst was over; he could face the others now. He could get through this day.

Elizabeth had her mother's sparkling blue eyes. She gazed at him with the same fondness she always had. She made no reference to the grey streak in his hair and it was only when the breeze shifted his fringe to reveal the wound beneath that her eyes widened. Full of concern, she studied his tired face and reached up to touch his scar gently with her fingertips.

"Oh, Robert what has happened. Does it hurt?" she exclaimed softly.

He shook his head. He had not even flinched; nothing hurt now.

"Do you think I have changed much?" he asked, his voice gruff and breaking, trying not to avoid the truth of the situation.

"Not to me. You're home. You're safe with us again. Nothing else matters," Elizabeth reassured him.

Instinctively she understood his doubts, and as she hugged him again and leaned gently into his shoulder, she felt his weakness and sensed his vulnerability. She was truly happy to have him back. She kept hold of his arm as they walked back to the house, the hounds following them. She smiled at him the whole time, as if to reassure him everything was fine.

From the house, an anxious face had watched the distant figures, their ensuing affectionate embrace and the alarmingly tender and familiar manner of their attachment as they began to stroll towards the building. Now horrified, the mistress shouted for help.

"John, John! Who is that man with Elizabeth? Fetch the master!"

"The master is gone out. He is still at our neighbours."

"Tell me instantly. Do you know who this man is?" she snapped, returning to the window.

John mumbled something about going to find out and disappeared quickly, intending to make himself scarce, anticipating the moment when her sharp anger would be replaced by an overwhelming tearful happiness.

Puffing from the exertion, Robert leaned on his sister as they climbed the steps up to their aunt's sitting room, he had forgotten how many stairs there were.

"Stop, I need to get my breath," he pleaded on the last few steps.

Elizabeth left him and rushed ahead, bursting to tell her aunt the good news.

"Aunt!" Elizabeth began, her face beaming and her eyes dancing brightly.

"Silence, Elizabeth. Who are you, sir? Explain yourself!" she bellowed authoritatively at the figure stood in the shadow of the doorway.

"Dear Aunt," he began softly, coming forward so she could see him clearly in the light. "I did not mean to alarm you. Excuse my shabby attire. I admit I am a little worse for wear."

Their aunt sat down sharply on the window seat, speechless

and shaking, her eyes staring at him, unable to believe it. Tears welled up in her eyes. At last, at long last, Robert was home. They were all used to his lengthy absences, his sudden departures and his travels, but for some reason this last period away had seemed longer than most and she truly had worried, without having any real reason for it. And now his tired, exhausted frame stood there and she looked at him again, only to gulp at her handsome nephew. The strange flash of grey in his hair startled her.

Robert understood her silent reaction and slowly sat down beside her, patting her hand and reassuring her that there was nothing to worry about. He was safe, in one piece and uglier than ever, he joked. She barely heard his words. All she wanted to do was to look at him. She took his face in her hands and smothered him with kisses before burying him in her arms. She held him for a long time, but he was well used to her prolonged displays of affection and waited patiently until she was ready to release him.

There was so much to tell them about the Haywards and their kindness. He owed the family so much. To take an injured stranger in when he was not their responsibility was beyond any normal expectation. His voice dried up at times, as the women anxiously questioned every detail, unable to believe he had survived such an accident. Although he had tried to make little of his injuries, he had to admit there was still the odd weakness in his elbow and other niggling aches and pains, but eventually he had satisfied all their concerns.

He was really tired now. It had been a long day, physically and mentally, and he could hardly keep his eyes open. It was obvious he needed rest and he almost fell asleep at the table, but he was determined not to be bundled off to bed until he could relate the whole story once more to their uncle when he returned.

“We must write to the Haywards,” insisted their aunt.

“Indeed we must,” agreed her husband, who had been equally overjoyed to see him again. “The next time you go that way you must deliver our letter, and we shall find a few things you can take for the children as well.”

When at last Robert reached his own bed, he slept the long, untroubled, all-consuming sleep that came from knowing he was truly home. And when he woke the next day in the comfort of his familiar room, the mellow warmth filtered through his every nerve, filling him with absolute contentment. Nothing was better than being here with his dearest family.

So it was that the household resumed its normal routine, Robert’s uncle, aunt and sister hardly noticing the mark to his hair any more. For them everything remained exactly as it had always been, with everyone pleased to have Robert home for a while. With no fresh instructions from his employers, Robert continued to enjoy this extended rest from his duties.

His first undertaking had been to walk towards the little churchyard at Luddesdown where his parents and sister were buried. His visit was overdue. He ran his hand over the top of their headstones and said their names aloud, thankful he had survived to be here.

As he walked back up the hill over Henley Down he stopped and glance back at the view. It was one of his favourite spots; the small valley remained unspoilt and the image of wild flowers amid the corn always stirred that sense of belonging which engulfed him here. Then he turned for home, with the softest smile on his face, comforted and reassured.

Not that he wasted his time at home. There was plenty to do about the farm and he was glad of any physical exercise to rebuild his strength and fitness. He purposefully exercised his horse every day to keep him in condition necessary for the long distances they travelled. He walked into the village or to see the neighbours, and volunteered to take the small cart into the weekly market to fetch any supplies his aunt required.

In between his chores and errands Robert spent his days outside making the most of the sunshine, often lying gently dozing at his sister's feet in the orchard below the house. The sun made him feel good; it renewed his sagging energy and even through his closed eyes it reached his very soul. Occasionally Elizabeth would engage him in conversation or nudge him playfully with her foot as he stretched and yawned.

After a while a foot nudged him again. He ignored it, only for it to gently repeat its interruption to his rest.

"Oh Elizabeth," he murmured, turning over to avoid her reach.

A man's smothered laugh made him open his eyes, but since the sun was in his eyes he could not easily make out the features of the visitor. He made to shield his eyes for a clearer view, only to find himself being hauled up onto his feet by a hearty tug accompanied by another laugh. The laugh was now instantly recognisable. The visitor was heartily smiling, holding Robert at arm's length and looking him up and down in amazement. Robert could only stare back, utterly horrified. Lord Rupert. Here! Why? He was never known to venture outside the privileged world of the high aristocracy. There was no precedent for such behaviour.

Robert glanced around quickly. He could see his sister playing with the hounds at the other end of the orchard. Rupert was apparently alone. What was wrong? For Rupert to appear like this, at their farm of all places, was unheard of. Never had their discreet association required such a drastic measure. Although the two of them were the best of friends, Rupert's position dictated a certain prudence. Their association hardly existed outside Hurl Place, Rupert's home.

"Do not look so worried," his friend smiled. "The man in the yard told me where to find you."

So Rupert had escaped the attention of his aunt, which was one blessing, otherwise his presence here would have become awkward to explain.

"But - what are you doing here? What has happened?" Robert enquired, glad to be able to speak freely.

"Nothing is amiss, my fair Robert. I only heard of your accident recently from London and I had to see for myself how you were," Rupert explained, too casually.

"Rupert, really! You should not have come," Robert insisted.

"And for you to be in such unusual casual attire. I cannot believe what I am seeing." Robert shook his head.

"Only for you, my dear friend, would I come incognito. But, what has happened to you?" Rupert asked, indicating his friend's hair.

"It was an accident," Robert said, still in a state of surprise at Rupert's presence.

Lord Rupert laid his hand heavily on his shoulder, shaking his head regretfully, his expression of concern hard to disguise.

"I never imagined you would come to harm by involving you in my stupid selfish requests," he said.

"Is that what you think? Rupert, I assure you, your errand was long finished. I was about my proper employment and on my way home, taking in the day. I had pulled aside to let some heavily-laden wagons pass more easily up the steep gradient of the track. Even the drovers were on foot, leading the horses. They had almost reached the top when the strain of the weight in the rear cart caused the main coupling pin to break. Separated from its central shaft and suddenly free of its harnesses and animals, the wagon body rolled back out of control down the hill. Toby was terrified by the noise, and he unseated me and fled. I was left in its path. That's all. It was an ordinary accident, nothing else."

"Ordinary! To have your bones battered in such a way can never be considered ordinary," Lord Rupert argued. He had clearly been informed of everything from London. Their report would have left nothing out; Rupert would have insisted on that.

It was Robert who suddenly put his fingers to his lips and nodded towards Elizabeth, who was approaching, holding the hounds back from bounding towards the stranger by their collars. Rupert understood his meaning.

"There is no need to alarm them with the full details," Robert whispered.

"Are you sure this is not in any way my fault? I would never forgive myself if I had been the cause of any harm to you."

"Honestly, it was nothing to do with your business."

His friend studied him closely, desperate to believe him and accept his reassurance. Robert had never lied to him.

"Come then, walk me to the horses. They await," Rupert concluded, apparently satisfied.

The word 'horses' instantly reassured Robert that his friend had not been foolish enough to travel all the way from his home without company. Robert gave a sharp whistle, clicked his fingers twice and pointed to the ground, at which the hounds instantly obeyed his command. Then, beckoning a reluctant Elizabeth to join them, he introduced Rupert as a friend from London, without even saying his name.

His sister, who was naturally shy of strangers, gave a slight curtsey, while Rupert beamed, bowing graciously in response. Rupert commented on how pretty his sister was, which made her blush. Then he smiled kindly and gently took her arm, linking it in his, for her to walk with them as he always did with friends. Thus the three of them headed back to the house, with the hounds at Robert's heels.

"I regret I am to attend my cousin in London shortly," Rupert sighed. "I cannot refuse him. Don't think I wouldn't prefer to spend time enjoying your company instead."

"I am sure you will amuse yourself in such circles. You have a reputation to maintain," Robert said, grinning.

"It is a fact, I am pleased you will not accompany me. I fear your distinctive hair would entice more curiosity and interest than is good for my ego. The ladies would not give me a second glance," Rupert joked.

His words were stopped by a warning glance and a loud cough. There was no need for his sister to know more than was good for her.

Their eagle-eyed aunt had watched the approaching group with displeasure and met them as they reached the house. She stood with her hands on her hips, her shoulders set and her eyes blazing intensely at them.

"How is it that visitors enter my home and grounds unannounced and proceed to roam its domain as if they own it? Who is this person, Robert?" she demanded.

Lord Rupert stepped forward to quickly save Robert from having to lie on his behalf.

"You must forgive me madam, for my bad manners. You have every right to be annoyed. But please understand, when I heard my friend had returned injured, I had to see him for myself, without delay. To make sure he was truly well," he explained, turning on the eloquent charm he was famous for and ending with a bow of profound modesty. Robert kept his smile, knowing just how far this friend had actually come on this journey, despite the misleading way it sounded.

"Am I forgiven, madam? I mean no harm and I will not stay a moment longer. I would not put you out in any way," Lord Rupert pleaded.

"You must not scold him, Aunt. It was a most welcome surprise," Robert intervened.

"It was my pleasure to have met Robert's family," Rupert insisted, graciously bowing again to each of the ladies in turn.

After which, to their continued astonishment, he swiftly backed out of the way, successfully leaving both the women ignorant of his identity. Robert quickly following behind him. The two men walked to the horses in the courtyard, where Rupert's personal escort waited fretfully. Robert was relieved to see them.

"Rupert, you are too impulsive to have come. I doubt your secretary sanctioned this visit," he said.

"The pair of you are always worrying too much for me. You may scold me for coming, but why should I not?"

"Because there was no need. You know that."

"I should not have sent you on my errands," Rupert murmured wistfully.

"Oh Rupert, stop this false remorse. Who else would you trust on your delicate missions?"

"I know, but I regret. You must come to Hurl Place again. You will come to visit me soon, maybe?" Rupert enquired.

Robert nodded; there was no need for clarification of a time or day. Nothing was planned between them. Their infrequent partnership had no rules. It would not matter.

"And immediately, if you need my assistance," Rupert added in a lower tone.

A firm handshake was exchanged between the two of them as they parted, leaving Robert to consider the imminent task of fending off the barrage of questions he would face concerning his visitor.

"Your friend is a foreigner. His accent is quite distinct," his aunt prompted on his return to the house.

"Indeed he is," sighed Robert, smiling to himself.

"He is not one of your usual acquaintances from London."

"No Aunt, he is not."

"He is not connected to your employment? Not one of your fellow colleagues?"

"No, he is not."

"Then who is he, Robert? He is doubtless one of the gentry, by his bearing. And he seems to know you particularly well."

"He is a good friend. But there is no point in asking more about him. I doubt you will ever meet him again." He did not want to be drawn into explaining further.

"He is such a gentleman. He had such fine courtly manners!" enthused Elizabeth, unable to hide her admiration for their visitor. This stranger was dangerously interesting. How could she not want to know more about him?

"Oh, Robert please, please tell me who he is," she asked.

"I don't think that would be advisable. He is a private man. He is a busy man."

His sister pouted at him, somewhat peeved at his refusal to tell her anything. With Elizabeth so overawed by this unknown gentleman, it would not do to encourage her, Robert decided.

"He has a lot of admirers, dear sister," Robert warned.

She shrugged, pretending that she was not interested in any such romantic fantasies, but Robert knew better. Her fondness for the neighbour's son was no secret.

"You are better to confine your affections to Michael," he teased, making her blush.

His uncle had readily accepted Robert's decision to preserve the visitor's identity, aware of the discretion required in his nephew's line of work, but his sister and his aunt refused to be satisfied. Over the next few days Robert was forced to laughed off the many attempts they made to question him. They had tried everything to find out more, but all their efforts were to no avail. Robert stubbornly refused to give up any information about Lord Rupert to either of them, until eventually he had to remind them that he could not be expected to discuss his important connections, even with his family. His organization would not allow it. They reluctantly gave up their pestering. They knew Robert was right, just as Robert knew they were safer not knowing anything about Lord Rupert. Indeed, Robert concluded, the sooner he resumed his employment and earn a living once more, the quicker the whole topic would be forgotten.

CHAPTER TWO

Robert was eager to return to work, and when his over-tolerant employers finally sent fresh papers for his next assignment at the end of July, he willingly set off back on the road. He was back in the saddle again, ever aware of his obligations. Robert thrived on the varied tasks of his interesting and unusual occupation, which took him all over the south of England. This month his instructions consisted of delivering confidential government instructions to regional headquarters and local authorities for magistrates, justices of the peace and mayors in Kent, Surrey and Sussex. He dealt with all ranks of society and had proved himself over the years. Allocated to different departments, Robert had displayed a natural talent and astuteness in completing all transactions smoothly and efficiently.

Likewise his two colleagues also allocated to the south had

been picked for their astuteness and trustworthiness. Occasionally when they happened to be at the office at the same time, the three of them would meet up in one of the London coffee shops which were the focus of debate. In London the public were well informed and content that the absent King did not interfere in their lives. Newspapers provided the latest gossip and people were keen to express their opinions, but the three of them tactfully never aired their views in public.

Edmund looked Robert up and down, very slowly and very purposefully.

"It is good to see you back. We missed you on the road," Henry commented. "How on earth did it happen?"

"It was an accident, pure and simple. A fluke." Robert shrugged.

They went on to discuss his recent replacement, Christopher. Apparently the keen youngster had been eager to prove himself, being determined to emulate Robert's efficiency. He had allowed little time for the usual socialising or the friendly banter expected by their clients. As a result there was talk of him being moved to East Anglia, where extra operatives were needed to combat the growth of the ports and illegal contraband.

"Just keep him out of my hair. He has a lot to learn yet," Henry concluded. With that topic dismissed, they went on to talk of more mundane matters before departing back to the Exchange.

Later that afternoon Robert was walking in London on a minor errand when he bumped into another colleague from the provinces.

"Catchwick!"

"Sutton!"

"How are you doing? Do you prefer your new posting in Suffolk?"

Catchwick beamed; the answer was obvious. He told Robert

he should try it, before he chirruped merrily away expanding the benefits of the different landscape and routine, the new towns, the small villages, the abundant farmland and agriculture. Then there was the vast, meandering coast, with its many small harbours and places where small boats could land an illegal cargo.

"A smugglers' haven?" enquired Robert.

Catchwick nodded and smiled, agreeing that there was plenty to be vigilant about. Like Robert, he enjoyed being out and about in all seasons. He liked being out on the road and the variety of challenges he was given. These officers of the Crown were all of the same breed.

"Will the new recruit Christopher be in your patch?"

Catchwick laughed. "Not if I have my way. They can send him to Essex."

They parted with a handshake and each happily went on their own way.

There was no explaining what hand of fate brought Robert to that Sussex town on business a week later, and straight into a potentially awkward encounter. He could not believe his bad luck to find an array of liveried carriages and a gathering of people in front of him. He recognised the lady at the centre of the entourage - Lady Arabella, of all people!

Robert swore silently. Bloody Rupert! His dear good friend was entirely to blame for eventually drawing him into that other elaborate world which contained such women. Lady Arabella, that wicked tantalizing creature, was one of Lord Rupert's many regular acquaintances, which was why unfortunately there was little doubt that she would recognise him immediately, despite his dull attire. There was no avoiding their meeting and he knew he must make the best of it and carry it off without causing any suspicion.

"Why Mr Robert Sutton, what are you doing here?" she exclaimed seductively, delighted to offer him her gloved hand.

Dutifully Robert performed the expected courtly gestures, bowing slightly and kissing her hand.

"Lady Arabella. I could ask the same of you," he smiled in return.

"Oh, you know my husband's obsession with horses, always after a better blood line. He is here to view a set of bays. Will you join us? He will be glad of a second opinion."

"I must decline. I would be of little use. I am no expert on horses, my lady," he countered.

"Oh, fie! I understand quite the opposite from more than one of my husband's acquaintances."

Robert made no comment.

"You are being modest, as always. Never mind. I would prefer your fine company for myself for the moment," she encouraged temptingly, slipping her arm in his and forcing him to walk a short way with her. Out of politeness he allowed himself to accompany her, although he was fully aware of the reputation of the dazzling and devastating beauty he was dealing with. He knew it was his own fault he had left such a marked impression on Arabella. His refusal to fall under her spell at the last spring ball held by Lord Rupert had made him a target of her more determined subtle intentions. It was clear she had not given up, and this afternoon's indirect advances indicated that she still sought to add him to her long list of admirers.

"It has been an age since we have seen you," she enquired during their sedate promenade along the street. "At the last ball, I believe. Is Lord Rupert with you?"

"No, he remains in London still."

"Such a pity," she sighed regretfully. "He would have made all the difference to this visit. We are staying at Goodwood House. Do say you will dine with us later."

"To my regret, I am on my way out of town. I have another appointment," he replied, gently detaching himself from her arm as they reached the end of the row. Surprisingly, she took his rejection without too much fuss.

"Your clothes may be lacking their usual grandeur today, but your charm is not lessened by their absence. Although I note you have gained a distinguishing addition to your delightful appearance. I can only wonder that a matter of honour has perhaps caused such a mark," she murmured mischievously into his ear as she finally let him go.

"My honour would never allow me to be so indiscreet as to respond to your unwarranted suggestion. You should know that any private matters concerning myself or anyone else will always remain private," he warned quietly, his eyes staring into hers, his meaning absolutely clear.

With the message fully understood, Robert turned sharply on his heels, leaving Lady Arabella to regain her composure. She was more than a little miffed at his departing words, but on returning to her entourage she gave no hint that anything unpleasant had passed between them. She refused to lose face in such society. It would not do.

Relieved to escape further difficulties, Robert slipped rapidly through the nearest archway into the cool arcade, only to be stopped suddenly in his tracks as he came face to face with Margaret, the eldest daughter of the Hayward family. Robert's uncle had instructed him several times since his accident to call on Mr Hayward whenever he was in that part of the country again. "I would hate him to think that we are ungrateful for his great kindness," he had said. He had always fully intended to do so, but he knew it would be a long time before he could. His schedule did not give him anywhere near enough time. And now here he was face to face with one of the family, herself far from home.

"Miss Hayward," he greeted her swiftly, confounded by her untimely appearance. He could not understand how she was here, in this part of the county.

"Why, Mr Sutton," she replied pointedly, acknowledging her own surprise at meeting him, but also at his much improved mode of attire, as she carefully looked him up and down, taking in every inch of him.

"You are looking well," she commented.

"I - how unexpected a pleasure," he offered, still slightly uneasy.

Thankfully Margaret did not refer to his meeting with Lady Arabella in the High Street only minutes before, which avoided him having to explain his association with the lady. Robert initially meant to pass on immediately, but he felt it would be impolite to be so brisk after all her family had done for him.

"May I enquire - you are here with the rest of the family?" he added.

"No. I am visiting with a friend," she explained, hastily glancing behind her and looking around for her companion.

"I will never forget the benevolence and kindness your family showed me. Please pass on my regards to them. They are all well? "

"Thank you, they are all in good health. I will tell them I have seen you." She turned to wave at an approaching figure bundled with many small packages.

"I will not delay you any further," said Robert, as her friend arrived.

He gave every impression of being fully composed as he set off to conclude his business elsewhere, yet he really hoped that Margaret had not seen him in the company of Arabella, nor the very courtly manners he had been obliged to display to her. His two worlds seldom overlapped, and on this occasion he definitely wished they had not. Although the event had been of little importance and should mean nothing, he hated the idea that his actions would have given the impression of any apparent fawning on his part over a titled lady. It would have presented him in a very detrimental way, and he would hate to have any of the Hayward family think badly of him.

As Robert travelled on in the afternoon, he was satisfied that he had easily completed his confidential business for the day. He regularly visited the suppliers of commodities, checked the quality and signed off the shipments for delivery. He was the most experienced operative they had and was authorised to renew contracts or instantly cancel them if anything was wrong. Today, after inspecting the quality of the goods at the merchant's premises, he was more than willing to add him to the list of official suppliers to the various establishments he represented.

With his task quickly accomplished and now ahead of schedule, Robert allowed himself a visit to the blacksmith, Thomas, and his wife. Thomas had his own living, making ironwork, repairing ploughs and making farm implements, as well as the usual farrier labour. Yet for years his smithy had also functioned as one of the many relay posts scattered over the organisation's network. The smell of his wife's cooking, the glowing forge and the ring of the hammer on the anvil welcomed Robert back to another of his favourite places.

Robert sat relaxed and comfortable by the fire with Thomas and his wife Jane, after sharing supper with them. As was his habit, Robert was staying the night with them, in their meagre home at the back of the forge. They had known each other for years, ever since Robert had started his obscure occupation.

"It's good to see you back, Robert," the large, homely woman told him.

"Your recent temporary replacement lacks your way with horses," Thomas murmured, leaning forward to stir more life into the fire.

"But apparently he has been almost as efficient in his other duties," Robert confided.

Both were discreet and trustworthy, so he had no worries about what he told them. Jane pulled a face; she had not been that impressed, she confessed. She enjoyed the company of their regular visitors, but some she just could not take to. And this Christopher was such a one.

Here the travelling couriers were welcomed and refreshed, here they could always stop the night or find a fresh change of horse, whichever was necessary. Robert preferred to ride his own horse on his assignments, attentive to its condition and never abusing its stamina. If something urgent required a much longer and harder pace, he would use the relay system, leaving his horse in Thomas's care and borrowing one from the team held in the accompanying stables and fenced paddocks. He would then change horses at other stations as required to complete the undertaking.

"Do you ever worry about the future after that accident?" Jane asked. "I know it's unlikely, but you can't afford any more like that one."

"To be honest, only briefly. Once I was back in my normal routine I easily forgot the scare it had given me. As long as I am fit to continue, the good pay will be put to good use. It supplements the farm and ensures its survival."

Robert shrugged philosophically. What more did he expect out of life? He had no grand plans in mind for his future; in fact he had never given his future any serious thought. For the moment he was content to simply deal with the business in hand. He had a long list of other commissions to complete before heading back to London.

A month later Robert had arrived at Hurl Place. He soon found himself and Lord Rupert in disagreement, which was nothing unusual, except that this turned out to be an exact repetition of the discussion at their first-ever meeting, with Robert once more representing a client who had some horses for sale.

"I will be advising my client not to sell them to you," Robert told his friend firmly.

"Robert! I don't think he will be pleased by your interference when I am offering more than good money," Rupert replied indignantly.

"Money is not the issue. After all the breeding and care in producing such fine animals, the last thing he, or I, will want is to see them ruined in weeks by your inept outriders. No, they are too good a quality for what you intend to do with them."

Lord Rupert glowered at the defiant Robert, because he hated being made to see sense in an argument. Robert was right again, he conceded, at which Robert smiled, satisfied that the livestock would now safely go to a more suitable establishment.

"So shall we have some wine, or are you also going to question my sources on that matter again?" Lord Rupert commented, a deliberate reference to their second meeting.

Robert shrugged, remembering the occasion when, soon after their first argument about livestock, there had been a disagreement over a consignment of wine. Lord Rupert had attempted to use his title to have the duty on the imported bottles waived. Robert, then an officer for Custom and Excise, refused, insisting the duty must be paid. Already seething, Rupert told him that in that case he would obtain his wine elsewhere, from a less scrupulous warehouse. At which Robert instantly warned him of the law and insisted that those who produced it and shipped it were entitled to a fair price for their efforts. Robert had prevailed again. Despite always sulking after being bettered, Lord Rupert, amused by his friend's strict code of ethics, had nicknamed him 'Fair Robert', which, although it was not originally meant as a compliment, was indeed Robert's philosophy in all matters.

Robert did not regret his involvement with Rupert, as their casual acquaintance had soon developed into friendship. Robert enjoyed the company of a man who rode well, made him laugh and entertained with a certain flair. Robert had never expected to be included or invited to attend the lavish functions Rupert hosted, but he soon found himself mixing amongst Rupert's circle of acquaintances, dining with his selective guests and appearing at the occasional ball.

Whilst his friend was famous in society for his soirees, Robert stubbornly refused to be overwhelmed by the glamour and temptations offered in those higher circles. Robert remained level-headed, even while performing the necessary refined elegant manners required in such polite company. He flattered and gently teased the fine ladies as was expected, and danced with many dazzling beauties. If he held them a little too long, they never objected or pulled away. He knew it was only a game, and made no pretence at being anyone special. He was no catch and he had nothing to offer them, but for some reason they just enjoyed his company, as much as he did theirs. Which, he sighed, was where he had unfortunately met the lady Arabella.

Robert rode on towards Hampshire, where he had two prospective buyers lined up. Of course Lady Arabella's husband, Lord Henry Wake, would have been the obvious choice to contact, because of his growing reputation for building up a fine stable of bloodstock. But although he liked the man himself, any proximity to Arabella ruled out that possibility. So instead he headed for the estate of Sir Eustace Tovey, with the next alternative after that being the home of Baronet Duskin. He was well used to the sight of various sizes of manor houses, in all states of grandeur, some with vast and prestigious formal gardens, other just a mass of glorious wild colour, scattered amongst the countryside. Sir Eustace's might be a modest residence, but the surrounding well-kept farmland spoke volumes for him and his tenants. The estate manager met him at the gates and escorted him up the gravel drive to the stable block where Sir Eustace himself waited, eager to show off his own stock and surroundings. A wide smile of welcome, combined with a direct, firm handshake, confirmed Robert's original impression of this landowner. He would enjoy doing business with him.

After the equine deal was settled, Robert made his own way back down the drive to the main road. He could not help casually noticing the ladies and gentlemen chatting on the terrace, their servants moving without command and children on the vast lawns chasing each other around the trees.

Then he saw a solitary figure misplaced in the setting, strolling away from the house. He was not quite sure who he was seeing at first. The height and colouring reminded him of Margaret, although it could not be. Margaret, here? He paused to shake loose his imagination, but his imagination was correct. It was Margaret - and not Margaret. The wild flowing locks he remembered were pulled back unflatteringly into a single plait. She walked straight and upright, formal and stiff. Her face looked paler than normal and her eyes were cast down. He could not believe the change in her.

He had almost decided not to attract her attention when she suddenly saw him and walked straight towards him.

"What are you doing here?" came her voice in a mixture of surprise and accusation.

"I had business at the house."

"What business would bring you to this place?" she challenged him, as if she did not believe him.

"I am brokering a deal for a client."

"You spoke with Sir Eustace?" she queried.

"Yes. In person. Face to face. Why should I not?"

She looked sceptical, wondering what on earth they could have in common, the gentry and this working man.

"Concerning horses," Robert enlightened her.

For some reason this made a difference, and she shrugged in acceptance of his story.

"What are you doing here, may I ask?" Robert countered.

She did not answer immediately. She gave a deep sigh. Then, pulling herself upright, she looked him straight in the eyes.

"I am in service, if you must know. My friend and I are both in service to Mrs Taylor. Not that it is any of your business." Her tone was different from that he had heard before.

"There is no need to be so belligerent. I was only asking! It is only natural I should," he reminded her quietly.

She turned her head away briefly, he guessed to compose herself.

"Mrs Taylor? She is here visiting her brother, Sir Eustace. The estate manager told me. I hope she is a good mistress," Robert ventured, kindly.

"You need not trouble yourself with bland polite social phrases on my behalf. I do not need them."

"Margaret!"

His eyebrows flickered at her sharpness to him, for she had never shown any hostility to him before. It shocked him, surprised him, although he forgave her immediately.

"And since when do you address me as 'Margaret'?" she snapped, glaring at him.

He always had, in his own mind.

They were interrupted by a raised sharp female voice from the terrace, enquiring where she was.

"Don't let me keep you. I wouldn't wish to get you into trouble," he murmured sarcastically. He bowed, deliberately low, whilst his eyes kept contact with hers until she turned away.

Robert was completely confused as he rode off. He was still puzzled and surprised at finding Margaret in service, as she was a country girl through and through. To be so far away from the farm and her family did not really make sense. And it was obvious from their brief conversation and her behaviour that she was not happy here. So why was she here?

Over the next few days he concluded his other business, first at Midhurst and then at Storrington, where he signed a completion document on behalf of his employers. Then he headed back towards home, intending to return via Dorking, where he intended to buy a present for his sister. In many respects, he acknowledged, he was lucky his work allowed a certain flexibility. They had always been allowed a certain freedom in their movements, to avoid making the regularity of their journeys too obvious to anyone who wished to disrupt their work.

For once he knew exactly what he wanted, a pretty necklace of pale blue glass stones. He had noticed it when he had been here before, on one of Rupert's special errands. Of course Rupert's trinkets were always much more elaborate and expensive, but this delicate simple necklace was so pretty and would be perfect for his sister.

He had booked into a good tavern for the night and as it was only late afternoon, he was content to sit outside for a while. The regular coach had just unloaded its passengers and their bags. Most of them were local to the area, as indicated by the array of carts and horses which stood waiting to transport them on their homeward passage. Other passengers who would be travelling onward the next day were heading inside to request meals and confirm the bookings for their rooms.

Robert did not take much notice until a large man strode towards him, offering his hand.

"Robert Sutton? It is Robert? How are you now?"

Robert continued to look mystified, until the man introduced himself as Arthur Dunhill, one of Mr Hayward's neighbours.

"I don't suppose you would remember me. I was at his home at the time of your accident. I am glad to see you are looking well."

Robert relaxed, thanked the man for his enquiry and took advantage of the moment to enquire after his original benefactors. "And yourself? You are well? And the Haywards? They are all in good health, all still at home?" Robert asked eager to satisfy his own curiosity concerning Margaret.

"They are much better now that spoilt old harridan has gone."

The man went on in great detail about how the wretched great aunt who had been the cause of Robert's departure from the farmhouse had been no end of trouble. Mr Dunhill paused, wondering if he should continue, and spoke again.

"The two girls are no longer at home," he said. "Margaret and a friend have both found good posts together in some household. Martha has been offered a live-in post, as an apprentice with a dressmaker."

Robert felt himself tense up. Both of them gone? This did not feel right at all.

"I believe Mr Hayward simply wanted them away from the awful influence of that dreadful woman and decided that the older girls should broaden their experience by leaving the farm for the time being."

Robert analysed the information. While he accepted that Mr Hayward would only have done what he considered the best for his family, even so it seemed quite drastic. Indeed he knew Mr Hayward must have given it a lot of thought before making that decision.

"It must be a terrible wrench for everyone," Robert offered.

Dunhill was more philosophical about the matter. "It won't be forever," he reassured Robert. "It may even do the girls some good. They may even find a suitor!"

Robert tried to smile. He made no comment. Put logically it made sense, but Robert preferred to think of the girls happily at home as they had been, as he remembered them.

Their words exhausted, Robert stretched himself lazily and buttoned up his faded old jacket before he bid the man his farewell.

Having bought the necklace, which was carefully wrapped and put in his deep coat pocket, he reported to his office and quickly headed home to Kent for his sister's birthday. Now Elizabeth was older, their uncle and aunt had arranged to hold a small informal country dance for people they knew in their barn, to celebrate her birthday. They had invited neighbours and friends for the evening, as well as persuading some local musicians and a caller to come. Everyone had eagerly accepted. The evening looked very promising and Elizabeth had been excited for days.

On the morning of the dance she was the first up, impatiently waiting to unwrap the presents, which had been left on the large sideboard. She gulped her breakfast down, while the others deliberately took their time, amused at her desperate attempts to hurry them into the other room. Smiling, they followed her into the sitting room and sat themselves down, as her curiosity exploded and she tore away at the large parcel which had been there for days.

She stood back, taking it all in, her face beaming delightedly. She was lost for words as she ran her hands over the material, and held it up before pulling it against her and swishing the skirts from side to side. Their aunt and uncle had paid for a new cotton dress to be made for her, in the palest blue with tiny flowers scattered all over it. It was so pretty. The older adults nodded to each other; it had been a pleasure to see her so happy.

Then it was the turn of Robert's present, which he had deliberately wrapped in many sheets of paper. It had taken him ages the previous night to make the parcel. He had collected every scrap of paper he could find and tied the top layer with a piece of string. It looked quite peculiar and a very odd shape when he had finished, but he felt pleased with the outcome. It achieved its purpose and it did not take long for Elizabeth to get frustrated by the endless task of unwrapping layer after layer and his accompanying smirking laughter.

"Is there anything in here?" she asked, suspicious of his gift. She would not put it past him to tease her by putting nothing in the middle. Maybe he was keeping her real present hidden somewhere else.

A little squeal of glee erupted as she finally found the object in the centre, and she rushed to show the other two adults her prize. It went so well with her dress, she exclaimed. She laid it on the dress, which was displayed across a settee, and rushed to throw her arms around Robert and kiss him. This was quickly repeated with her aunt and uncle, thanking them over and over again for their special gift. She could not help herself; she skipped happily around the floor and hugged and kissed them all again and again.

John and Robert spent the morning clearing the small barn, brushing the dirt floor and stacking the hay bales to one side for seating and putting some planks on others to form tables. Their fellow neighbours and friends would each bring a plate of food for the evening, to add to the dishes being prepared in the house. His uncle returned with several barrels of ale, to be set up in the corner. That just left the lanterns to be hung on the beams and the uprights to be decorated with sprigs of greenery, including wild flowers and herbs.

His sister was so animated that it made everyone smile. She would dart in and out all the time to see how it was progressing.

"You'll wear yourself out before this evening comes, if you carry on like this," their uncle joked.

The evening came, with a merry band of people arriving to wish Elizabeth a happy birthday and present her with lots of small gifts. Robert noticed that Michael had given her a bunch of blue hair ribbons, at which she had blushed. There was no mistaking the way things were between them; they were nervously fond of each other. Robert watched as his sister, carefully holding her treasured tokens, hurried away to put them somewhere safe in the house, so that she could return quickly to his company.

The informal evening was soon in full swing, and the fiddler, the flute player and the jolly caller were encouraging all to dance to the catchy tunes. The dances were energetic and carefree, with partners often changing as they moved around the floor. And whilst Robert danced with his sister a couple of times, it was obvious who she really wanted to dance with, as she kept looking around to see where he was.

Eventually the tired assembly were ready to go home, having greatly enjoyed the evening. Elizabeth was almost asleep on her feet, but she refused to go to bed until she had thanked everyone for coming as they left.

"Thank goodness that's over," their aunt sighed exhaustedly

as they saw the last of their guests depart. Tomorrow the place and their lives would be back to normal, they did not hanker after too much excitement.

The birthday celebrations over, Robert's uncle tackled him before he left again.

"Really Robert. It is not good enough. When are you going to visit the Haywards? It has been months. I am sure you could have managed to fit it in before now. I cannot imagine what they must think of us. It is the height of bad manners not to have delivered our letters and presents by now."

"I had intended to when I learnt that the two girls had found employment away from the farm. It seemed a little awkward to just turn up."

"Rubbish! Excuses. Either you do it soon or I will make the long journey myself and apologise on your behalf."

Robert had been carrying the letters from his aunt and uncle and the small packages for the boys in his saddlebags for an age. The envelopes and wrapping were getting more battered by the week. He should have made the effort before now, but he seriously had not wished to impose on Mr Hayward after hearing his treasured girls would be absent.

Put to shame, Robert made the request to the establishment on his return to London and rearranged his schedule to allow him to visit the Hayward farm. Naturally they had no concerns about his changed timetable and in fact they had wondered why he had not done this before. He was usually so correct about doing the right thing.

At long last Robert headed towards the South Downs on his mission to find out how the Haywards were really managing with part of their family missing. He patted his saddlebags, confident that the contents would soon be delivered and hoping they would be happily received.

He was only a few miles from the farm when Robert came across another traveller on the same route. It turned out to be Joseph, their steward. Apparently he had been on an errand for his master, he explained to Robert as they rode side by side. Robert was eager to enquired after the family, hoping to learn that Margaret and Martha would soon be returning home. The man pulled his horse to a stop and shook his head.

"It could be better for all of us," he said.

Robert waited patiently for the man to explain further, expecting it to be some minor complaint which, once aired, would make him less pessimistic. What Robert heard, however, shocked him immensely. Apparently the Haywards, together with their neighbours and friends, were suffering an unexpected and disastrous financial loss through no fault of their own. Although the wheat crop had more than made up for its poor harvest last year, the prices they had been offered were well below the normal rate. The new corn merchants had told them that the abundance of wheat had created a huge glut in the market, which meant it would fetch less.

Robert shook his head; he could feel himself frowning. There was always a demand for wheat, and he, more than most, should know. As an agent for various government agencies, he knew the current prices being paid around the country. He did not like the sound of this at all.

"So what did Mr Hayward do?" he asked.

Joseph explained that they had considered looking further afield for a better price, but the cost of transporting the grain would have defeated the purpose. Thus they had taken the best offer they could get. The price offered from these new merchants.

Robert felt his stomach tighten. The Haywards and their neighbours had been deliberately cheated. There had been no serious fluctuation in the market.

"It must have been difficult."

"We made small sacrifices here and there. A few of our neighbours sold items to help them get by, until things pick up again."

Robert was suspicious, and quizzed Joseph as much as he could.

"Had anyone known or heard of these new merchants before?"

Joseph did not think so.

"Do you know their name?"

"Er – Redick and Company."

Although he made no further comment, Robert was incensed. The Haywards and their neighbours were good, hard-working people and did not deserve to be swindled. A fair price for a fair crop - how else would anyone survive?

He changed his mind about riding over to see the Haywards. He did not wish to impose on their hospitality or upset them with lame idle conversation when they must be worried. He thought it better to turn back, and handed the letters and parcels to Joseph to deliver for him.

Robert could not ignore this news. It had to be investigated, and for once it was within his influence and jurisdiction to actually do something about it. At last he might be able to repay the enormous debt he owed them.

That evening in the tavern, having settled into a secluded corner, Robert nursed his tankard and stared at the dark liquid, his mind churning, mulling over the best way to sort this out. As an officer of the Crown, he had every authority to instigate his own investigation into the merchants in question. But on reflection he decided it would be better to remain impartial and report this to the Exchange in London, allowing them to complete an unbiased, independent assessment. He was too personally involved and he did not want to be accused of influencing the case. That would not help anyone.

It was not just the merchant's behaviour which bothered him. Mr Hayward had sent the two girls away from home for one reason, but a financial reason now forced their continued absence. It seemed his two precious girls would remain in service to ease the economic burden.

He must have nodded off, because the jerk of his head falling forward woke him. Whatever he had been dreaming about rapidly disappeared from his memory as he tried to go over his previous plan of action. Ignoring the rest of the room and the other travellers who had filled it, Robert buried himself in thought once more.

Until some words caught his attention.

"Will the marquetry will be at Hurl Place tomorrow night?" said a voice.

There was no answer, but the mention of Lord Rupert's home, had Robert suddenly alert and listening for more. But who had spoken, and had he heard correctly? What did he mean, marquetry?

He peered over the corner of his wooden settle and looked around, expecting to identify some master craftsman proudly discussing his work. The general conversation in the room made the person impossible to identify. Everyone looked like normal rural travellers, and the time passed with nothing more being said other than the odd order of more ale and food. He decided to ignore it, convinced that no one in this remote place would have any knowledge of anything being sent to Hurl Place. Why should they? No one here would even know where Hurl Place was – except him, of course.

He shook his head. He was tired and headed off to bed, convinced he must have had misheard whatever was being said, or had maybe even half dreamt it.

Outside the wind had risen for the predicted storm, rattling the shutters noisily, and as he looked out of the window at the bottom of the stairs, he noted people hurrying for shelter. Two such people were stood by the door unwilling to brave the weather.

"I'm sure the dinner at Hurl Place will be the perfect place to broach our venture," said one. "The discreet private residence is ideal. A little subtle conversation should find out if there is any interest in our financial scheme. If we can encourage any of those influential guests to invest, it will encourage others."

"What does Lord Rupert know of this?"

"Nothing. But if we can somehow also suggest a link to Hurl Place, the proposition will attract considerably more support."

Robert stayed in the shadow of the stairwell. The back of his neck went cold. What in heaven was going on? This furtive conversation indicated that Rupert was about to be unwittingly involved in something not to his advantage. Who were these people, and who were they in league with? Someone attending tomorrow's dinner was all he knew for certain.

The outside door opened and closed quickly and the two furtive, whispering figures had gone. No doubt in different directions, Robert assumed from experience. Not that it mattered, since he did not have time to chase after either of them, because he was more worried about warning Lord Rupert. There was no point in going to bed; he would have change his plans immediately. He had to go this minute. As he threw his belongings together again and went to the stables, he was already planning the change of horses necessary on the route.

Robert rode as fast as he could from the South Downs, battling against the storm which had frustrated him at every turn. The rain had lashed the countryside relentlessly for the whole of his journey, until after a long night and a longer day he at last arrived in the early evening, sodden to the core. Lord Rupert's splendid residence was already dazzled by light and activity, making Robert wonder if he was already too late. Had they started dining?

The sound of his echoing gallop on the cobbles startled the stable lads. He had never ridden so far in one continuous prolonged journey. After many changes of horses, he was already stiff and his legs ached and buckled briefly as he swung down immediately he entered the stable yard. He could not delay; he tossed the reins in the air for them to catch and snatched off the saddle panniers, which he never let out of his sight, and headed indoors.

The air of urgency was evident on his face as he rushed through the many corridors, scattering his wet outer clothes on the floor and letting the dripping panniers leave a trail of small puddles as he went. Unseen hands were swift to gather his discarded garments behind him and wipe the floor, while doors opened and closed for him in his progress to the private apartments. All those within Rupert's private court were aware that he was Rupert's personal friend, an ordinary man with no rank or title, but whose status was beyond that definition; an emissary and a prudent diplomat in Rupert's personal matters. Accordingly no one barred his way or delayed him.

Ellis, Rupert's private secretary and personal valet, was startled at this unexpected arrival and even more alarmed at Robert's gushing report. He explained that Lord Rupert was already dining with the assembly and it would be difficult to interrupt without alerting the unknown conspirators.

"Who knew about this dinner?" Robert asked.

"It wasn't a secret," Ellis replied.

"Hmm!"

As the pair of them approached the great hall, the doors were open and the stewards were retrieving the various plates and trays of food from the first course. What were they to do? How were they to draw Rupert away from the room and his guests in order to warn him, without causing too much interest?

Then Robert had it. There was only one plausible way, only one thing serious enough to allow the host to leave the room without any excuses being necessary. Taking the head steward aside, they gave him instructions.

Seconds later the steward re-entered the dining hall, very upright, very correct. He walked to the head of the table and bowed to Lord Rupert. Rupert glanced at the servant's face and nodded.

"Forgive me, my Lord," he announced quite audibly, "there is a messenger arrived from Richmond Lodge, who insists he must deliver a letter to you personally. It has the royal seal and may need an immediate reply."

There was a reverent gasp of astonishment as the impact of the words fluttered around the room.

"Of course," Rupert replied, rising slowly. "If you will forgive me, gentlemen." He followed his man out of the room. Robert smirked. Who was going to argue? Richmond Lodge meant a royal command, and none here were going to question that.

Robert was looking through the small lattice panel into the dining hall as Lord Rupert hurried towards Ellis.

"What is this all about Ellis?" asked Rupert. Then he caught sight of a dishevelled Robert.

"Robert! What the devil are you doing here?"

"Saving your neck, I hope. I do not have time to explain

fully, just listen to me. For God's sake, be extra careful what you say tonight."

"What do you mean?"

"I don't know what's going on, that's the problem. I only overheard part of a conversation, but it did involve your dinner. One or more of your guests intend to propose some financial project tonight. Please Rupert, avoid getting involved. No rash comments or flippant opinions on anything that is suggested. Pretend indifference, tiredness, anything which may prevent being drawn into a speculative mistake."

Lord Rupert tried to take it all in. "I had better get back..."

"No. Wait. I want to watch them for a moment."

Nothing untoward had happened in those brief minutes while Rupert had been absent from the company. No one seemed concerned, nervous or too confident, and none of them showed any indication that they were in league together. Instead all of them seemed greatly interested by the message which had interrupted their dinner. There was a merry banter about such a private communication from Richmond Lodge, although they were fully aware that they could not ask their host about it.

Robert had another suggestion for Rupert. "Later in the evening I want you to mention that you will be attending the court in the next few days, where you will be pleased to tell them about the wonderful guests who are enjoying your company this evening."

Perplexed by all these instructions, Rupert returned to the guests whilst Ellis and Robert continued to watch the assembly from their secret location. As they waited, Robert asked Ellis if Rupert had received any recent gifts - a tray, a box, anything that had the pretty inlay. Had there been any item of marquetry?

Ellis shook his head. He was sure nothing like that had arrived recently, and besides he himself always kept a detailed inventory of gifts, in case they had to be returned. Robert frowned deeper, wondering if one of the guests had brought something with them.

"I don't see how a piece of marquetry fits into any of this. It does not make sense," Robert confessed.

"Only if it was a box which held documents," Ellis suggested.

"Maybe it was too risky to bring or be left lying around for anyone to see."

Nevertheless the pair of them intended to search the outer reception rooms and supper room later.

Within a few minutes of seeing the last guest to the door, Rupert had rejoined them, grinning, proud of his performance and thanking Robert for his warning. As the three of them sat down, Robert explained all that he had heard, including the reference to this evening, but for all their combined thoughts, none of them could guess or imagine what had really been planned for tonight. There had certainly been no mention of finance or conspiratorial huddles anywhere. As Robert had hoped, Rupert's ramblings about visiting his distant royal relation had been enough to deter any attempted scheme.

"How well do you know any of them?" Robert enquired as he and the secretary studied the various cards left against the guest list.

Lord Rupert shrugged. They were all acquaintances he had met over the years and the informal dinner was simply one of the normal social events he put on now and again. He lived a pleasant life there and enjoyed an uncomplicated life in society. His family's exile and retirement to England decades before from Holland had left him with no desire to reclaim any estates or allegiance to his homeland. They could not believe anyone would misuse this hospitality; it was a shocking idea.

Though they were far from satisfied with their lack of evidence over Rupert's intended predicament, there was nothing else they could do. Worn out by their inconclusive theorising, Rupert eventually went to rest, while Robert and Ellis went to take a look for any unnoticed gift which might have magically appeared in their absence, before they did the same.

Robert was tired to the bone as he hauled himself back into the saddle the next morning and Lord Rupert was sombre at his going.

"However can I thank you? I disrupt your life continually," he admitted as they parted.

"That's nothing new," Robert joked.

Slowly Robert headed towards London, satisfied that at least Rupert's reputation was apparently no longer at risk. Rupert did not need his help, whereas the Haywards and their neighbours did.

CHAPTER THREE

Robert rode straight to London and his office, and the issue concerning the corn merchants' behaviour niggled him for the rest of the journey. He was hardly containing his annoyance by the time he reported the suspected fraud to his colleagues. They were as appalled as he had been, aware that no legitimate merchant would have had the audacity to commit such a deliberate act of exploiting their customers. It seemed a stupid thing to do, as when all monies had been paid, both the buying and the selling figures would be on record somewhere. The merchants would surely have realised they would eventually have been found out and would face serious questions. Nevertheless, the appropriate officers would certainly investigate fully.

Robert knew the procedure. The authenticity of Redick and Company would be checked out and officials would be sent to take statements from the community where this had taken place. The prices given to Haywards and their neighbours would be compared to other prices paid elsewhere. Enquiries would be made to see if the same thing had happened anywhere else in the country. Any unfair trading could result in arrest once the evidence was found, although Robert regretted it would still take time. It was late autumn already and he wondered how the families would manage until everything was put right. He hated to think they would struggle through the winter, for he was concerned for their welfare.

Much as Robert wanted to be involved in the background and push the investigation along, those in charge reassured him that the matter could safely be left in their capable hands. They promised to keep him informed as to progress on the matter. He had no choice except to leave it totally to them. He frowned as he left. He wanted things done quickly, but that was impossible. Frustratingly, he would have to wait for the results he wanted.

Robert liked to be kept busy, so when his employers proposed a special commission to add to the rest of his workload, he willingly accepted. The unusual assignment involved him in inspecting suitable properties for a junior minister. The minister in question would be leaving the government at some point and retiring from London life. He was interested in acquiring a suitable property in the country and Robert's task, while criss-crossing the southern counties, involved looking out for any establishment which would suit the man's specific requirements. Robert would be required to investigate if the owner would be likely to sell, evaluate the condition of the buildings and give his opinion on the value. It was an important, responsible and mammoth task, yet Robert had no doubts he could manage to fit it into his other schedules.

His next assigments took him through the countryside he knew best, across the North Downs in his home county of Kent. He had papers for Captain Ben at Dover instructing him to collect merchandise from France. Their brief exchange was as cordial as ever, and Robert had caught up with all the latest news from the continent and further afield before the seaman set off to put the ship in order.

The journey back through Kent allowed him to visit once again his oldest childhood friends, Samuel and Becky. With beaming smiles and enormous hugs welcoming his every arrival, he always felt at home there. None of them had changed that much; they might be older in years but otherwise they remained, totally at ease and relaxed with each other. They always found themselves reminiscing about the childhood they had all spent together and picking the hops and getting thoroughly dirty at Rebecca's grandparents place, near Faversham.

Robert always marvelled at the ongoing improvements both inside and outside their cottage. It changed all the time, because Samuel loved working with his hands. He had worked in London as an apprentice furniture and cabinet maker originally and now had his own small business in the centre of the village. He had never cultivated the more prestigious career offered in the city, because he wanted a proper, comfortable home with Becky.

Robert was constantly teased that he might have won Becky's hand if he had not been so dedicated to his work, which he knew was true; he had made his employment the most important thing in his life. But seeing these two together, Robert admitted he would never have made her as happy as she was with Samuel.

As they sat on the bench overlooking the rear garden and the village, finishing the last of the home-made beer, Robert mentioned his latest commission and asked Samuel about local properties. As he was in demand as a cabinetmaker to some of the grand mansions, he wondered if he had heard of any that might be coming up for sale. Samuel shook his head, explaining that very few ever came on the market. Most the old houses and estates had been in the same family for generations. It was doubtful that the owners would ever consider selling.

This task was obviously not going to be as easy as Robert had originally thought. So far he had found nothing. He had approximately five months to put together a short list for the minister to consider, after which he hoped he could hand over the responsibility to his lawyers to represent his client during the proposed transactions.

On reflection, Robert had been flattered by the request for his assistance, but he was aware that he was not doing very well. Surely some land agent would have been better suited to the project. He had never questioned his employer's instructions and had always done exactly what they had expected of him before, maybe he should actually query their decisions once and a while. Still, for now he would carry on the search for a property.

It was late November when Robert heard the good news he had waited for. The company of merchants involved in the corn fraud had been found and questioned. Redick and Company had claimed that they had been persuaded to cheat their customers by other people, although no one believed them. Their attempt to shift the blame elsewhere had failed.

Meanwhile notices of their unscrupulous behaviour had been posted in the guildhalls all over the area, for the public to read. Their licence to trade had naturally been withdrawn and official letters were sent to the Merchants Guild notifying them of the incident. The local Mayor, the Justice of the Peace and the Magistrate had also been advised of the crime.

More importantly the merchants had been made to reimburse all the people they had swindled. Their own goods and belongings had been confiscated and sold to pay what they owed. Yes, Robert smiled to himself, the Exchange had rectified the matter. Now he could stop worrying about the Haywards. And with any luck Margaret and Martha could soon return home. The family would be complete again for Christmas. That was good. That was a relief.

Winter had come and gone. Robert had not seen Lord Rupert for months, but he had heard via his office that the royal court and ministers alike had recognised the potential of Rupert's home. They considered it to be very suitable accommodation for any confidential visitors and dignitaries, much to Rupert's disgust. So far Lord Rupert had refused their suggestions. His home would remain his home and nothing else, he had argued.

Robert smirked broadly and decided that after completing his next few assignments he would enjoy visiting Rupert to hear his exact views. So after checking out the credentials of a visiting diplomat, arranging a shipment of cases from the docks and valuing another potential property for the minor minister, Robert found himself once more at Hurl Place.

Robert had never been able to shift that nagging uncertainty about the marquetry mentioned in connection with Hurl Place last year. Nothing further had ever come of the strange incident and everyone else concerned was satisfied that the matter was over and almost forgotten. Yet Robert had never voiced his concerns about the other two conspirators he had overheard at the tavern. Had they really given up, or would they try again at a later date?

Robert did not like to worry Rupert, but the beginning of any visit always started with the same question to Ellis about the marquetry, and Robert always received the same answer. Nothing had appeared, and similarly no specific rumours concerning any of Rupert's guests had reached their ears. Accordingly the two of them were still left wondering.

That topic was soon brushed aside once Rupert entered in a flourish of exaggerated gestures, because he could not wait to refer to the request he had recently received from certain ministers and his own royal relation. This was quickly followed by a complaint that he was far from pleased that Robert was responsible for this. Robert was astonished.

"This is your fault, Robert," said Rupert. "You are too good at your job. Having refused their initial requests, I am asked to play host to a visiting ambassador, because you have checked him out."

"Well what's wrong with that? You like entertaining. You have a great talent for being the perfect host. Your guests thoroughly enjoy being in your company. It would not hurt you to actually consider the proposal," Robert argued.

"What! I never expected you to support their ideas. How fair is that?"

"Rupert, have you ever thought you could be of some use to your cousin? This could be your opportunity to prove your worth. He allows you to stay here in England, in this fine home, out of kindness. How have you repaid him? By entertaining and pleasing yourself, all the time. How fair is that?"

Lord Rupert was shocked at his criticism; he had never been scolded so openly before. It made Ellis smile, because only Robert could have got away with being so honest. The subtle comments he had tried in the past had always failed.

"You are admired amongst your fellow peers, and there is no suggestion that this would compromise your ideals," said Robert. "Maybe you should have something worthwhile to do with your days."

"Worthwhile? I am hurt by your words, Robert. That I prefer the uncomplicated task of protecting my home is quite sufficient for me. Unlike you Robert, who has too many talents for you to settle down. What do you specialise in doing?"

"Helping you, normally," came Robert's calm quiet reply.

Not that he minded the occasional unexpected requests from his friend. He did not mind acquiring a special gift for a lady, or the discreet delivery of it. Such little adventures involving the return of a souvenir or a private letter were always entertaining.

Rupert huffed and puffed, a sure sign that his friend had made a point that he did not like. Despite the request coming from a highly impeccable source, Rupert insisted he would steer clear of anything even vaguely connected with politics.

"The problem is, you only prefer the hint of intrigue when it is associated with ladies of your acquaintance," Robert joked.

It had been some time since Robert had learnt that the matter concerning the Haywards and their neighbours had been officially settled satisfactorily. With Robert being in the area in March, he had no hesitation in riding over to find out how his former friends were faring these days. Without wishing to intrude into their day, he remained at the top of the hill by the battered oak tree at a discreet distance to satisfy himself all was well below. He was pleased to see that the farmhouse and outbuildings were in good repair, that the fields were fertile and even the small herd of cattle in the far pasture looked very healthy. Life looked to be running on its familiar pattern, although as he waited, watching the farmyard, he saw no sign of Margaret or Martha.

Suddenly he found himself being tugged to the ground, and childish giggles announced that he had been discovered. The boys were both exactly the same, excitable and full of energy and questions.

"I knew it was you," Matthew boasted.

"We saw you earlier," Mark added. "What are you doing here?"

"Just resting on my journey," Robert explained.

"Are you coming to the house?"

"No, not this time. I am on my way to Chichester."

They pulled faces at him, disappointed briefly, before rapidly launching into the whole history of what had happened over the last year.

"It all went wrong from the moment that horrid aunt came. We were pleased when she left," said Mark.

"Then there was trouble with the corn prices. No one knew what to do. It was awful. Then miraculously recently it was put right. We had com-pen-sation," Mathew finished, struggling with the last word.

"Father said we have a guardian angel looking after us."

"But everything is all right now? The farm looks as if is doing well," Robert enquired tactfully.

"I suppose so," Matthew answered thoughtfully.

Robert looked at them both, already wondering what was else could be wrong.

"Father is very quiet and thoughtful," said Mark.

"Are Margaret and Martha home now?"

"No, I wish they were. We all miss them."

The news that Margaret and Martha were still in service came as a surprise. He did not understand, but just as he was intending to try to quiz them a little more, they were summoned by their father's booming voice from the yard below. Robert let them run off, fully understanding their eagerness to report their meeting to their parents, besides it was simply a casual encounter, that was all it had been. No one would read any more into it.

Although Robert was pleased that the disreputable merchants had reimbursed the families, he sensed that something else might be bothering Mr Hayward. Had the farmer, an astute man, begun to think like himself, that there could be more to the recent events than first appeared? That these merchants had suddenly been tempted into such a fraud had never sat easily in Robert's mind. Had they been put up to it by someone else with the promise of being paid well for their trouble, as they had claimed soon after their arrest? But who would do that?

Fortunately the incident had not been bad enough to cripple anyone. No one had had to sell up, which ruled out his other wild idea, that there might have been some vague scheme to acquire land. On the surface it would seem that the attempt to defraud and make a profit was nothing more sinister than that.

Robert's days were certainly hectic as he continued his complicated and varied employment for the various departments which combined together in the government agency. Whilst the operatives tactfully referred to their employers as the 'Company', the official title in London was the 'Exchange'. The beginning of April had seen him making checks on the business practices of companies who had submitted quotes to the Exchange. Hence the reason for other clothes he always carried in order to remain inconspicuous in his discreet enquiries into all aspects of their enterprises. Robert was a master of blending in with whichever set circumstances he found himself dealing with, including the less savoury side of human existence.

Eventually Robert returned to London and took the chance to study the relevant documents in the corn case personally. He was not quite satisfied with this yet. He intended to question the merchants, Redick and Company, to find out more about the others they had claimed were involved. With no one being found with the names they had been given, everyone had assumed their whole story was fictitious. It was understandable that they had not been believed, but Robert could not help wondering if they were also victims in this. Robert could not help being suspicious.

After losing their livelihoods and their reputation, Robert would not have been surprised to find that they disappeared completely, gone to ground or changed their names. In fact Robert had no trouble in finding his quarry. A casual remark to the clerk when he handed the papers back had the man relay their present whereabouts. Apparently, after having paid the deficit money, the compensation to the farmers, the heavy fines imposed by the Merchants' Guild and the court's fines and costs, they had had nothing left. Destitute, they were both in a debtors' prison.

Now Robert was convinced these new merchants would not have defrauded the farmers on their own initiative, unless they had been sure they had financial support from somewhere.

And so a few days later Robert presented himself at the prison gates, having already made an appointment and gained permission to interview the men. There in the room allocated for his purpose, he showed them the official documents which indicated his authority in the matter.

"Good afternoon, gentlemen," he began in a friendly manner. "I wish to speak to you about your recent misdemeanour concerning corn prices."

The men looked tired and perplexed; they had already paid for their crime. They were still paying for it. They sat dejected, as they had already answered all the questions imaginable. There was little else they could say. It was time to come to the point, rather than bewilder them any more.

"I have a few queries. I am more interested in what you claimed after you were arrested."

The merchants exchanged a glance, a desperate hopeful glance that someone was willing to believe them at last.

"You stated that some other party was behind this."

"Yes, yes, yes," They both answered together. "The authorities did not believe us," added one of them. "I don't think they even made much effort to look for them."

Robert could not help asking how on earth they had been persuaded to do anything so foolish. They explained that they had been struggling to build up their business. With surplus produce, they had lost money. They were desperate. Someone must have known they were in difficulties to promise to reward them handsomely if they could obtain the corn cheaply.

"They wanted the corn, to sell on? They had a market ready?" Robert queried.

"No. They were not interested in the corn at all. In fact they disappeared completely once we had bought the corn."

From a simple case of a little fraud, they discovered they had been set up. And no one believed them. They shook their heads, not knowing exactly what else to say. It appeared quite foolish to admit how gullible they had been. Their main concern had been simply been for the chance to recoup their losses.

"Why did they suggest you went to that area?"

They shrugged. They did not know.

Robert half closed his eyes. He could not fathom this at all. He had already discounted his earlier theory about the land itself being the key. Besides, there was nothing special about the land; it was ordinary farmland, the soil adequate but nothing else. It was some distance from any commercial centre. It had no specific advantage.

"They said they were connected to a firm of financial advisers in Surrey. It was Ash and Hawks," said the second man.

Robert did not believe for a minute that these men were financial advisers. And whoever they were, he doubted Ash and Hawks were their real names either. Any firm willing to commit a felony or pay others to do so would use false names to protect themselves.

They had been shown phony documents as proof of identity, so they had nothing in writing to prove their story, said the men.

"Swindlers can be very clever when it comes to preserving their own immunity," Robert acknowledged.

"Is there any chance they could be found?"

"I doubt it. Not after all this time."

Even if they were located, these elusive fraudsters would insist they were innocent and that the merchants were lying to protect themselves. There was no point in giving these two false hope, because, tragic as it was, these men were to stay here. They were lucky they had not been transported to the colonies. Many other minor crimes had seen the unfair results of such punishment.

Robert left them to their plight, acknowledging that if it had not been these two men some other poor struggling concern would have been found to commit the same crime. Robert did not understand why 'Ash and Hawks' would be so interested in an area which had nothing to do with them. He concluded that they themselves were acting for and being paid by someone else. There were new villains in the frame, although Robert was shrewd enough to accept that tracing them would be impossible.

Everything indicated a conspiracy, and quite a complicated one. But why? It made his head ache. Nothing made sense. This situation was getting worse with every new discovery.

What could he do? Common sense told him the impossibility of resolving this to his satisfaction, but he hated not being able to solve problems, especially those he felt personally involved in. Annoyed at being unable to get any further, he tried to put it to the back of his over-active mind, but it was difficult.

He resumed his travels for the London office the next day, attempting to put his full concentration back into his work. Keeping busy was the answer. This month he was responsible for providing reports for contracts and licences, but the niggling doubts and unanswered questions refused to go away.

It was Thomas the blacksmith's casual remark on Robert's next visit there that stirred it all up again.

"I can't believe how the time has flown," he said. "Do you realise it's a year since your accident? And here you are back in your routine as if nothing had happened. Have you seen much of the Haywards?"

Robert reported the tale of their misfortune with the corn prices and the restoration of their finances after the arrest of the merchants, but little else of his other, darker concerns.

"That's good to hear. I like a happy ending," Thomas concluded.

Happy ending? If only! It might seem like that to Thomas, but it did not feel like a happy ending to Robert when the two girls were still away from home. He had no idea of how long their periods of contract would last. And remembering the changes in Margaret the last time he had seen her, he dreaded the effect her continued absence from home would be having on her. No doubt it was the same for the shy Martha. He wished it had been different. He might have no idea where to find Martha, but he certainly knew how he could find out how Margaret was faring. He would be visiting Sir Eustace shortly, to check that he was satisfied with his acquisition of horses from last year. It would be easy enough during their casual conversation to find out exactly where his sister-in-law lived.

Armed with the information that Sir Eustace's sister, Mrs

Taylor, and her staff had rented a place in Surrey whilst her own house was under repair, Robert duly arrived at the front of the house. Here he tethered his horse to a tree and settled down on the stone bridge opposite the gates, to wait for the opportunity to speak with Margaret on her own.

Carts passed him by and people trudged the track, some acknowledging him with a mere grunt as they went on their way. He felt sorry for Margaret. Should he have come? Then, before he could change his mind, she appeared around the corner of the lane carrying a small parcel. He had never seen her look so thin and so lethargic. It stopped him in his tracks as he was about to speak.

"Why, Robert. You appear in the most unusual places," she commented quietly.

"Since when do you call me Robert?" he scolded jokingly, remembering her similar words the last time they had met. Instantly he wished he had never spoken so carelessly, for her jaw dropped and her eyes lowered to avoid his. He stepped forward to reassure her, but she jumped back away from him.

"I am sorry. I didn't mean to upset – I was teasing."

"What are you doing here, Robert Sutton?" came her tired voice.

"I happened to be in the area. I heard Mrs Taylor had taken temporary residence here. I wondered if you were still in service."

"Well now you know." She gathered her parcel tighter to her and made to go.

"Wait!" Robert pleaded, reaching out to stop her. She flinched again to avoid his touch, which hurt him.

"I waited here to see how you were," Robert confessed.

"Why? What does it matter to you?" she snapped, now glaring at him.

"I thought we were friends or at least good acquaintances."

"Did you? Well I would never know whom I was talking to, would I? You who have the freedom to be anything you want to be. Are you here as labourer or as a gentleman this time, I wonder?

"I must fit in to work wherever I can," came his perfectly plausible excuse.

"Evasive as ever. Whichever it is, I find you displaying the same light-hearted and carefree attitude as you do in your conversation with certain other ladies of quality."

"What other ladies?" came his automatic response, despite knowing immediately to whom she referred to.

"The Lady Arabella."

Damn it! So not only had she seen him with Lady Arabella that day, but she had been astute enough to find out the name of his acquaintance. No doubt Mrs Taylor had pointed her out at some point during their travels. He could not help wondering what else she knew about him and what other false impressions she might have formed.

"No doubt you were also on good terms with the Marquis Tree as well," she sneered sarcastically.

"Who?" Robert genuinely had no idea, but he was astonished by her next revelation.

"Why surely *you* know! He is Lady Arabella's cousin and the owner of the mansion on the hill."

"I do not move in such exalted circles," he said, laughing. He could only try to bluff it out. She raised one eyebrow sceptically and shook her head at him. Clearly she didn't believe him, but she did not have the energy to argue. She shrugged, and then she was gone. He had never known exactly what she thought of him before, but it was obvious from her attitude today that she did not like him much, having assumed the worst of him because of his over-gracious manner towards Arabella.

He decided to return the next day, in the hope of getting the chance to talk to her again. He wanted to make it better between them. He did not want to leave on awkward terms. If necessary, he would wait there all day. Yet as the morning passed without any sight of Margaret, he began to rethink his plan. Surely she would have further errands which would bring her outside again. Or maybe not. He sighed.

The day was hot and the water rippling beneath the bridge was inviting. He slid down the slope and scooped clear water into his cupped hands, allowing it to cascade over his head as he stood in the steam.

"I did not want to see you here," came her voice from the river bank.

Her words were softer than yesterday, her whole demeanour more resigned; there was no anger, no resentment. He flexed his tired muscles and dragged himself up the bank, and this time she did not cower away.

"Why not?"

She did not reply immediately, yet as they stood simply looking at each other, he sensed the sadness in her silence. She was utterly miserable being here. In her heart she was longing to go home, and her next words hid nothing from him.

"Because the sight of you torments me. You have the freedom to go anywhere whenever you please, while I am bound by the restrictions of being in service. I have no choice except to do as I am bid every day," she gulped.

"Oh Margaret!"

"You always remind me of home. Robert, please go. You are making it worse." Then, with the swish of her skirts in the grass, she was gone.

He let her go, feeling depressed and inadequate. He had only made her feel more wretched. This had not been one of his better ideas.

Robert had collected an exquisite green and gold trinket box for Lord Rupert on his way through Guildford and was showing it off to the others in the office before going on to Hurl Place. It was so pretty that it had to be another intended present for a lady, they all agreed. Robert could not keep up with Rupert's romantic dalliances; no doubt he would find out soon enough.

A few of the officers went on to discuss the latest news in London over the past months and bring Robert up to date with the details. A new company, the Pavilion Trading Company, had been set up, the city had become excited and individuals had eagerly invested expecting to grow rich quickly. As expected the demand for shares rose, but the lack of sound financial funding and the company's own vulnerability soon became apparent. Just like the South Sea Bubble of 1721, investors panicked, prices tumbled and the company collapsed. The failed venture had left men ruined, whilst those responsible for establishing the scheme had vanished, presumably having fled the country. Those in the Exchange were relieved that none of their own clients had become victims.

Lord Rupert was delighted to see Robert and the beautiful little box he delivered, but Robert was in a playful mood. As Rupert went to pick it up, Robert withdrew it swiftly from the table, to deliberately torment him by passing from hand to hand, unwilling to let Rupert take it.

"Am I to know who it is for?" he teased.

"No, you do not," Rupert sulked.

"You don't normally keep secrets from me."

Rupert huffed and puffed and walked the room, shaking his head. Then Ellis entered to check over the wine order for a forthcoming gala dinner. Robert's eyes gleamed wickedly as he wondered if the guest list would include this object of his latest affections. Was this merely another of Rupert's romantic dalliances, or had he sensed that this time it might be different?

When Rupert returned, he gave Robert one of his blank-faced, no-nonsense glares and calmly held his hand out for the box. Robert had his answer; this was a very different matter. With the faintest of smiles, he handed over the gift without another word.

Robert felt like being mischievous and enquiring if he was inviting Lady Arabella to the event, but remembering what Margaret had said, he changed the topic completely. To satisfy his own curiosity, he asked both of them if they knew anything about Arabella's cousin. Neither of them had any idea as whom he meant; they had not even realised there was a cousin. Rupert asked him to repeat the title Margaret had mentioned slowly to make sure.

"The Marquis Tree," said Ellis.

Robert suddenly felt a cold chill up his back as the words he had just spoken sank in.

"Oh, my God," he exclaimed loudly, his face frozen in shock. All this time they had wasted in trying to associate a gift with that evening!

"What?" Rupert said, anxiously looking around as if expecting to see something awful.

"It wasn't 'marquetry', it was the Marquis Tree," Robert explained. "I misheard. There was no inlay box, there was no gift. It did not exist. It was a person. It was the Marquis Tree who had come here that night."

"I do not know a Marquis Tree," stated a puzzled Lord Robert.

"You forget surnames are different from their titles, so the Marquis would be known by another name," Ellis explained.

All three of them looked at each other.

"Where is the list of guests from that night again?" Robert demanded. Were they about to solve part of the puzzle?

The papers were soon found, and they hastily read and re-

read the names. But there was no Marquis Tree on the list; the title had not even been added against another name.

"This country of yours is full of dukes, earls, baron, baronets and viscounts. You have such a vast extravagance of peers," bemoaned Rupert, disappointed that they had failed, after expecting so much.

"There may be another difficulty. It could be that the man has never used his title at all."

"How do we find out?" Rupert sighed.

"With a little patience," Ellis counselled.

"Patience is not something I have much of," Rupert admitted.

"We all know that," Robert and Ellis both said at the same time.

Robert was reading the list over and over again, as the connection to the failed Pavilion Trading Company struck home. Robert gulped. Had that been what was intended that night, to somehow imply that this new company had Rupert's blessing, to encourage wealthy investors? He closed his eyes and silently thanked God that that had been avoided.

"What are you thinking?" Rupert interrupted.

Robert paused to allow himself time to think properly.

"Well - we don't know what was really intended that night. And since nothing came of it, do we actually need to worry any more?"

Ellis gave him a curious glance, confused by this sudden lack of interest.

"All we know is that this Marquis Tree and an unknown associate came to your dinner. What if they had second thoughts and abandoned their whole scheme? Whatever it was might have come to nothing. In which case we will never discover what they were involved in."

"Robert, for someone who rode the width of the county to

warn me, I would have thought you would have been as determined as myself to find out who they were."

"I am. But how important is it really, if the threat was not as serious as we supposed?"

"Serious or not, I do not like the idea that people think they can use my hospitality for their own ends. For my own satisfaction I would like to have words with them," said Rupert.

Robert gave Ellis a look and shook his head, indicating that this was not a good idea. Ellis understood the message.

"I will have to find out who this Marquis Tree is, I think," Lord Rupert continued firmly.

"Rupert, even if you discover his other name, you are not exactly subtle when it comes to dealing with people who have upset you. I would prefer it if you let Ellis and me deal with it in our own time. I still think it was just an unlucky chance that your invitation coincided with some opportunity of promoting a deal. It could have happened at any time, at someone else's dinner."

"Why should any of my acquaintances be in need of making deals? How ridiculous!" Rupert scoffed.

Robert and Ellis exchanged another sceptical glance.

Somehow they managed to change the conversation around to the gala dinner again. This left a much happier Lord Rupert sitting in his favourite chair, delightfully contemplating the next forthcoming function whilst holding the pretty green and gold trinket box tenderly in his hands.

In another private room much later, where it was quieter, Robert took Ellis aside to confide all he had heard concerning the financial scandal reported in the city recently. Ellis now became equally worried that the financial fiasco might be connected to this Marquis person. If it was, he dreaded Lord Rupert's reaction. An incensed Lord Rupert would be particularly hard to handle. Heaven help them.

"I dare not let Rupert suspect that there could be any connection between the two," he said to Ellis

"But you think it is a possibility?"

"The longer I pondered it, the more I believed so," Robert admitted regretfully.

They had to find out this Marquis's other name. There was one obvious answer - to ask Lady Arabella, his cousin - but neither Robert or Ellis were keen to air such a suggestion. It would be exceptionally difficult and awkward to approach her or ask her any questions without the whole of society becoming interested. They just hoped that Lord Rupert would not think of it either. The only other way to find out was see if any name on Rupert's guest list also appeared on papers connected to the Pavilion Trading Company. Normally the names of those who had set up and instigated the venture would be printed amongst the headings on the first page of the documents. It was up to Robert to see if he could approach the Treasury to view the seized articles, while Ellis would try everything he could to prevent Rupert from hearing about the failed business scandal.

The next day Robert returned to his employer to collect the details of his next assignment, and while he was there he mentioned his curiosity about the disreputable trading company's failure. Everyone was quite open about expressing their views and those assigned to the Treasury had no qualms about sharing any details between governmental departments. Besides, there was nothing that secret about the matter, since the whole scandal of the recent disaster had become public knowledge. Thus Robert found himself allowed to read through the papers at his leisure, and with no one looking over his shoulder.

He had taken a copy of Rupert's dinner list with him and soon began the unenviable task of comparing one list of people against the other. As he studied them carefully and methodically, he realised that in essence he should be looking for two people. When the Marquis attended the Hurl Place dinner, he would have needed at least one other accomplice to attempt the necessary conversation. He would not have come to the dinner alone.

As it turned out, the only name on both lists was someone called Phillip Brimley. He had to be the person they were looking for. Nervously Robert double checked. He tried to find a second name on both lists, but there were no others which matched. There was no way to discover who else was involved. So he was left with one important question. Where was the proof that this Brimley was also the Marquis Tree?

Tentatively he broached the question to the other official clerks who dealt with these confidential aspects. Since he was a fellow government official they had no reluctance in showing him the various peerage listings, together with genealogy and biographical dictionaries, which confirmed that Phillip Brimley was definitely the Marquis Tree.

Robert pondered the next step. Now he had the information, what should he do with it? Inform Ellis of course, so that he could do his best to keep the information from Lord Rupert, but little else. Something which looked entirely possible by the rest of their disclosure. His spirits were further lifted on being informed that the Marquis Tree, who never had his title bandied about, because of the bad reputation associated with his father, had disappeared, apparently overseas. There was no trace of him. Desperate to raise money as the company foundered, Brimley had quit his lands and property and sold what he could in a rush to buy a passage abroad. His home,

Stour Park, was now empty of every stick of furniture and furnishings and was in the hands of the official receivers.

A relaxed Robert rode off to Kent on his next round of duties. He would let Ellis know his findings on the way back; there was no panic. Logically, Robert had thankfully assumed that Brimley's unknown accomplice at the dinner and the other two participants at the inn would also have fled the country.

He smiled to himself. Lord Rupert could remain in blissful ignorance. Thank goodness for that.

CHAPTER FOUR

Throughout June, Robert dragged himself around various large country houses and period mansions in between his other tasks. He had been given a specific brief to fulfil, and he was determined not to settle for anything other than what he felt would be absolutely right for his client. So far he had not been satisfied, although he had several more appointments lined up with land agents and property owners. Most of all he was looking forward to seeing one of the two on his remaining list, because it took him to the part of the county where Mrs Taylor was still in residence.

It was not she or Margaret or the property on his list which interested him on this occasion. No, it was more his keenness to visit the location. It was the house on the hill, the one which Margaret had so kindly mentioned, which was important. Known as Stour Park, it was Phillip Brimley's deserted home.

The house had been cleared of all furniture and other articles by Treasury officials. As yet the authorities had not decided about its future, although it would eventually be sold. At the moment it stood empty and uncared for, which gave Robert the perfect opportunity to search the building.

How diligent had the authorities been? Had they missed anything? Were there any relevant papers still there? It wouldn't hurt to make sure there were no documents hidden somewhere mentioning Hurl Place or making use of Rupert's name. Not that this was his only concern. If Brimley had left in a rush, if he had been careless, there just might be something to identify his companions and co-conspirators. Just what might he find at Stour Park?

Robert had no qualms about breaking in. Technically he was breaking the law, but who would know? With the house empty, it would be easy enough. He smirked to himself. So much for the exemplary record the Exchange expected of him. They really did not know him as well as they thought. He particularly enjoyed the cloak and dagger aspect of his work, but they would never have believed him capable of deliberately doing anything criminal. He knew they would not have approved of his actions, but then he was never going to tell them what he was about to do, was he?

Arriving in the early dawn, he slipped around the boundary of the lower house where Mrs Taylor and staff were still staying and made off in a wide loop over the fields to reach the house on the hill. The splendid period mansion and its outlying structures looked devoid of life as he cautiously approached the rear quadrangle. There was always the possibility that the Crown might have installed a caretaker to protect the site, so he was particularly keen to see if anyone was around.

"Hello?" He called out, announcing his arrival. He was

ready with the excuse of looking for employment, in case someone appeared, but there was no answer. He called out again, just in case someone was slow to show themselves. No one did, and Robert felt himself relax. There was no need to rush. He could take his time and be methodical.

He poked around the exterior for a while, checking around the outbuildings. The stables were empty and the coach house too; not a cart, bucket or harness had been left here. The reports were correct. Even the contents of these outbuildings had been confiscated and removed by the authorities.

As he turned his attention towards the main house, he heard the unexpected sound of voices approaching along the driveway. He had no idea who was coming, but he did not want to be discovered. He darted into the nearest empty building and hauled himself up into the meagre loft space. Keeping in the shadows, he risked peeking out through the gaps in the planking.

A small band of people ambled through the archway, casually making their way towards the former kitchen garden area. He could not imagine who they were or what they were after, although they had brought spades, barrows and handcarts with them. They did not even bother to look into any of the outbuildings, and as they passed below Robert caught the odd smattering of their disgruntled chatter. They turned out to be former employees left unpaid and locals who were owed money. They had got together and were now determined to plunder the walled kitchen garden, to dig up all they could to sell at the village market. Robert could only remain in his hiding place, while they were in no particular hurry to complete their task or leave.

Eventually, after what seemed ages, they had collected their spoils and left, happily pushing the loaded produce over the stony track. But still Robert waited before moving. He did not want any other unwanted visitors turning up. Only when he was sure that he was totally alone did he make his move towards the kitchen area, considering this his best point of entry. There, try as he might by wiggling the small knife he had between the casements, he was unable to slip the catches of any of the windows. He had seen others make it look easy, but for him it was not. He was useless. He would never be any good as a burglar, he admitted. He scowled and stared at the building.

He had already wasted too much time because of the delay caused by the recent scavengers. What should he do? The scullery door rattled loosely when he tried it, and rather than waste time on attempting to pick the locks, another talent he knew he did not possess, he had no option except to kick the door in. The splintering sound as the lock snapped in its frame echoed in the empty yard, making him pause briefly. Then he was inside, pushing the door back into place and jamming it closed at the base with a piece of the broken wood.

The once splendid house was reduced to a shadow of its previous existence, the emptiness and silence giving an eerie feeling as he crept around the interior. The floorboards creaked with almost every step as he went from room to room. Without any furniture, chests or bureaux inside, there would be few places to house any relevant papers. He nervously checked the walls for any sign of hidden panels or priest holes, but for all his tapping and knocking, there was nothing there. Even the grates were empty of any burnt papers.

That only left the attic. Forcing up the trap door to the attic, he encountered a face full of thick, dusty cobwebs, forcing him to wave his arms about frantically to brush them out of his eyes.

He glanced about, slowly adjusting his eyes to the low light. There was nothing up here, absolutely nothing; no boxes, no blankets or old furnishings. The loft was completely bare, and there were not even any tell-tale footmarks on the dirty floor. No one had been up here for years.

Slamming the hatch shut as he descended, he was showered with more dirt and bits, on his shoulders and in his hair. After shaking the worst off, he retraced his way back through the house, pausing again in every room, aware he could not afford to miss any clue. This might be his only chance to investigate.

Even the library had been emptied of books. The mass of empty shelves looked strange, although one solitary volume had been left to lie on its side in a corner. Obviously the book had been considered totally unimportant to the owner and the authorities alike.

Curious to find what it might be, he reached up and pulled it down. Bigger and heavier than it first appeared, it landed at his feet with a thump, the crumpled dog-eared pages opening into a fan shape. It was a family bible.

Closing it to put it back, he stopped and took a quick glance at the names recorded on the inner flyleaf, below the family coat of arms. Phillip Brimley was indeed the Marquis Tree. All the Brimleys were listed, including Phillip's father and Arabella's mother, who were brother and sister. What a shame that no one thought enough of it to pass it on to the next of kin. Although Robert disliked Arabella, he felt a little sad that this had been left abandoned here. It should have been sent to her. It was a family heirloom, something to be treasured, but he could not very well tell her about it himself without disclosing that he had been here.

Robert noticed that the stiff endpapers normally glued to the back of the embossed front cover had come unstuck over time and the edges were worn and tattered. It would be the perfect place to hide anything secret, his suspicious mind acknowledged. He peeled one edge back slightly, to discover there was quite a gap inside.

The hairs on Robert's neck bristled. Holding his breath, he carefully forced the gap wider to see a small piece of paper inside. He prised it out. It proved to be a blank corner torn from the rest of the page, which must have been removed in a rush. It was thicker than normal paper, almost like the stiff parchment used for official documents. Turning it to the light, he scrutinized it on both sides, but there was no watermark or any indication of what it might belong to. It could have been anything, but it had been important enough to hide and then remove. What was it?

His mind churned. Could it be connected to the plan to have Hurl Place connected to financial venture? Why couldn't he let go of that theory? Why did it haunt him? Because he knew the worst of men.

Quickly he inspected the back of the book for a similar compartment, finding another gap between the endpapers and the back cover, but he found nothing inside this time.

Well - he had done his best. Dusty and dirty from poking about, he sighed with relief, content that for all his efforts he had found nothing. There was no evidence of any kind here, which meant that there was nothing for him to worry about. Which was a blessing.

Replacing the book where he had found it, he left the house, again securing the scullery door by wedging the top and bottom with slivers of wood. Satisfied that the broken lock didn't appear too obvious, he gave it one more glance before making his way back to the seclusion of the barn. His plan was to wait there until much later; he intended to reach the village and collect his horse in the dusk to avoid anyone taking much notice of his dishevelled appearance. Most people would be heading indoors to settling down for the evening, which would allow him to leave the area unnoticed.

Robert hadn't taken but a few steps across the yard when fireworks went off in his head. A burst of colours scattered his vision, and then came only darkness.

When he eventually stirred, his head was ringing. Without opening his eyes, he felt the sensation of being in a crumpled heap. Nothing wanted to move. His limbs were limp, but he found himself being shaken gently. He barely opened one eye, to see who was disturbing him. It was Margaret. Smiling, he closed his eyes again to let the comforting illusion continue.

"Robert, please wake up!" the soft voice pleaded. "I'm sorry, I didn't know it was you. Robert!" This time the voice was louder in his ear.

It really was Margaret. She was actually there, holding his hand, squeezing it, rocking back and forth on her knees beside him. He did not understand what was going on, but as he tried to sit up, intending to rest his back against the wall he discovered he couldn't. The pain in his back was crippling, his neck and shoulders ached and when he leaned on his arm for support, it collapsed. He had always ignored the occasional weakness in his elbow since the accident, but this time he could not.

"What – you - here?" he mumbled, his mouth unwilling to work.

"Ssh. Don't talk. You hit your head when you fell. It's bleeding."

He flinched as she dabbed a wet cloth to his head. Falling? He didn't remember falling.

"Keep still."

"I can't lie here forever."

Margaret instinctively tried to prop him up, but he quickly stopped her, warning her that he was too heavy and it would be better if she left it for him to do in his own good time.

"Let me get help," she said.

"No! It is not necessary." He must not let anyone else know he had been here.

"But…"

"Margaret, please!"

He gripped her hand a little too tight, and she bit her lip.

"Just let me get my breath," he murmured.

"I didn't mean to hit you so hard."

"You did this?" he was shocked, wondering what she had used to floor him so easily.

"I hit you with the broken wooden paddle lying outside the laundry," she confessed, before going back to the pump in the yard to soak her handkerchief again.

Heavens, she must have put all her strength in that blow, he thought, wincing again.

"I thought you were a vagrant. What were you doing here? You weren't going to steal anything were you? You aren't in such difficulty that you would do such a thing?"

He shook his head. He could hardly tell her that there was nothing left to steal anyway without incriminating himself. This was going to be awkward. He could only lie.

"I hoped to find temporary work. Assisting a caretaker. The place could certainly do with extra help, judging by the gang of plunderers I saw on my way here."

"There is no caretaker," she told him.

He shrugged. "Then I wasted my journey."

He asked her why she had come there, to be told that she had merely wanted to look at the place before the household returned to Balcombe tomorrow.

"We have an early start in the morning." She paused. "There, the bleeding has stopped."

The cold water was working wonders, and having begun to regain his wits, Robert could not lose the opportunity to question this reliable source. Margaret had provided a vital clue before. Had she seen anything else useful? Could she unwittingly know more?

"Is this where you saw Arabella and the Marquis Tree?" Robert asked.

"No. Mrs Taylor pointed her out earlier in the year, she was in a carriage with her cousin at Arundel." She had obviously misunderstood his reason for asking. "Were you hoping she would be here?" Margaret challenged as she sat back from him, glaring.

Robert had not expected her to think that. This could go horribly wrong.

"God no. Of course not."

"Just as well, no one would look twice at you, looking like this," she told him.

He waited for her next comment, but the expected confrontation never materialised. Instead he found himself sitting there in silence, smiling weakly at her, glad of the chance to keep still and rest his bones for a long as he could.

Then he saw her shoulders sag and her hands drop into her lap. She hung her head, unable to look him in the face any longer.

He did not understand. "What is the matter?" he asked, puzzled.

His softer words acted as a catalyst to the emotion she struggled with. Her frame trembled as she fought to get her words together. Then she could not help herself; she had to tell him, and it all came bursting out.

"That night at Sir Eustace's after first seeing you again, I hated the way you made me think of home. I had managed to put up with my circumstances until you appeared. And every time after that, when you came suddenly from nowhere, all I wanted was to go home."

Suddenly she was sobbing his arms, there for the world to see. It was the first time he had ever held her or had her whole body pressed into his chest. She was desperate for some comfort. He wrapped his arms around her, gently at first and then gradually tighter, despite the pain it caused him.

"I have never been so miserable," she sobbed. "All alone in my room and very late, I often cry myself to sleep. I hate the restrictions I am forced to obey. I want the freedom of being myself again. I want to go home, but I know I cannot."

Poor Margaret, he knew how she loved her home, their land, just as he loved his own. He shook his head and sighed. He knew that longing too well. At times it could eat away at you. How often had he paused on the last part of his journey home to look over the familiar views. His own affection and sense of belonging had never dwindled. How his heart went out to her! He did not know what else he could do except hold her.

Slowly she recovered from her tears and pulled herself from him, to sit staring at the ground.

"I'm sorry. I did not mean to get so emotional."

"I'm sorry I cause you such upset. I wish I could help," was all he could offer, taking her hand in his. Neither of them knew exactly the right thing to say.

"I'd better go," she sighed, standing up and letting her hand slip from his.

"So must I," he added, preparing to push himself up.

"Can you stand? Can you walk?"

"It's only a couple of miles to the village. I'll be fine," he reassured her.

Gritting his teeth, he knew he was looking pale as he forced himself to move to prove it. There was no way he would let her know how bad he felt, for she would be devastated to know how much she had injured him.

He hauled himself into an upright stance and leaned against the wall to catch his breath. It was enough to convince her, and returning his weak smile, she slowly walked off, kicking the dirt as she went, once more reconciled to her present existence. A sight which made Robert sad. What could he do?

Brushing himself down as best he could, he began his return

journey, knowing it would be advisable to make the same wide detour as he had done on his way there. Yet the few miles to the village seemed more like ten. He felt awful, every jarring step sending pain into his back. His arm ached and his head felt so dizzy that it was a wonder he stayed on his feet. He could not walk far without having to stop to recover before pushing himself on again.

When he reached the main road, his back was screaming at him and he slid to the ground to rest against a tree. If he just closed his eyes for a while…

"Mr Sutton. It is Mr Sutton? Whatever is wrong?" a woman's voice asked.

He opened his eyes to see a carriage had stopped in the road in front of him and an older, well-dressed lady of some quality had descended to speak to him.

"You are in a terrible state. I cannot leave you here like this. Edwards, John, help him into the carriage."

"No no, there is no need," Robert hastily protested. But before he could argue the point further, two footmen had descended and lifted him off the ground. He groaned loudly.

"Careful," the woman instructed.

"This is very kind of you. Is it possible you could take me to the village? My horse is stabled there."

"Nonsense, I will not hear of it. You are in pain. You must come to the house and rest."

He was gently lowered into the plush carriage, where Robert looked at her, wondering at her obvious recognition of him. As if realising his uncertainty, she explained.

"I am Mrs Taylor, Mr Sutton. Sir Eustace's sister. He has pointed you out on several occasions."

Damn, this was Margaret's employer, and he was being taken back to the very house where she was in service. What would she think? What would she say when she saw him openly sharing the carriage with her mistress? He was supposed to be out of work, and here he was conversing on equal terms with Mrs Taylor.

"I am pleased to be of any assistance Mr Sutton, when my brother holds you in such high regard," she whispered, bending closer so that no one else could hear her words.

"Yes I have heard of you, Mrs Taylor, from your brother. I visited him recently."

There was no point in not mentioning it; it might come up in future conversation between brother and sister.

"I feel I should offer some explanation for my present condition," he said.

"It is not necessary. I am aware of your special status in certain places," she continued quietly. "I may be curious, but I will not ask any questions of you."

"It would be bad manners of me not to confide a little of why I am in the area," he replied. "I have been looking at a property for a client and for that reason I was remaining incognito. When I heard the place on the hill was empty, I decided to take a private look, but a rabbit hole prevented that. I twisted my back as I fell, which is where you found me." However discreet Mrs Taylor might be, there was no need for her to know everything. Although she was a relation of Sir Eustace, a man he respected, he meant to make light of his journey here. He really did not want to excite too much curiosity.

"I do believe I have hurt my back more than I had thought," he said. "I would be grateful for somewhere to rest tonight, Mrs Taylor. I do not want to inconvenience you. A bale of straw in a barn would be sufficient."

"Sleep on a bale of straw? Of course not! Out of the question. The house may be in some disorder as we are packing up ready to leave in the morning, but you will have a good meal and a proper bed. I will see if Edward can find any liniment to ease your back."

As they entered the driveway, Robert desperately looked out for Margaret. Then there she was, stopping in her tracks, just as he expected, wide-eyed and open-mouthed at the sight of him in the company of her mistress. Keeping his eyes fixed on hers, he shook his head slightly, hoping she understood. He could not afford for her to expose their earlier encounter. Unnoticed by Mrs Taylor, she nodded and turned back to complete her duties. His instinct told him that somehow she would find a way to speak to him alone much later when there was no one else about.

Washed, refreshed and a deal more presentable, Robert was housed in a small room on the first floor. Although he was settled into a good bed, he remained awake, waiting for his visitor. Not that the pain in his back would let him sleep in any case.

It was very late when the door opened and closed softly, and her footsteps on tiptoe rushed to his side. She bent over him.

"Robert! Robert! Why has Mrs Taylor taken you in?" she whispered anxiously.

"It was a strange coincidence. She happened by in her coach. She recognised me as being acquainted with her brother Sir Eustace. You remember I called at his home about a horse deal." He hoped his words would satisfy her.

"Yes, but…"

"Presuming I was still employed in a similar status, she offered me a bed for the night and refused to take no for an answer, despite the fact that I looked the worse for wear. To be honest I was struggling by then. I did need to rest up properly."

"Oh Robert. You said you were all right," she gushed.

"Margaret, I will be. I'm going to be fine."

"You said that before."

"Listen, I mean it. I have come through worse, haven't I?"

He tried to joke, but in the darkness he could not see if she appreciated his efforts. She did not answer, but she remained sitting by his side.

Robert had yet to find a way to make her keep his visit to Stour Park a secret. He had to choose his words carefully.

"Margaret, I would hate Mrs Taylor or Sir Eustace to know I am between jobs. Although temporary, my present situation may give them a poor opinion of me. An opinion I may be glad of, if I am to stand the chance of finding a better post. Please do not tell anyone of our meeting at the Brimley house this afternoon. Please keep my being there a secret, promise?"

"Of course, if it means that much. Not that I am likely to converse with the gentry about anything, the way you do."

He squeezed her hand in thanks, wanting to say more, but he did not. She pulled her shawl closer around her and shivered slightly. She was getting cold and he knew it was time she left. She sighed and stood up slowly.

"I don't know when I'll see you again," Robert offered at their parting.

Margaret paused on the way to the door. "I wallowed in self-pity, this afternoon, because I had a friend to confide in. I shall miss you, Robert Sutton."

Then she was gone.

The following morning Robert convinced his host that the liniment had helped considerably and that he was quite able to continue his journey, once he had collected his horse from the village, where it had been stabled overnight. Mrs Taylor was quite willing to take his word amid the whirlwind of activity, as she eagerly kept an eye on matters. The house was in confusion, boxes being packed, staff were rushing here and there and a series of carts were being loaded in the yard.

"I must thank you Mrs Taylor for your immense generosity and hospitality," Robert said to his hostess. "I regret I have been much inconvenience to your household at this particular time."

"Think nothing of it," she purred back. "If you are still interested in Stour Park, I can tell you that it has been empty for some time. There are many rumours as to the reason."

"Do you know much about the house, or the owner?" he asked, genuinely interested.

"The Marquis Tree. Phillip Brimley. A waster, just like his father, who gambles his inheritance away and fails to take care of his property or his staff. I believe there has been some kind of terrible scandal to do with money, although I don't know the details. Some say the house was repossessed by the Treasury to pay off his debts."

"Then I shall not bother to see it. Any messy long-drawn-out legal matters would hinder my client's plans."

"I believe he managed to remove most of his valuable trinkets before that happened," Mrs Taylor continued, ignoring his comment.

She paused, and making sure no one else was near, she beckoned him closer to whisper.

"I expect they are hidden away at his secret little lodge on the coast."

"He has another property?" Robert was intrigued.

"Oh yes. I caught one of his servants sneaking the items away from there a few months ago. I forced him into admitting where he was taking the parcels, or be accused of theft and arrested. I doubt many know of its existence."

So Brimley might not have left the country, because he had somewhere else to hide on the coast. Robert wasn't sure if this was good news or bad. He would have to discuss it with Ellis.

Certainly he would have to keep this information to himself for the moment. He could hardly report it to the correct authorities without disclosing where he had been yesterday, or that Mrs Taylor was the prime source.

"I don't suppose you would know where exactly where the lodge is?"

Unfortunately she did not; she knew only its rough location, which was a shame. Still, it was enough for him to store in his memory for future use.

"And you will keep this conversation to yourself?" he said.

"Certainly, Mr Sutton. You are a government official after all. I realise it may be important and may need to be acted on. I am only too happy to help. Can I be of any other further use to you?"

"Thank you no. But I…" How was he going to put this tactfully, without causing too much interest from her? "I recognised one of your maids in the courtyard yesterday. Margaret Hayward?"

"Margaret, my maid? I am perplexed Mr Sutton. You have not visited my establishment before. How is it you are acquainted with one of my staff?"

"I am in debt to her family after they took me in after a serious accident last year. She is a country girl through and through. I was surprised to see her here."

Mrs Taylor rose, her hand ready to ring the bell and turned to Robert.

"Do you wish to talk to her?"

"No thank you."

Mrs Taylor looked surprised, curious and more than a little amused. She had assumed he had meant to pass on his regards.

"Then?"

"Like most country girls, I think she misses her family. I do not know how long she has been in service, but I expect she would like a few days leave to go home. I doubt she would ask you herself, in case she loses her position with you."

Mrs Taylor nodded eagerly. It was a small thing to request.

"Of course she may have time off. I will speak to her later."

"Thank you. You will not mention I spoke to you about her?"

The elderly lady smiled. "You have a good heart, Mr Sutton. I presume the family are unaware of who you actually represent?"

Robert's eyes flashed merrily and he smiled back. She had her answer. It was entirely understandable that a government operative would not advertise his position.

Thanking her again for her assistance, he was driven into the village to collect his horse. Having paid for its stabling and feed, he waited to watch the convoy of carts and carriages make their way along the road. He saw Margaret snatch a look back at him. He gave her a gentle wave, and she smiled. He hoped she would go home soon.

Home? He did not dare to go home in this condition, his sister and aunt would have a fit and neither could he return to the office yet for them to discover his injuries, or the cause of them. He would be in serious trouble if they knew he had broken into any property, empty or not. This time he did not have the law on his side and he would have to be careful not to let them suspect what he had been up to. Maybe he could beg a bed at Hurl Place for a couple of nights.

A dirty, dishevelled Robert arrived at Hurl Place, this time stiff and uncomfortable as he walked through the house. His intention had been to talk to Ellis, his co-conspirator, hopefully before he encountered Lord Rupert. It was a great relief to find that his friend was away at Richmond Lodge, which allowed them to talk freely.

He immediately confessed that he had been to Brimley's home at Stour Park, where he had searched and found the place empty. Sticking to the same reason he had given Mrs Taylor for his back injury, he left out the real cause, and the fact that Margaret had been there. He spoke warmly of the meeting with Mrs Taylor, since it had proved to be a blessing because of her other important revelations, namely the existence of the lodge on the coast.

"So there were no incriminating papers at Stour Park? Nothing to link Hurl Place with the financial fiasco? But you are still worried?" Ellis queried.

"Now I know Brimley may still be in the country, there is always the chance he might do something desperate. Unfortunately, I do not know what he is capable of. None of us do. I would dearly like to take a look at this lodge at the coast."

"Oh, Robert, is that wise? Is it necessary? Why risk another surreptitious journey? It could be dangerous. It is not worth letting a suspicion put you in trouble."

"Except that it is a suspicion which might yet damage Lord Rupert, if it is left unresolved."

"I think you are worrying too much. I am sure if there had been anything, it would have surfaced by now. I would advise that we let the proper authorities know where Brimley has gone and let them catch him."

"And how do we do that? I can hardly explain the source of my information without indicating my presence near Stour Park. They would suspect something, and to be honest I would prefer to keep my job for as long as I can."

"Be assured I'll do my best to keep your social call at Stour Park and the new developments from Rupert," Ellis muttered.

Robert's back still hurt. Liniment was applied and hot towels, and he rested, but he could not sit still for long. He tried sleeping on his side with a pillow at his back. Nothing was working.

"This is going to take longer than a couple of days," Ellis concluded.

"In that case I had better try to catch up on my schedule. The Jeskyns property is not too far to ride to. I can manage the journey if I take it slow."

Robert examined Mrs Jeskyns' house thoroughly. Although the widow and her staff had been quite obliging in answering questions and allowing him access anywhere, he felt less than convinced about the property. The location and size were acceptable, but the place had a strange atmosphere about it; exactly what is was he could not put his finger on. It was a fine house but half the rooms were unused, and it was obviously too big a place for her and the small staff she had.

In addition to that, there was something about the woman he simply disliked, although he knew he should not let that influence him. She had a weird appearance, with her hair drawn into a bun sitting on top of her head and decorated with a mixture of coloured feathers and long beaded pins. He tried not to judge people on sight, but her voice, a sharp rasping sound, aggravated his ears. He found he disliked her secretary, Cosmos, a narrow-faced weasel of a man, even more. His eyes darted about and he never looked anyone straight in the face when he spoke, a trait Robert recognised. In his experience it pointed to the man being untrustworthy and devious. This was not a man he would like doing business with, even if he was assisting his mistress.

The valuation price Mrs Jeskyns had wanted had been fair, he agreed, but the lady herself seemed unsure as to whether she really wanted to move. Apparently she had dithered and changed her mind from day to day as his visit came closer. This gave him the perfect excuse to move the property to the bottom of the list. He could consider it later if necessary, depending on what other places he looked at. To be honest he was getting fed up with this quest, wondering if he would ever find a suitable place for the minister. He wished he had not taken on this search.

Robert was pleased to take his leave of the stifling building and immediately took a deep breath of the fresh air outside. This is what he liked the most, the freedom in between his assignments.

Returning to Hurl Place, Robert was pleased to hear that Lord Rupert was taking his new role of host ambassador for visiting dignitaries most seriously. His royal relation had complimented Rupert on the recent impressive formality, respect and protocol he had shown his visitors. Lord Rupert was, despite his earlier objections, enjoying his new role.

When Lord Rupert returned, Robert was about to offer some words of congratulation when he was stopped short. Rupert glowered at him, his jaw set, his eyes wide. He was clearly far from happy.

"I am glad you are here Robert, because I will have words with you and Ellis. I am not pleased with you. Either of you. Did you think I would not find out eventually?" Rupert stormed.

The pair exchanged a mystified glance. Robert and Ellis were not quite sure what was coming. Just what had he found out?

"I do not think it was fair of you to keep me in the dark concerning what you have discovered. Were you ever going to tell me? Were you? You don't even look repentant."

They remained quiet, wary of saying the wrong thing. They could not alert Lord Rupert into learning any more than he thought he knew.

"You found out that Phillip Brimley was the guest at my dinner, the same Phillip Brimley who has the title of the Marquis

Tree. And what is worse, much, much worse, is that this same Phillip Brimley is connection to this financial failing, the Pavilion Trading Company, which is the talk of the city. At least my relation had the kindness to tell me the details. Details which you have both kept from me for some time."

Robert relaxed and smiled casually.

"I thought it unnecessary. So I found out his name and the rest, but I also knew you would get yourself in a state on learning of his attempted business venture. There is no way you can be associated with his scheme, but I knew your reactions would be extreme despite the fact that it is not important."

"Whether it is important or not, I am angry because you should have told me. You are my closest friend. It is not for you to decide if I need protecting from unpleasant revelations."

"I am sorry Rupert. I am. But I acted for your best interests and you do need protecting from yourself. You can be quite irrational, you know. You get hot under the collar and rant and rave, imagining goodness knows what and going off at a tangent. Why should you worry about this Brimley anyway? You were nothing more than casual acquaintances."

"I fear any association with him will reflect badly on myself. He was a guest in my home, prior to this scandal."

"I expect he was a guest at a good many dinners, hosted by many other important people, prior to this. Are they behaving like this? Are they?" Robert argued.

Rupert shook his head, reluctantly admitting he had no knowledge of any such behaviour elsewhere.

"How dare he even think he could offend me like this, at my table, at my dinner. I would strongly like to wring his neck, if I could get hold of him."

"Rupert, how has he offended you? Nothing happened that night. You are fretting over nothing. There is no need for all this."

Lord Rupert showed no signs of calming down; in fact he

was getting more and more agitated. Robert and Ellis glanced at each other. This was exactly what they had wanted to prevent.

"The law will take care of him," Robert mention softly in an attempt to reason with him.

"How, when rumour has it he has already fled the country? He has escaped justice, Robert. I don't like it."

Robert shook his head. Rupert was not so much annoyed that the man had escaped justice as about the intended use of the dinner to promote that scheme. Robert didn't have the words to deal with Rupert in this mood. He looked towards Ellis for help, although Ellis seemed equally at a loss for the best thing to say.

"To think he is Arabella's cousin. I would like to shake her as well."

"Rupert! Honestly. You cannot possibly blame Arabella for his actions."

"Why not?"

"All this wild conjecture. You are imagining too much. How could she know anything about Brimley's plans?"

"The quickest way to find out the truth is surely to ask Lady Arabella, face to face. Is it not?"

"It is not!" Robert yelled, horrified at the idea. This was getting worse. How on earth was he going to reason with him?

"How do you know what she is capable of?" said Rupert.

"Arabella would never be stupid enough to upset you. She adores coming to your impressive gatherings. She likes to be admired. She would never ruin her social position in society. It is too important to her."

Rupert huffed and puffed and strode about the room looking back at both of them. His mind was still racing with theories.

"I shall have some course of retribution, indeed I shall. Right or wrong, I am of a mind to leave her and her husband off any invitation in future."

Lord Rupert's tone had changed as he considered the extent of his influence over other functions and how Arabella could be excluded from them. It would be a torment for her to miss all the fashionable gossip and elegant company, he told them. The sight of Rupert's slight grin allowed Robert to relax again and flop into a comfortable chair, immensely relieved that everything had calmed down.

"And talking of future events, there are the arrangements for next week to be finalized," Ellis reminded Lord Rupert sharply.

The next morning Robert was shaken awake by an anxious Ellis with the news that Lord Rupert had stormed off alone, intending to ride to Lord Wake's residence. Rupert had apparently fretted about the situation all night and had now against, every advice and pleading from the Ellis, gone to challenge Lady Arabella. Even his escort had been to slow to stop him, although they were now in pursuit.

"Damn it. Why doesn't he ever listen to us?" Robert exclaimed, already pulling on his boots. He still hadn't fully recovered from his back trouble and it was all he could do to force himself into action. Luckily one of the fastest horses was being saddled for him as he hurried to the yard. But how his back ached as he leaned and ducked below the overhanging branches, cutting across country, twisting and turning through woods and across fields, flying at the rails and hedges without thinking. Rupert would have stuck to the main road, which meant Robert had every chance of catching him up by taking this madcap route. He soon did, and having raced along the track parallel to the road, he swung through the open gateway, came alongside and swung his horse in front of Rupert's steed, making him pull up frantically to avoid a collision.

"Get out of my way!" Rupert thundered at him, his face contorted, his anger unabated.

"No!" Robert bellowed back. He had to stop him, which meant continually making his animal twist and turn at an angle in front of Rupert, as Rupert tried to edge past.

"Get out of my way!" Lord Rupert repeated, the authority edgy in his throat.

"No," Robert replied, quieter this time.

"I will knock you out of my road."

"You can try," Robert said firmly, doubting his friend would injure either horse by forcibly barging his way through.

Lord Rupert looked at him for a while in silence. He recognised his friend's expression, his composure, the way he sat. He could see that his friend was prepared to do anything to prevent him from continuing his journey.

Robert waited until Rupert had stopped glaring at him before he began reasoning with him.

"What the devil do you think you're you doing, riding off in a fit like that? Where is your common sense?"

"You are suggesting, as you did yesterday, that I do nothing?"

"Yes, precisely that. You have been working yourself into a fine state, just as I warned you you would. And for what? Nothing came of Brimley's scheme at your dinner, did it?"

Rupert pulled a petulant face, which worried Robert, for although Rupert gave every indication of taking his advice, he did not promise to.

"Sulking does not become you. And as for riding out abroad without your escort, since when have you been so stupid?" he scolded.

Lord Rupert shrugged. He did not like being told off by Robert, especially when it was valid.

"Remember you have become an important ambassador for this country. You have more important duties to concentrate on than to be bothered by petty incidents like this. Making a scene at Lord Wake's will not help your new status at court. You cannot afford to act so rashly."

By now the escort had caught up and circled around the pair of them, to wait for their orders. Were they to continue the journey accompanying their master in the orderly manner expected, or were they turning back to Hurl Place? Even Robert was unsure of what a stubborn Lord Rupert would decide to do.

Then Rupert sat up straight in the dignified posture of a gentlemen and turned his horse towards home. It appeared that he had begrudgingly accepted what his friend had said.

"Will you join me for breakfast, Robert?" he asked.

Neither of them made any reference to Rupert's earlier intentions as they rode back together. Instead they were content to comment on the passing countryside. Robert himself was mindful to keep his friend fully distracted, because he was unwilling to risk a repeat of their confrontation. The next time, Rupert might not listen to him. What he needed was a serious diversion to keep him occupied, and a very pretty one would be the answer. If only he knew who the green and gold trinket box had been for.

CHAPTER FIVE

Robert made his way criss-crossing the southern counties, delivering an amended town charter to one mayor and collecting documents from another. His progress eventually ending at the port of Dover, where he needed to check over a shipment waiting to be sent to France. Captain Ben greeted him as usual with his jolly voice and merry beaming smile. Their business swiftly completed, the pair of them retired to the nearest inn for a meal, where Robert listened to his recent travels and tales from the overseas colonies. The man was a mine of interesting information.

Later that week Robert had escorted a precious crate containing a fragile clock, carefully packed in straw, all the way from London to its destination. It was a personal gift from a French diplomat, Louis Gaboriau, to a country gentleman, Sir Francis Caslon.

Robert had stayed for the unpacking, to make sure it had survived the journey. The recipient, overwhelmed by the expensive token he had been given, could only stand and stare at it. He looked at Robert, looked at the clock and shook his head.

"Are you sure this is meant for me?"

"Definitely. My orders were to deliver this to you in person."

"Well, it is too generous. I merely lent him my coach to complete his journey, when his coach ended in a ditch after it lost a wheel."

"He must have considered his timely arrival in the city important. Not to be delayed or inconvenienced obviously meant a great deal. You know what some of these foreigners are like," Robert surmised.

The clock had been placed in the centre of the table and the man walked slowly around it, not knowing what to say, still in awe of the gift. Robert bent forward and slowly turned the key at the back. The mechanism twirled into life and when Robert moved the hand to the hour, it chimed a short tune. The elegant music instantly drew the rest of his family into the room, all of them curious to see what it came from. After they had all inspected and marvelled at it, they could not bear to leave it, and brought their chairs from the next room to sit and simply enjoy its design. They had been about to dine, but that was forgotten.

Robert smiled at the pleasure gained from the gift and made his way back towards the hall, intending to leave. Sir Francis came after him.

"Forgive my manners. You must dine with us, before you journey back. I must write to thank Monsieur Gaboriau. Would you take the note to him for me?"

"The letter I will take, but not the meal, thank you. I should leave soon."

The man took him into another drawing room, where Robert was bade to sit while the letter was composed. It was a delightful room; in fact the whole house and its people were delightful.

Suddenly Robert caught sight of a gold and green trinket box on the mantel. Casually he got up to study it closer. He doubted there were two the same.

"This is an elegant piece," he commented casually.

"Yes. It was a present for my daughter from an admirer."

Robert glanced at the pretty daughter swinging her little sister and brother about in the other room. She was fair and small featured, her laugh had a soft mellow lilting sound and when she turned her head to the window, where the sun caught every detail of her sweet face, Robert understood the attraction. Robert grinned to himself. This girl was the special secret his friend had kept from everyone, and Robert understood why. Rupert naturally meant to keep his interest and feelings for her from them all until he was sure of a favourable response. This was no casual attraction.

"He seems quite serious, but I feel she is too young," said Sir Francis. "She is not used to the grand society he moves in. I think he would spoil her too much."

Robert nodded; indeed he would. Rupert would court her with a passion and do everything he could to make her happy. Rupert's instinct would be to shower presents on her. But in this case, such an abundance of gifts and attention might overwhelm her. Lord Rupert might lose her without thinking.

"Dare I ask how she feels about him?"

"I don't think she knows. She is flattered, she did not seek his attention. She is too young."

The letter in his pocket, Robert headed home for an overnight stop, happily mulling over this discovery. Rupert's secret wasn't a secret any more. This girl could make a difference to Rupert's life, but he did wonder how on earth Rupert had met her. The Caslons were a quiet country family; they did not move in the same social circles as Lord Rupert.

Having taken time to view the livestock and enjoy the Dorking Fair the day before, Robert had travelled south to Chichester and was having a late breakfast at the inn the next morning. He was sitting there contemplating his next journey and idly gazing out of the window when he saw Mr Hayward.

He watched as a very glum farmer entered the magistrate's office. To have Mr Hayward come so far from home to Chichester indicated it must concern an important matter. Puzzled by that in itself, he was more curious when Mr Hayward left some time later. The man's head was bent even lower, his shoulders sagged and he walked down the street completely oblivious to anything around him. Robert could not imagine what could have caused Mr Hayward to be in such a state. If they had been on closer terms he would have chased after him to ask the reason, but unwilling to pry into his private business he felt obliged to enquire from the other source. Accordingly Robert entered the same office and presented his official papers.

The magistrate did not mind discussing the previous appointment. The dreadful event needed to be aired. Apparently Mr Hayward had intended to acquire a small loan from the bank to acquire some new cattle to improve the herd on the farm, but when asked to produce his deeds as collateral for the loan, he could not find them.

"The poor man. As if being cheated the other year wasn't enough to deal with, he has misplaced or lost the deeds to his property. He can't remember when he last saw them. He has never needed to refer to them before. He came to ask if any records or copies of the original land transactions were held here."

Robert knew Mr Hayward to be a very careful, methodical man. He would have kept such documents safe. They would have been locked away somewhere in the house. To lose such documents was very unlike him.

"The bank naturally required his documents as proof of ownership, as security against the loan."

"Of course."

"Maybe it was never recorded," the magistrate suggested.

"Please don't say that!" Robert gasped.

"The original title deed passing the land to his family in the last century has disappeared. Their whole inheritance could be in question. If he cannot prove his ownership, he could lose everything his family has worked for, for generations."

"What!" Robert exploded. He stared at the official, his mind whirling. "You will instruct your clerks to look thoroughly?"

"Naturally, I will do everything I can. Mr Hayward does not deserve this. But I am not sure we would have them. They could be anywhere. Not all land transactions are mentioned in public records. Manorial records have registers of transactions, dealing with transfer and tenancy of property. At worst they could be in some parish or church archives, long forgotten and buried in dust. Besides we do not know how far to go back to begin the search. With no date, it could be an impossible task."

Robert fully understood the problem, although for the moment he could not find any useful suggestions to help.

Whilst Mr Hayward had not seen Robert, Robert had not seen Joseph, who had accompanied his master to town. Joseph was curious about Robert, and after waiting until Robert had left, he entered the same building.

"The gentleman who has just left - who is he?" Joseph asked the clerk at the front desk.

"A courier from London."

Joseph looked puzzled. The clerk smiled.

"He delivers and collects important papers from London."

"Oh."

So Robert had another job, his employment obviously changing with the need to keep money in his pocket, Joseph surmised. Well, at least he was in work and looking well.

While the magistrate began the slow search, Robert began his own quest for results elsewhere. He would begin by visiting every local public office around the Haywards' home area to ask them to search their rolls of old documents. It was time to call in a few favours.

It was barely a week later when the same magistrate urgently sought out Robert the moment he arrived back in town. The news he had to give was far from good.

"The bank officials have passed the query about Mr Hayward's deeds on to other legal authorities," he reported. "They have since been in touch with Mr Hayward to warn him that if the documents are not found soon, his ownership of the farm may not be legally binding. He has asked my advice about finding suitable lawyers to help sort this out and represent him, if it comes to court. There are experts in that field in London, but their fees are beyond his means. I wish I knew how to help."

Robert was stunned. He could not take it in. That it had come to this! And so quickly. There was no way that Mr Hayward could manage this latest catastrophe on his own. He was in dire trouble, and somehow Robert had to help him. Such matters were definitely beyond his own expertise or jurisdiction, but there were those in the Exchange who could certainly advise him and recommend the best way to proceed. It would require the proper legislature administration to ask the right questions and to take on the case. It was also obvious that Robert himself could not afford to hire such lawyers, but he knew exactly who could, and he wasn't afraid to ask him. Lord Rupert was his only choice; he would have to ride to Hurl Place.

The ride gave him time to go over all the frustrating thoughts churning in his mind. Robert hated difficult problems, his philosophy having always been to get them sorted out immediately, so he could move on. Except recently he hadn't been able to resolve any of them.

Any stranger would have been surprised at the unchallenged ease with which Robert Sutton marched through the sumptuous apartments. Despite his appearance his arrival raised few questions, indicating the familiarity with which he was accepted in these respected halls of priceless extravagance. His was a direct access, bypassing secretaries and awaiting dignitaries without fuss, whenever necessary. Today it was necessary. He had to see Lord Rupert immediately.

Rupert was surprised as Robert strode into the room after a single knock without waiting for the invitation to enter.

"Rupert, will you fund a good lawyer, for me? Only the best will do. Do you have the contacts and means to hire such men? I shall need the finest legal minds to sort this problem out," Robert began instantly, disregarding the normal social greeting.

"I cannot believe you have need of a lawyer in your occupation," Rupert joked, very surprised at his request.

"It is not for me," Robert stated firmly, in no mood for frivolity.

"As I suspected. You never ask for things for yourself, Fair Robert, so it must be important. Who needs this help, who means this much?"

"A man with a good heart. The man who took me in and cared for me after my accident. A man who believes that to help another is perfectly natural, in the hope that some day another would do the same for one of his own family if necessary."

"Ah, the man we are to thank for your recovery!" exclaimed his friend."

Robert nodded.

"Then by all means. Whatever you need will be done."

"He must have an expert team of associates. It will require an extensive search of parish and church archives to find any record of the missing documents and land deeds from decades ago. The case will be expensive. I cannot have him lose his home."

If there was one thing Rupert was passionate about, it was the protection of one's home. His own home was precious to him. So he understood the serious nature of this request.

"I know just the man who will act for you," Lord Rupert chuckled.

Within a few days the details were arranged and the eminent lawyer Lambert Hampton, primed by Robert, wrote to the family. He informed them of his interest in the peculiar situation, explaining that he liked to challenge himself with unusual cases. His firm, Hampton and Williams, would be acting on their behalf, at no cost to themselves. Despite any protests from the Hayward family, they would receive the best of help. Thus with Lord Rupert's blessing and the loan of his carriages, the lawyers set off to meet their new clients.

No doubt Mr Hayward would not believe this turn of good fortune and would have many questions, but Robert knew he would remain ignorant of his benefactor or who had instigated this miracle. Robert felt much better now, as it allowed him to concentrate properly on his normal assignments. The Haywards were in safe hands. He could do nothing more himself.

A two-week lull in his work allowed Robert the opportunity to finally set off on his other secret quest without telling anyone what he intended to do. Since Lord Rupert was being so generous as to pay for the Hayward's case, for people whom he did not know, then in all fairness, Robert was bound to return the favour. Robert had to see if any possible threat to Rupert actually existed. He had no doubts about his actions. It had to be done. All he knew from Mrs Taylor was that the lodge was near the Purbeck Hills, which was way out of his jurisdiction and an area completely unknown to him. Was he wasting his time? What if the lodge was somewhere completely different? The carrier, when challenged by Mrs Taylor, might have said the first thing that came into his head. What if the carrier had lied to her? There was only one way to find out.

With no idea of the name of the property or its precise location, Captain Ben had advised Robert to talk to the local coastguard station, for they would have maps of the coastline and other local details. Accordingly Robert visited the coastguard station to ask for their opinion on suitable isolated locations in the area where a boat might slip in and out unnoticed. He had not expected that there would be so many on this rocky coastline.

He then enquired about any buildings with access to the sea. Most of them were owned by local tenants whom the coastguard knew personally. There were a few other empty buildings dotted along the map, their ownership unknown. Not that Robert expected any property to be registered in Brimley's name.

It seemed a daunting task. Yet the seaman doggedly worked his way around the map, discounting one place after another, either because of its unsuitability or because it was a ruin or too open to observation. Finally there was just one left, a stone lodge which sat on the edge of a cliff, in an isolated spot and facing out to sea.

Robert was sure this was Brimley's hideaway. He studied the map, asking the coastguard for some information about its surrounding geography. Apparently the building lay in a slight hollow, perfectly protected from any neighbour's curiosity on the landward side. There was a thin line of trees which hugged the steep coast edge close to the lodge on one side and an inlet cut into the rocky cliffs on the other. Both would hide any unusual activity from any locals. Not that there were likely to be many locals interested in picking their way up the long open slope from the nearest village. The long open slope was beneficial to the occupants, since anyone approaching across the open grassland on the downs above would be easily spotted, standing out isolated and silhouetted on the skyline. Brimley had chosen his spot well.

The map also indicated a rugged coastal footpath from a small gentle valley to the right, and Robert concluded that this appeared the best way to reach the place unseen. So later that day, with his horse safely hidden, he set out on foot to embark upon his mission.

He had not realised that the path would be so rocky underfoot, nor that it would have such steep slopes up and down. Ahead he saw the man-made caves of some old mine workings cut into the dark rock face. It looked foreboding, but the path led past the little inlet in front of them to the stone steps cut into the side of the cliff. Halfway up he found the steps suddenly stopped, the rock being too hard for any further cutting. He would have to struggle up the remaining uneven surface, knowing that one slip would have him bouncing down the cliff face into the sea.

He took every step very slowly, carefully placing his feet squarely on the surface and keeping his balance. Going up would be better than coming down the other way, that was certain, which made him realise there was no way he could retrace his journey. When it came to it, he would have to find a different path back, if he could.

At the top the path resumed its route towards the pinnacle, and luckily it still kept him in a dip from the house to allow his progress to remain unseen. He paused the moment he caught sight of the building. The stone-built lodge sat on a slope, and had ample windows for a perfect view in every direction. This would not be easy.

Flattening himself in the low scrub of bushes and brambles he watched and waited. He could see people moving about inside, and a couple of men came out, looking out to sea at regular intervals. Was there a boat waiting out there? Was Brimley here? How many of his friends would be in there with him? The two from the tavern and other colleagues involved in the company, plus Brimley and the co-conspirator, who had attended that same fated dinner at Hurl Place? He faced an unknown number of men. He would not stand much of a chance if they caught him. He had come alone; only the coastguard and Ellis knew of his rough plans. He was risking his own safety, to say nothing of his whole future career if he survived this. Why was he here, he asked himself again? Of course he knew the reason. For Rupert and for his own peace of mind.

Robert looked for the best way into the building. There seemed to be two doors, one at the front and one further round at the side. How could he get inside undetected?

He decided to withdraw to consider his options, and carefully made his way back along the path at the top of the cliff. There was no way he could attempt going down the dangerous route by the caves. That would be suicide. He was stuck here. He would have to hunker down somewhere close by to hide until it was dark. Then he could decide whether to abandon his idea of getting into the building or sneak around the lodge, keeping to the bushes and hopefully make his escape across the downs.

There was a hollow in the earth bank at the side of the path which he had not noticed from the other direction, and as he huddled down into it to rethink his plan, he felt the very soft earth underfoot give way. Testing it, he stepped on it harder, to see the earth fall away into a hole. As he tugged at the tuffs of grass around it, it became larger and larger until he found what appeared to be a small tunnel or an old water duct to drain the rain away. It was wide enough to crawl into, and as he pushed himself forward, it appeared to lead downwards. Would it lead to the caves? It was worth a try. Another route of escape later would be invaluable. Anything to avoid that frightening climb he had taken before.

He began by pushing the fallen earth aside and wriggling forward carefully on his stomach, feeling the sides with his hands as he proceeded. Occasionally the earth fell into his face, causing him to stop to brush it away, but generally the tunnel seemed sound enough as he persisted in his descent.

He slid out of the other end to land on the rock floor of the man-made caves below. The caves remained dark and luckily uninhabited, although he could see boxes inside the cave entrance, boxes which had not been there when he had passed the opening earlier. He was puzzled by their presence. They could not have been carried down that precarious rock face, nor through the tunnel he had just crawled through. Which meant there had to be another way into the caves from the direction of the house. Would it mean there was another way into the house itself?

At the furthest, darkest end of the cave he found the passage he was looking for. The sides were chipped out of the rock, with earth and rubble packed into floor of the roughly-hacked base to provide a twisting slope leading upwards. He made his way up, listening all the time for any sound indicating that someone might be coming in the opposite direction. He did not want to come face to face with any of them.

At the top he found a door, a door to the unknown. He leant against it to listen. All was quiet the other side, so he slowly turned the handle and gently pushed it open. It moved easily and without any noise, indicating frequent use. Inside was some sort of basement with several doors, a flight of steps and more boxes stacked nearby. They obviously had not finished moving everything.

Quieter than a mouse, he crept up the stairs to the next door. Again he listened, but could hear nothing. His hand reached for the handle and stopped. His heart was thumping. Ellis was right, this was sheer madness. He should turn back before it was too late, but he had come this far. Just do it, just open the door, he told himself. Otherwise this was all for nothing.

Opening the door a fraction, he took a quick look through the gap. He was looking into the hallway of the main building. There were several doors off the hallway, but no sign or sound of people. He stepped inside and waited, until his courage allowed him to move on again or to retreat if necessary.

He looked into the room to the left. There was hardly anything inside; a few pieces of basic furniture, a table and chairs, a couple of beds, nothing else.

Then he heard the voices in the middle room and felt his stomach tighten. An unknown number of men were still here. Flattening himself against the wall next to the door, he could hear the conversation in detail.

"It has been reported that someone broke into Stour Park recently."

"The place is completely empty. Why should they bother

when there is not a scrap of incriminating evidence left anywhere?"

"All the registered company papers were seized, which makes me think they were looking for a clue as to our whereabouts. That worries me, because most people think we've long fled the country."

There was a long pause. Robert held his breath. The conversation had clearly indicated that Brimley was amongst these men, but which one was he? Somehow Robert had to risk looking through the crack left between the door and its frame.

"Maybe it could be because of these," said one of them, "Although who would suspect their existence?"

Robert saw him tap his jacket pocket, indicating there were papers in the inside pocket. Now he knew which one was Brimley. He ducked back against the wall, wondering what on earth those other papers contained. There had been no reference to Rupert or Hurl Place in the conversation. Dare he finally accept that Rupert was safe from any incriminating connection to the Pavilion Trading Company?

"Well whoever it was, they will be unlucky to find us. Tomorrow we shall be gone," said one of the men.

"Even so I would be happier knowing who it was and what he was actually after," said Brimley.

"I will just be pleased to get out of the country," one added.

Then Robert heard footsteps returning from outside. There was nowhere to hide. He could not get back to the basement in time. There was a shout, and seconds later he felt the cold end of a pistol barrel against his throat. He knew he was done for.

He was ushered unceremoniously into the room, and those inside were utterly shocked at this unwelcome arrival. Robert realised that the cobwebs and dirt on his clothes, hands and face must have made an odd picture, but it would also make it obvious how he had found his way in.

He stood perfectly still and offered no resistance as they searched him for weapons and identity. Robert carried neither.

"There are no papers on him. Does he know who we are?" one asked.

"Why else would he be here? Having found out about this lodge he has obviously been clever enough to find the way in from the caves," Brimley himself concluded.

"Who are you?"

Robert did not answer.

"Maybe you are the one who broke into Stour Park," One queried.

"The authorities do not usually send single operatives to investigate buildings they have already emptied," Brimley observed thoughtfully. "Who told you we would be here?"

Robert remained silent, wondering how long it would be before the verbal questions changed to something more physical, because of his refusal to speak.

Brimley looked Robert up and down, trying to read the character of this stranger. He took in every feature, just as Robert did of him. Robert looked him in the eye, unflinching, his expression fixed. He noted every mean line on his adversary's thin face, the grim jaw set firm, the clenched cheek muscles and the harsh glare from those narrow eyes. There was no way Robert would forget this face. It was quite distinctive, yet Robert could not place him amongst those attending the dinner at Hurl Place.

"Who are you working for?" Brimley asked.

Robert said nothing.

"I accept that there are others in the government who are a little more shrewd as to our intentions. They would naturally be interested in what we have done with the rest of the money," Brimley pointed out. "Is that why you have come?"

Still Robert was silent.

"We are wasting time. Whoever he is, I doubt he came alone. There could be others on the way as we speak. We must finish getting the boxes down to the caves ready for the boat. You two go watch the road for any other visitors."

Brimley had tired of the confrontation. He had more immediate and important matters to attend to. "Lock him in the cellar, until we decide what to do with him," he concluded.

Robert could not believe his luck. He had feared he would end up dead and thrown into the sea, with only the coastguard to find and identify him later. As it was he had been left bound hand and foot in the dark, to listen to the men moving boxes past the door.

After a while they had finished, and his eyes had slowly adjusted, allowing his mind to concentrate on the problems ahead. First he had to get free of these ropes, then get out of the door, before even considering his escape.

How was he to untie himself? He stared at his stiff leather boots, which had prevented the rope from being too constricting. If he jammed the backs of his heels against the floor he could wriggle his feet out of his boots.

It worked. Soon his boots lay empty, still tied together on the floor. His arms were still tied behind him. Could he curl his back enough to bring his hands under his bottom and then forward beneath his knees?

The process of bending his back into a ball was pure agony as he tried to stretch his shoulders downwards at the same time. It also hurt his weakened elbow beyond belief, but it had to be done. Taking a deep breath, he concentrated on pushing and stretching every muscle further and further. Then, taking another deep breath, he tried again. The rope tore at his wrists, but it was stretching.

Eventually his arms were under his knees; that part was over.

His body was trembling at the excessive effort he had used, forcing him to rest and let his aching limbs recover. Then another breath and twisting his legs sideways and up tight into his chest, he slid them through his arms until his hands were in front of him. Now he used his teeth to pull and tear at the rope, spitting out the bits from his mouth at intervals. Eventually the knots loosened enough and he was free. It felt exhilarating. Quickly he removed the rope from his discarded boots and pulled them back on.

Now he had to get out of this room. The air was stale in here and Robert had begun to sweat. The effort of his struggle with the ropes had already made him hot and his next plan would demand even more physical exertion. He had to battle with the door, and there were only a couple of broken pieces of wood in the corner to help him.

The door was locked, with no key left in the outside. He looked at the hinges; they were not rusty. That made a difference. He forced one of the bits of wooden planks under the gap at the bottom of the door and lifted it slightly. Then, finding a nail left in the pallet, he waggled and bent it back and forth until it came out. His hands were sore, but he pushed the nail into the bottom of the barrel part of the hinge to lift the pin which held the hinge together, and slowly it levered up and came out. He repeated this for the other hinge. He tested the door; it moved. It was only held in place by the lock.

He was tired and thirsty as he considered how to open the door without anyone hearing. Using brute strength - not that he had much left - would create the noise of the splintering door, bringing the others to investigate. Instead he would have to bend the door little by little, splintering the wood around the lock slowly, making less noise, until the gap was enough for him to slip through.

Robert stood in the basement, breathing the fresher air from the open door to the caves. Common sense told him to get out of there. He did not need to stay. Robert was satisfied by the lack of references in the conversation upstairs that Brimley had nothing to use against Lord Rupert or link him to the scandal. Otherwise he would have boasted about it. There was no evidence to link Lord Rupert to the scandal. Thank goodness for that. The relief was tangible, and Robert felt it ease his whole tired body.

And yet he hesitated. Brimley clearly had more important papers on him, papers concerning the money which belonged to the investors. Robert noticed that the rest of the cases had gone, a sure indication that they meant to leave soon, probably on the first high tide once it was light. He could walk away and let Brimley leave with his papers and keep his ill-gotten gains. But that would not be fair. None of this was his responsibility, but there was no one else around to prevent that happening.

It was the early hours when Robert climbed the steps back up to the main floor. Outside the lookouts would be patrolling around the lodge while their colleagues slept safely. He could hear the snores of the men scattered in the different rooms. All were sound asleep. He looked into each room to see them lying sprawled asleep with old blankets wrapped around their bodies, a disarray of arms and legs protruding from the cots. Brimley, as expected, was with them, but his jacket containing the papers was folded and tucked up under his head to make a pillow. Damn! How he would have loved to push him off the bed, grab the jacket and made a run for it. But that was not going to happen. He needed to remove the papers quietly and put something else in their place, to prevent Brimley noticing they had gone.

He crept into the kitchen, looking for something to use in their place. There were a few torn and crumpled pieces of paper used to wrap the bread, tossed on the top by the sink. They would have to do. He folded them flat as best he could and creased them to fit into an inside pocket. With any luck Brimley would not need to check them before he left. He would only pat them reassuringly to make sure they were still safe inside his jacket.

Suddenly Robert heard someone stir in one of the rooms behind him, making him dart back to hide behind the open door in the hallway. He did not want to be trapped inside a room with no exit. From here he could watch what was happening, with the option of escaping down to the basement if necessary. It was Brimley himself, who having rolled over, was wide awake and sitting up. Yawning and stretching, he stood up, at which point Robert dived back through the kitchen and into the pantry to hide. The chance of the jacket being left unguarded was a possibility he did not want to miss. However Brimley had picked up his jacket and was carrying it over one arm as headed past the kitchen for an exterior door. He leaned outside, exchanged a few words with someone, closed the door quickly and returned to the kitchen.

Robert held his breath. Leaving his jacket draped on the back of a chair, Brimley went to the sink to pump the water for a drink. The jacket was temptingly close, but so was its owner.

Then Brimley went to the water closet, leaving his jacket on the chair. This was Robert's chance. He swiftly stepped out of the cupboard, took the jacket from the chair and removed the handful of papers, quickly replacing them with the substitute bundle. Then he dived back into the pantry, folded the retrieved documents even flatter and firmly pushed them well down inside his boot as far as they would go, without looking at them. He could do that later.

Brimley returned and took his coat, to casually rejoin his sleeping companions. Robert allowed himself to breathe properly. For the moment he was safe.

Later, Robert made his escape, using the route he had planned. It was still dark, and even darker in the passage from the basement. He had to feel his way down by touch, but he reached the floor of the cave without hearing the sounds of any unwelcome company, either behind or in front of him. He edged forward to the opening, concerned by the lack of boxes to give him cover. A boat was already tethered in the tiny stone-cut dock; it bounced steadily in the slight swell. Most of the packed boxes were already loaded on board.

Now it was time to run. He hurried along the twisting, rocky coastal path, often stumbling to bang his limbs against the hard stone in his haste. He did not stop until he had reached the place where he had left his horse hidden in the trees. Toby had peacefully been chewing the grass from his long halter and was far from bothered at his master's sudden appearance. Robert gave him a gentle reassuring pat, allowed himself to take one last look towards the way he had just come; then he was riding steadily towards London.

Robert doubted his captors would waste much time looking for him, as they were so eager to get away themselves. They would be taking the boat on the first tide. As for Brimley, would he even check his papers? They had no reason to suspect that Robert had done anything other make his escape from the basement. Who would have guessed otherwise? There had been no reason for him to return up the stairs to the main rooms before he left.

Robert arrived at Hurl Place feeling very pleased with himself. It had taken two days since leaving the lodge. Safely installed with the secretary Ellis, Lord Rupert being absent again, Robert described his adventure, his nerves still on edge as he remembered every detail.

Finally he withdrew the pages from his boot. He gave them to Ellis to read and leaving the man to study the contents thoroughly, he poured himself a drink and sank into a comfortable chair.

Ellis let out a sharp gasp and looked up, his expression far from the jovial one Robert had expected.

"Robert, do you know what you have here?" His voice had a note of concern.

"No. I just grabbed what was in his pocket. I did not have time to look."

"What did you expect these to contain?" he asked tapping the documents.

"Maybe some false papers to help him elude justice. A bank draft. A receipt. Some indication of where the money has been put."

"Oh Robert, they do that all right."

Robert stared at one of the pages he was holding up. It had a corner missing. It matched the piece of torn paper he had taken from the Brimley family bible. Whatever it was had been hidden there before its removal to Brimley's personal care.

"This is a bank draft to be presented at a bank in the West Indies. Plus, a bill of sale for a plantation. It seems the transfer of ownership and the deeds of the property await his arrival there. It would appear Brimley expected to begin a new life well away from England."

Ellis paused, shaking his head. "In one desperate moment, your determination for justice and fairness has deprived him of most of his money and his future livelihood. You have ended any chance of a comfortable of any comfortable existence in exile.

Without this he cannot deposit or access money anywhere. He has nothing left. You have made him penniless and homeless. God, Robert! I cannot imagine what Brimley will do. He won't forgive you for this. He will seek some retribution."

"What can he do, when he's halfway across the ocean?" Robert scoffed, but he could not hide his alarm at this revelation.

Ellis looked at the last piece of paper. "Except that he might go to Europe first. There is a confirmation letter of other money already transferred to a bank in Calais. He could easily extract his revenge from there."

"Thank you, I feel so much better for your theory," Robert gulped.

"I am sorry Robert but that is no theory, it is a real probability."

Robert sat drained of his usual poise, struggling to digest this catastrophe. "Do you really think he would seek me out? Do you think he would risk coming back to England himself?"

Ellis nodded. "France is not that far away. He has nothing to lose. He may want revenge at any cost. He could be a vicious enemy."

Robert buried his head in his hands. This was worrying. All he had wanted was to have the money restored to those who had been cheated.

"Does he know who you are?" asked Ellis.

"He only knows my face," said Robert glumly. Indeed they had looked at each other long enough to easily recognise each other again.

A worried silence followed as the two of them looked at each other. Robert had made a terrible mistake. It made his head ache. He stared at the papers he had so carefully taken and silently cursed them.

"So what do we do with these?" Robert asked. Not that he really cared now.

"We must hand them into the authorities. They need to recoup the funds and deal with Brimley - if they can catch him."

Robert pulled a face. "How do we do that? I don't want to have to explain how I obtained them, or why I was there."

"They will not know you were involved. I intend that they will arrive anonymously. I will take the responsibility," Ellis reassured him, showing the experience of a diplomat.

Robert left Hurl Place feeling totally dejected, the burden of his actions overwhelmed any other thoughts. The fault and the responsibility were his alone. His life was suddenly getting worse, not better, and there was no one to blame except himself.

CHAPTER SIX

Robert returned home completely demoralised. He could not get his head to accept this predicament. Inside his stomach was in knots. The whole idea of the threatened repercussions ate away at him.

He had come home as promised for his sister's birthday again, at the end of August. He had bought her a pair of white lace mittens this year, but he was running out of ideas. Elizabeth was not a child any more; she wanted pretty things. They had celebrated the event this year by inviting their neighbours to a fine supper, which everyone had enjoyed, especially Elizabeth, since Michael had been one of the neighbours attending. Robert had watched the event as if from a distance, although he had been in the same room and part of the same merry conversation. Somehow he found it hard to concentrate. Every time he thought he had pushed the fear away, it returned to haunt his mind.

Within days he was sent to Faversham, to tour the local brewery and check and complete paperwork. The brewers in Kent had the hop market highly organised, proved by their ability to meet the demands of the navy at Chatham and Deal.

"What do you think of the new beer?" the owner commented as Robert signed the last page. "Porter. Have you tried it? The combination of three beers is a wonderful taste. And very popular. It's all the rage with the masses in the cities."

"It should make the hop industry very wealthy." was all Robert could manage to reply.

As he stepped out of the door having finished his business, Robert found his arms suddenly grabbed from each side. His heart missed a beat. He could not believe his enemy had struck so soon. They had appeared from nowhere. He had not begun to resist when the grip had softened into a nudge. Henry and Edmund were either side of him, grinning from ear to ear.

"God, Robert! You looked like you had seen a ghost. You went quite pale. Did we frighten you that much?"

He did not have time to find an answer.

"Come on Robert."

"But…"

They laughed, not letting go of him. They were going to make the most of the day and they were taking Robert with them. They were both off duty and as he had finished his work, there was no excuse. Edmund tapped his pocket reassuringly to check his flute was still at hand as they wandered off. He never went anywhere without it and today seemed exactly the right occasion to play one or two tunes.

The beginning of September heralded the end of the hop-picking, and the established local custom was a celebration. People were adorned with hops around their heads and hats. There was a small market in the town square and the street and shops were decorated with coloured ribbons and bunting, while in every tavern, the population made merry sampling the various brews. The three of them joined in, and by the end of the afternoon they had consumed enough to make them feel quite heady.

"They should develop this into a proper hop festival," sighed Henry.

"You mean to allow more drinking?"

"Not necessarily," Henry scoffed unconvincingly.

A dance at the tithe barn in the evening with story-telling and singing normally completed the day, but none of them had the energy to drag themselves there. They were all thoroughly tired and yawning, and sensibly abandoned the entertainment in preference for a good night's sleep. They were officers of the Crown after all, they had responsibilities. Tomorrow they would have to return to their respective duties.

Robert continued his scheduled errands, determined not to let fear get the better of him, but he could not help being wary of groups of strangers on his travels. He could feel his whole body tense up instinctively as they rode towards him and he could not relax until they had gone by. This was ridiculous, he scolded himself. He could not go on like this. Although he sadly recognised that the initial scare caused by Henry and Edmund in Faversham had proved his inability to react quickly enough to defend himself.

He slumped in the saddle as he headed back home for the Harvest Festival. He could have hidden away, kicking his heels in some obscure hole for a few days and become more dejected. Instead he made an effort to be with his family, hoping for some semblance of normality for a while to shake him out of this mood. The family were glad to see him and he readily followed their routine of the day, which began with joining them and the villagers for the thanksgiving service. The church had been decorated with flowers and greenery as was the custom, fruit and vegetables were on display and a plough had been brought inside for the blessing. Robert sat with his sister, aunt and uncle as everyone prayed for next year's harvest to be plentiful. The joyful service passed quickly, although he did not listen to the sermon and merely mouthed the words of the communal hymns, unaware that Elizabeth had been watching him intensely.

His vagueness continued at the Harvest Supper that evening. Feasts were held at farmhouses and barns throughout the county, garlands of flowers and ribbons decorated the interiors, corn dollies had been made from the last sheaves and hung up. Games were played and the whole community, especially those who had helped in the harvest, revelled in the event. Robert smiled and nodded to those he knew, and found he ate with a hunger which came from nowhere. He did not remember much of the evening except for making his sister blush at his insensitive probing concerning how far the romance had blossomed between her and Michael. Regretting his questions, he was quick to save her further embarrassment by suggesting they should take a picnic with them to the fair next week.

The carts carried the family and neighbours to the fair, which was being held in the grounds of the crumbling remains of Allington Castle. It was a large affair, with all types of noisy amusements and crowds of people. Because of the throng they had eventually found it easier to remain perched on their carts to share their picnic, the food and drink being passed from one to another as they took time to decide where to start exploring.

As Robert strolled around the stalls, Elizabeth slid up to him and grabbed his arm, squeezing it and then tugging him excitedly along one of the wide gangways. She stopped in front of a brightly-decorated tent where a gypsy sat dealing cards on a table. Elizabeth was fascinated by the sight of the woman dressed in bright colours, with beads and shiny bangles around her wrists and neck. But Robert's spirits sank, and what brightness he had forced himself to pretend for their sakes vanished immediately.

"Don't you want to know the future?" she persisted.

That was the last thing he wanted. He already knew his future, and he did not want it broadcast to his sister.

The wizened woman who sat outside waiting for customers looked up at the young man. Usually she would have encouraged potential custom, but she did not need to look at him for long, because she could see here was someone who already knew his fate. For that reason she did not offer to read his hand or ask for money from him. The young lady was quite different. She smiled at the world and would enjoy her life. The woman didn't need to look into the cards for that either.

Robert unwrapped her arm from his and offered to wait if Elizabeth still wanted to have a sitting with the old lady. But his sister had gone off the whole idea now. It was supposed to be a bit of fun, something they could do together, she told him.

"You old misery. What is wrong with you lately?" she pouted.

If only they knew. If only he could tell someone. Only Ellis shared his secret problem, there was no one else he could confide in. He would have to learn to live with this shadow hanging over him. He could not protect himself from harm. He would ultimately pay for his innocent mistake. He was tired, tired of remembering his conversation with Ellis. He did not want to spend his days looking over his shoulder, listening for any warning sounds, or seeing if he was being followed. The isolation and freedom which he valued as part of his occupation would now also make him more vulnerable.

Robert took his usual solitary walk over to the top of Henley Down and sat in his favourite spot looking down at Luddesdown Church below. He remembered his father telling him to make the most of his life. On reflection, he was forced to admit that he had not come anywhere close. Look at the mess he was in now! He had done his best to put a brave face on in front of everyone, but it was becoming more difficult with every passing day under their close scrutiny. He had noticed the odd curious glance and frown from his family, although so far they had not asked the reason for his strangely silent mood. The sooner he was back on the road and taking his troubles with him, the better.

"God, what a mess," Robert fumed, burying his head in his arms.

"What is?" asked the soft voice from behind.

Elizabeth! She sat beside him and leaned gently against him. He put his arm around her shoulders and rested his head on hers. There they sat for a long time without talking. Occasionally she would turn her head slightly to look at his sad face and then look away. Whatever was troubling him was buried deep as he stared into space, and she knew better than to try to coerce it from him. If he would not confide in her, he would not tell anyone. This wasn't like that stubborn teasing refusal to tell her about the foreign gentleman from last year. This was different.

Robert eventually stirred and pulled her to her feet to walk home with him. He had been glad of her closeness and the quiet comfort he gained from her being at his side. Elizabeth accepted his unusual reticence without judging him or asking any more. His sister was a blessing, and tomorrow he could cast off all their worried concern, because he would be leaving. At least it would be easier to mask his personal concerns from his employers.

His new instructions sent him through his home county of Kent again to Dover. It was usually one of his favourite routes because of its familiarity, but now its normal appeal was lost on him, the villages, farms, even the sight of cathedral spires of Canterbury leaving no impression. He passed them by without a second glance.

Arriving at Dover, he went to the courthouse to introduce himself to the new magistrate. He carried the accredited paperwork to prove his own authenticity and authority for the man, but found it was unnecessary since his reputation had preceded him. Nevertheless Robert made him take the papers; they were official and he knew the rules.

After that he rode to the docks to check the accommodation which had been organized for a visiting dignitary en route to London. The gentleman was expected on tomorrow's crossing and Robert booked himself into a modest lodging for the night, ready to greet him on his arrival and escort him on his journey. He had learnt to be thorough in all his assignments.

Robert woke in the morning to find wild winds battering the town and everything in its way. It buffeted the buildings and kept all inside as things flew into the air and crashed around the streets. The gale lasted all day, with no let up. There would be no boats leaving or crossing the Channel today. The harbour was deserted and the boats inside banged against the harbour walls, the rigging rattling and the pennants tugging on their masts as the boats pulled against their moorings. Beyond the harbour the small boats had been pulled high onto the shore, where the waves crashed on the shingle and dragged it back out with a loud swirling sound, threatening to rip it into the ferocious sea. All cargoes remained in warehouses, with the means of transport, the wagons and horses, securely stored inside, safe from the horrendous weather. The port was like a ghost town.

Most inhabitants were sensibly sheltering, whilst Robert was forced to make his one journey of the day to the harbour office for the latest news of any expected crossings. He had never experienced such a difficult walk, it was hard to stay on his feet, and the fine sand carried in the spray from the distant beach stung his face. As expected, he was told the conditions had made it difficult to predict any landings. He would simply have to wait in Dover until the boat arrived with the diplomat.

Making his way back through the dull grey drizzle, he noted a man here and there, bent against the wind, and two men huddled under an arch for shelter. Apparently others had business which forced them to brave the outdoors. Head down and collar pulled up around his neck, he turned a corner, and bumped into the solid figure of a man going the other way. Robert hesitated, but the man didn't even pause or look up; he merely hastily mumbled his apologies and hurried on.

The moment was enough to frighten Robert, for it could so easily have been an attack on him. He could not control his fear as he stood there, taking deep breaths and trying to pull himself together. He was all alone, with too many shadows threatening to harm him. He walked on cautiously, listening and watching every doorway until he had made it back to the inn in one piece.

As night fell, the weather still had not eased and Robert lay in his bed listening to the relentless noise of the wind howling around the town. How long could it last? He did not feel safe here in the dark, despite the door being securely locked. His nerves were pounding and each loud thump against the rattling windows or the bang of a door somewhere would make him jump. His was a fitful sleep, as the noises woke him on and off through the night.

Although he was tired, daylight made him feel much better. He had things to do, and he was always better when he was active. Too much thinking was bad for him. This morning the wind had died down, but the rain now took its place. Beating heavily straight down, it meant few people would venture outside.

Regardless of the rain, Robert braved the walk to the harbour once more, where he was told the boats were still delayed. Even the larger vessels remained inside the harbour. As he viewed the tremendous waves, he realised the diplomat would need time to recover his stomach and his legs when he arrived. He would be in no condition to make the ongoing journey immediately, so Robert took the initiative to extent the booking for a couple of extra nights in case it was needed.

A pale-faced foreign dignitary and his aide arrived the next day and were most appreciative of Robert's thoughtfulness, both of them swiftly going to their rooms to recuperate. This left Robert with the day to fill. He roamed around the port, kicking his heels. He had nothing to do. All the arrangements were made; he was just waiting for the diplomat to feel well enough to travel.

Most people were now getting back to their livelihoods and stalls were set up, shops were open, carts rumbled over the cobbles and supplies were being delivered all over the place. Robert soon found himself in the tavern, where he was pleased to see his friend Captain Ben puffing away on his pipe. Naturally they spent the next few hours together discussing the effects of the last few days' weather. Captain Ben was a mine of information, having an ear for all the gossip from overseas, and it prompted Robert to ask him about the plantations in the West Indies.

"The West Indies? A different world. The sugar trade has made many men rich, it has made England rich. But anyone heading for Jamaica will find it a very different society from England. It was different in the beginning, indentured servants served their contracts and returned home. These days it is more economical to use slaves, since the slaves remain slaves forever. The hotchpotch of nationalities demands more slaves, but to control the vast numbers the landowners enforce a reign of fear. It's a nasty business. You wouldn't believe the cruelty I have heard of. There will be trouble there eventually, mark my words."

Robert allowed himself a self-satisfied smirk. Even if Brimley had reached the West Indies, he would not have found the easy existence he must have predicted for himself. Casually their conversation faded out and each sat quietly supping the beer from their tankards.

Robert wandered back to the inn. The foreign gentleman and his aide were looking much better and after a meal, they were at last prepared to set off for London. Robert heard them chattering away as he escorted the coach as far as Greenwich, as arranged. There two other dignitaries greeted the visitor and they took over the hospitality. Another assignment had been completed, and Robert was eager to make a quick call at Hurl Place.

As Robert walked into Rupert's home he sensed his friend was entertaining, because he could hear several voices as Rupert guided his guests around the numerous rooms. He would not disturb him. He would have a quick word with Ellis and leave, he decided.

Robert was met by a questioning expression from Ellis, desperate to know how he was faring.

"You are looking tired Robert. I hope everything is still well? There has been no sign of trouble?"

"None." Robert shrugged. "No dire consequences have occurred. No cruel hand of fate has struck me down. I was at Dover recently, the closest point to France and Brimley. It would have provided the perfect opportunity for any successful assault, especially in the dark ferocity of the gale."

"Providing he had known you were there, of course."

"Which is the one flaw in this whole affair. He has no idea where I come from or who I am. Realistically, how would Brimley or any others he sent expect to find just one man in the whole of the country? Would they bother to search the length and breadth of England for a man whose only distinguishing feature is the splash of grey in his hair? It could take them forever. And how would he know where to find me at any specific time?"

"Maybe we have misjudged the situation. Brimley might have left France already. He might begrudge using his funds to hire someone to hurt you."

"I can only hope so."

Their conversation drifted away from the subject, and Robert made to leave.

"Lord Rupert is presently entertaining the Caslon family," said Ellis. "He is showing them around his home. He appears to be very attentive. I do not know how they are acquainted."

Robert was smiling now, a wonderful wicked smile. He sat down and made himself very, very comfortable. He was going to enjoy this.

"In that case I think I will definitely stay a little longer," he said.

Ellis was puzzled by this sudden change of plan. Robert winked at him and then put him out of his torment.

"The beautiful gold and green trinket box I collected for Rupert was a gift for Anne Caslon."

Ellis's eyes widened, his mouth dropped open a fraction.

Robert nodded. "Oh yes. Rupert is smitten."

The tour of Hurl Place eventually wound its way into the room where Robert sat. Rupert stopped, surprised to see him there.

"Robert. I wasn't expecting you today, was I?"

"No, Rupert. I merely called in to rest for a couple of hours, on my way home."

"And will..."

"Mr Sutton, how good it is to see you again," Mr Caslon interrupted, beaming and coming forward to greet him.

"And you again, sir," Robert reciprocated, shaking the hand offered to him. Rupert frowned and looked from one to the other, unsure of this apparent connection between them. "You know each other?"

"I had the pleasure of calling at Mr Caslon's home recently," Robert offered, deliberately remaining vague.

"You remember my wife and my daughter Anne?"

"Of course. Ladies, it is a pleasure to see you again." He bowed graciously.

"That clock was so beautiful," Anne acknowledged.

"You gave Miss Caslon a clock?" Rupert challenged Robert, struggling to remain calm in front of his guests. Robert could see his friend was suspicious and jealous at this news, and he longed to prolong the torment. But he was not given the choice.

"Goodness no. It was a gift from a French diplomat to myself. Mr Sutton was good enough to ensure its safe arrival," Mr Caslon explained. Rupert relaxed.

"I doubt Miss Caslon has need of such a clock when she has such a beautiful green and gold trinket box, to gaze on," Robert added.

Anne blushed and Rupert stared at Robert, who beamed directly back and mischievously raised his eyebrows, awaiting clarification. Rupert made no such mistake. Instead he diverted his attention back to his new acquaintances.

"Mr Caslon, Madame, Anne. If you would care to be seated for a moment, I will send for some refreshment," Lord Rupert announced.

As they settled, Rupert bent down by Robert's shoulder to request a quiet word in private, nodding his head towards the other room. Robert shook his head.

"Later," Robert replied quietly. Lord Rupert's eyes narrowed and his jaw clenched as he glared at his friend. How dare Robert be so difficult?

"Why are you so upset that I am acquainted with the Caslon family?" Robert asked him later, when his guests had gone.

"I am jealous that you are so at ease with these people. I wish to make a favourable impression. I intend… to ask for their daughter's hand," Rupert confessed.

"Dear Rupert. You do not need to flatter them or impress them. None of them are used to such fine surroundings or the rich society you mix with. Do not overwhelm them or expect them to enjoy your fine elaborate functions. No grand gestures. You must allow them more time to see your potential as a suitably caring husband. They are aware of your affection towards Anne, but they are concerned that your social position may be too much for their daughter to adjust to. She is still young. They only want Anne's happiness."

"How am I to court her, Robert? How do I convince her she will be my first and only consideration? I am indeed worthy of her consideration, am I not?" Rupert sighed wistfully. He looked rather lost.

"Yes, you are. There must surely be something about you she likes already to have persuaded her father to agree to this visit. Maybe it is your kind heart and good nature. And I have never known you to be cruel or mean."

Rupert looked a little brighter at the unexpected compliment. Indeed it prompted him to be inspired. He would invite himself back to Sholden Hall for a few weeks so that he could visit the Caslon family on a regular basis.

"A few weeks? Rupert, that is abusing anyone's hospitality."

"Whinney will not mind. There will be much encouragement. He has a soft spot for romance. While I'm there I shall ask Mr Caslon for permission to visit them every day. I shall be considerate to what is expected. I will be modest about my home and its treasures."

"You are so enamoured that I fear you show every sign of spoiling her completely. Please listen to me, you must not lavish grand presents on her. Just find small things she will appreciate."

"Books? A puppy?"

"That is better. Just not one of your hounds."

Lord Rupert nodded and smiled broadly. He could see the sense of Robert's suggestions. Indeed he was feeling better about the whole prospect.

"Please take time to find out what she likes and dislikes. You must confide in her, make her laugh over mistakes you have made, make her feel you trust her. Share things, little secrets. Show you value her opinion."

Robert could not believe he had voiced his opinions on such a delicate matter, for he was no expert on romance. The very opposite. He had only a sister's feminine preferences as a guide.

"All this advice from one who has neither a sweetheart nor a wife," Rupert quipped.

Robert shrugged. He had never thought he wanted his life to be any different.

"I am too set in my ways. I am bound to my career. I am content enough. Besides, it would not be fair on any female to put up with the demands of my occupation."

"Are you indeed content? Always the same excuse. I think it a shame, you will not be as happy as I."

Robert had been curious for ages; he wanted to know how they had met.

"I was staying at Sholden Hall one weekend when I saw this

bright young thing appear racing her horse across the heather ahead of her siblings. Her radiant smile, dancing eyes and lilting laughter as she encouraged them to catch up quite took my breath away. I did not expect to see her again, but then when I accompanied my host into town, there she was. She and the rest of her family were attending the same theatrical play at the town hall. Don't ask me what play it was. I could only look at her. I persuaded Whinney to introduce me to the family during the interval. She was so quiet and polite and I was tongue tied. It was not a great beginning," Lord Rupert lamented.

Robert rode home, smiling the whole way. He had been amazed at the depth and openness of Rupert's feelings. He had never been known to share his deepest emotions before. He had never seen a man so happy or so eager to express the love he had for this charming girl. Robert was pleased for him.

After spending some well-deserved time at home, Robert was back on his travels. At Milford he entered the council office building, to ask, as he did everywhere he went, about the possibility of any deeds being kept there. He was giving the details to the clerk when a former mayor who had overheard the enquiry beckoned him aside.

He had information. Very curious information, as it turned out. Apparently over a year before a couple of lawyers had come to his office to ask the same thing. Robert was puzzled, because it was only a few months ago that anyone had realised that the deeds had gone missing. Robert did not know what to think; it did not make sense.

"They said they were acting for Mr Hayward. We did delve into the archives, but with no specific date to go on it was a useless search. We found no records of any kind."

"Damn!"

"They left convinced that no such document existed here.

They did not seem greatly concerned at the failure to find anything and I do not think they intended to go elsewhere in their search. After they left, nothing more came of it and I presumed that Mr Hayward must have found the deeds, otherwise he would have been desperate for them to continue."

Robert was thinking. Perhaps the first enquiry made by Hawks and Ash might have been for a client who was interested in the property and discreetly wanted to check the legal ownership before they made an offer to purchase it. If the client had been put off by the initial lack of official documentation, it would seem quite plausible that no one had bothered to pursue it any further. But why say they had come on behalf of Mr Hayward unless it was to allay any suspicion?

"Did they give a name?" he asked.

"Er, yes. It was Hawks and Ash."

Robert's memory bells were churning. This was remarkable. The Redick merchants had been approached by two men calling themselves Ash and Hawks.

"Not Ash and Hawks?" Robert queried.

"Oh no. It was definitely Hawks and Ash."

Having thanked the man, Robert left to consider this development. These men had to be the same men as those who had involved the Redick merchants over the corn prices, although he could not believe they had simply reversed their names. This was more than mere coincidence. Robert was positive the two names connected the two incidents. He urgently sent the information on to the experienced gentlemen in London who were already dealing with the case.

Lambert Hampton was inclined to agree with Robert's instinct. It was very suspicious that Hawks and Ash had been associated with both events. There had to be more to this than first imagined. He agreed that it did begin to look like a conspiracy, so much so that they might change the way they presented this case when it came to court. They were going to insist that Mr Hayward was obviously a victim of some unknown intrigue and suggest that his deeds had been deliberately stolen, for some reason yet to be discovered. Would it make a difference?

Other reports left by the company of Hampton and Williams, acting for Mr Hayward, were not encouraging. Their team searching for proof of ownership of the farm throughout Sussex had had no success so far. But they had not given up. On the positive side Mr Hayward had been able to supply several previous wills legally passing the farm from father to son through the generations, indicating that the property had been in the family's ownership for a considerable time. Hampton was convinced that this would be a good argument in their favour, despite the missing deeds themselves. Hopefully they could do enough to stop Mr Hayward losing his home.

Robert was well aware that the stature of Lambert Hampton would make all the difference to the outcome, and after the court case they would certainly recommend investigations should be made in tracing the fictitious firm of Hawks and Ash. Although everyone, including Lambert, had accepted the unlikely prospect of finding them or real culprit behind this.

Of course this did not stop a turmoil of questions invading Robert's brain. Why would anyone want to put Mr Hayward and his family out of their home? No one had shown any interest in wanting to purchase his or any other farm in the area. Had the land been unimportant? Had the idea been only to ruin the Hayward family? Was there a grudge against Mr Hayward? All these notions seemed ridiculously unlikely. Whilst he could hardly approach Mr Hayward to ask him outright, maybe Margaret would have some personal insight to the matter, if he had the nerve to ask her.

It was beyond comprehension, beyond sanity, but a few days later Robert had ridden out of his way to head back to the parish of Balcombe, where Margaret should still be in service. He was halfway along the lane when an open coach came into view, but to his disgust, it contained one of his least favourite people. Why did Arabella always appear at the wrong time? There was no way she could not miss him, and sure enough, she leaned out of the carriage to engage him in conversation.

"My dear Robert, you do appear in the most unusual places!" she called, waving and making her coachman stop her chaise.

"My Lady Arabella. I did not expect to find you so far from civilisation. I presume your husband is here looking at bloodstock once more?" replied Robert, slowing his horse.

"He is, but I am so bored being dragged about these rural surroundings. Why he insists I have to accompany him I really do not understand," she complained with a deep sigh.

Was she really that naïve? The whole of society knew the reason. The unfortunate connection to her cousin's scandal had proved enough for the nobility to ostracise her. Besides which, Lord Rupert had made it plain she was not to be invited to any function he attended. Thus devoid of other entertainment and amusement, she was forced to attend to her husband's interests.

"It's about time you curbed your frivolous, selfish nature and gave your husband the support and loyalty he deserves," offered Robert.

Arabella looked astounded at his personal attack. She could not believe he had the nerve to criticise her behaviour, especially in front of her servants. Her maid could not resist a hidden grin - like most servants, she knew the rumours - but as she turned away to mask her expression, she accidentally knocked Arabella's drawstring purse from her lap. It fell to the floor and then out of the open sides of the chaise and onto the roadway, scattering several of its contents as it landed. Robert instantly leapt to the rescue, his gallantry well rewarded, for he spotted a green-crested notebook among the items.

"What an unusually pretty notebook" he said. "This device is not your husband's crest." He smiled gently, offering it back to her.

"Indeed not, it is from my own family," she boasted indignantly, holding her hand out for her belongings.

"Yes, I know. I have seen it before. The crest also belongs to your cousin Phillip Brimley, the Marquis Tree. The man who has fled the country with creditors on his heels."

His face had turned to stone, his eyes dark with anger and his sudden grip on her arm like iron. Normally he would have handled what could have been a tricky situation with more care, but he was not in that mood. Instead he pulled her closer.

"Mr Sutton!" she whimpered, trembling and frightened at the lightning change in him.

"Lord Rupert is under the impression that Phillip intended to promote his dubious scheme while a guest at Hurl Place. He is not in a forgiving mood."

"What are you talking about?"

Robert retained his cold stare, determined to scare her. It would not hurt.

"Rupert is the least of your worries. The authorities may like to have this memento as proof of your family connection. Your cousin's victims will be delighted to arrive at your door as the nearest relations, demanding financial satisfaction," he growled harshly, before putting the notebook in his own pocket.

"Oh God, no! That fiasco has nothing to do with me. We will be made bankrupt, ruined... My poor husband!" came her desperate and sincere plea. Her face was ashen. She was genuinely horrified.

"It is about time you began thinking about your husband for a change," continued Robert. "How he tolerates you and your antics I do not understand. You should be grateful he cares about you so much. I would not have been so tolerant. I would have brought you into line or had you turned out of the house ages ago."

"Robert Sutton, you are no gentleman." She had never had to endure such stark criticism from anyone before. It came as a very unpleasant shock. How dare he!

"I never pretended I was!" he snapped as he released her in disgust.

The coachman and maid had been too astounded to attempt any help to their mistress, and even Arabella had forgotten their presence, concerned only for what Robert would do now.

"Please Mr Sutton, let me have the notebook back," she pleaded.

"Not yet. I haven't decided what to do with it. I can only pray that our paths will never cross again," he retorted, urging his horse briskly on.

Robert rode straight on, hoping to find Margaret somewhere beyond the attention of her mistress. Which he soon did. She was standing outside the main gate, as if she was waiting for him. While he had calmed his anger, in anticipation of a more welcome and kinder conversation, Margaret did not reciprocate his demeanour.

"I see you are obviously well employed these days and still on familiar terms with ladies of high quality," she remarked. Once more she had skipped any pleasantries, coming straight to the point, it was becoming a habit to put him on the spot.

"I think you are mistaken," he replied.

"I think not. I saw your confrontation with Lady Arabella.

Your behaviour towards her was not that of a mere acquaintance."

Robert was not going to explain or make excuses.

"The gentry do not generally consort with mere soldiers," she continued.

"I never said I was a soldier."

"You never said what you were. You are constantly evasive."

His dark eyes looked intensely at her as he answered. "I am your friend. Whatever else I may be, I am your friend," Robert insisted.

She had lowered her head, but he tilted her chin to make her eyes level with his.

"Please believe me. I came all this way to see how you were. I heard about the court case."

Robert wanted to reassure her somehow, without betraying his intimate knowledge of the whole affair. He could hardly tell her of the latest development, and it stayed unsaid.

"I heard that there were some prominent legal gentlemen working on your father's behalf. Surely that is good?" he asked. Robert was sure Mrs Taylor would let her have a leave of absence under the circumstances, especially if he spoke to her. But Margaret's next words made that unnecessary.

"Oh Robert, Mrs Taylor has been so considerate. She is willing to let me go, with no demands on my return. I won't be in service anymore. I shall be home next week."

That was a blessing he had not anticipated. Things were looking better.

Her annoyance with him had vanished. She seemed quite glad to be able to confide in him again. It always made a difference to have a friend to talk to, she told him. She had not liked him seeing her so unhappy.

"Every time I saw you, all I really wanted, hoped for was –

I know it was silly, but I desperately wanted you to take me home."

"I did not know."

"Then by some miracle the day you left, by some strange coincidence Mrs Taylor decided to allow me home for a while. Tell me Robert, honestly, were you responsible for that?"

"Me?"

"I thought it would have been nice if you had." She smiled.

He waited for a moment before tackling the topic he had come all this way to ask her about. "I wondered, I am sorry to be so curious, do you mind if I ask you? Would anyone have benefited by the deeds going missing?"

Margaret was so relieved to be able to talk honestly about the whole matter that she gabbled on for several minutes, anxiously pouring out every theory she could think of. Her mind was racing, as she argued with herself and then dismissed her suggestions. She had no idea. In the end she was as confused as he had been. So Robert remained as ignorant as he had been when he started.

Robert was confused by the silent grins and sniggers of staff he passed on his next visit to the Hurl Place. He could not imagine what was happening. He soon found out as he entered the main drawing room, for Lord Rupert was prancing around the room, smiling and laughing, unable to keep still. He had never seen his friend so animated and so deliriously happy. He seemed to want to hug everyone who came in reach. Once was enough for Robert, who carefully backed away. These foreigners were much too free with their excited expressions.

"Oh, Robert! I am to live a calmer, less extravagant life," his friend began. "I no longer need the grand social gatherings of the nobility. I am to have a wife at my side to fill my days."

"The young lady has accepted your proposal then?" Robert teased kindly.

"We are to announce our engagement on her next birthday."

Robert had returned from Greenwich with a set of sealed documents for the Exchange. It had been a dusty journey and he was looking forward to the day off he was due. On arrival he was handed an elaborate invitation card and a note which had been left there for him from Lord Rupert. As expected there was to be an informal celebration of Anne's birthday and the announcement of their engagement. It had been arranged for the beginning of November and was to be held at the Caslon home, with a minor ball at Sholden Hall the next evening. A note with it confirmed that Rupert's friend Whinney would be delighted to be the host to Rupert and his friends for the occasion. Rupert expected him to attend, and had already instructed his employers to that effect.

Robert managed a tired smile as he returned to the courtyard to water and feed his horse. That was typical of Lord Rupert, to expect the government office to comply with his wishes. Although his status as an ambassador to visiting dignitaries might have influenced the matter.

He was busy tending to the horse, removing the saddle and giving him a brush down, when he heard a familiar sound close by. He turned to see Edmund lazily sprawled across the wide rear stone steps, playing his flute. Edmund finished his tune and casually came to talk to him.

"I heard you were expected. I have an errand in Bermondsey, would you care to join me? I really don't like the area."

Robert understood his apprehension. Edmund did not like crowds and Bermondsey and Deptford were a huddle of warehouses and wharves and immigrant housing along the river.

The hustle and bustle of casual and unskilled labour associated with the docks filled the streets. Robert nodded his agreement. To be honest, even he preferred to be there in the daylight rather than in the intimidating grey and damp of the night.

They led their horses through the street market, weaving through the stalls and the bickering people. There were small pickings for the poorer inhabitants, who were reduced to begging or trying to sell trinkets or hand-made items.

Robert suddenly handed the reins of his horse to Edmund and turned back.

"Where are you going?" Edmund gasped in panic.

"I won't be a moment. Just wait here."

Robert approached two children, who stood boldly by a tray balanced on a box. Apparently well used to their surrounding and unafraid of the adults, they shouted out the prices for their goods, hoping to attract customers. Robert was impressed by the small simple carved animals on display, although they obviously had not sold many by the amount left on the tray.

"Did you make these?" he asked. They both nodded.

"I will take four."

They let him pick the ones he wanted and smiled at him when he paid them. He returned clutching his purchases to Edmund, who was waiting impatiently and fidgeting nervously. "There was no need to do that," he said.

"It might encourage others to buy, they deserve to sell more. Look at these, they are beautifully carved."

It was then that Robert promised himself he would return to the market soon to see how the children were managing. Robert did not often make promises, but this was one he had every intention of keeping. Meanwhile he was going to put the carved animals on his window sill at home, knowing that they would make him smile every time he looked at them.

CHAPTER SEVEN

As the weeks passed, nothing happened to alarm Robert, despite his nervous apprehension, and life seemed to stay normal. All his previous anxiety gradually subsided and he really believed that both he and Ellis had indeed misjudged the whole situation concerning the danger from Phillip Brimley. He relaxed and enjoyed his journeys across the countryside once more.

At the end of September Lord Rupert was hosting a special reception for some foreign diplomats, with a lunch and entertainment provided in the grounds in the afternoon. Robert had been invited to attend, and because he had nothing else planned for that day, he thought he might as well. Rupert had drifted through his official guests with polite conversation, but once he had done his duty he was eager to talk with Robert and Ellis. Lord Rupert was glad to see Robert again. It seemed ages since he had been to Hurl Place. There was no stopping his endless enthusiastic chatter; he was still making plans for the future. Anne should choose the rooms she wanted as her private domain, and would redecorate as she wished. He could already picture soft green upholstery and white furniture, he told them.

It was obvious to Robert that he would no longer be able to arrive unannounced and whenever it suited him at Hurl Place. It would not be proper. It would no longer be a bachelor's domain. It was to become a home, with Anne at its centre. A soft, warm and gentle ambience would filter through its interior, without Lord Rupert even noticing.

Lord Rupert was eager to confide his latest idea to his friend. He wanted to buy Anne something really special and personal for a wedding present. He had seen a magnificent ivory inlaid cabinet at Ham House, the prize possession in the house. Although it had been made decades ago, in Antwerp, Rupert was so impressed that he was determined to employ the same company to make one similar if they could, even if it meant traipsing to Europe. He asked if Robert would accompany him on the journey. It would be like old times.

Robert shook his head, explaining that such a journey would not be necessary because his childhood friend Samuel, an expert furniture maker, would do an excellent job. Although not in ivory, Robert was sure he could produce a similarly delicate piece equally as fine, with an inlay of other woods as decoration. There would be no shipping fees and Samuel would be able to keep him up to date on the progress and let him view it to his satisfaction at any stage. It sounded much better all around.

"It would be unique and less opulent, as Anne would prefer," he said.

Lord Rupert was instantly agreeable, and insisted that once he had consulted the owner of Ham House to make the arrangements, Robert should escort Samuel there to view the item. He preferred that Samuel should see the item before he took on the commission. Robert already knew Samuel's response; he was highly skilled and enjoyed new challenges.

"A meeting must be arranged soon," Rupert insisted.

With that Rupert made his way back to resume his role as host. Ellis returned towards the house and Robert wandered off to look at the various attractions. There were many people, both nobility and businessmen. Some Robert knew by sight from Rupert's other grand dinners and balls, while others he was not acquainted with.

There was a display of archery on one of the lawns and most people were heading in that direction. Robert followed.

"Robert! Look out!" Rupert yelled at the top of his voice.

Situated where he was, Rupert was the only one who could see the danger. But his warning was too late, for even as Robert turned, he felt a violent thump as the bullet hit him. He fell back against a tree and slid down its trunk into a sitting position at its base to stare blankly in front of him, in shock. He was unaware of any pain or of the blood which was beginning to pulse from the wound. He did not understand the strange sensation which held him fixed in this position. He could not move, speak or see properly.

"My God, Robert!"

Ellis had never seen his master move so quickly as he covered the ground to his friend, shouting for help even as he ran. Oblivious of his guests, his own safety and where the assailant had gone or if he had gone, Robert was his only concern. Whilst others took on the chase for the culprit instantly, Rupert sank to the ground beside his friend, staring at Robert's white face, saying his name softly over and over. Lord Rupert was devastated at Robert's plight, not knowing what to do, until Ellis gently intervened.

"We must move him," Ellis instructed softly, nodding towards the figures behind him. "You must let them attend to him. I have sent for a doctor."

Rupert looked forlornly at the men around him and reluctantly let them gently help Robert to his feet. With their arms supporting him, took him back towards the house. By the time he was taken inside, Ellis was glad to see the physician running across the lawn.

The rest of the house guests and the afternoon reception were now unimportant, for Rupert had only one thing to focus on - his friend. Robert was bleeding profusely. It was hard to look at. Rupert felt quite squeamish at the idea of what might be necessary. He did not think he could watch the removing of a bullet.

As it was, he did not have to. The physician informed him that the bullet had passed cleanly through the flesh. There was no serious damage, but the wound would be stitched and bandaged to stem the blood flow. Once it had has eased, it would need a clean bandage and occasional bathing. The physician proceeded to attend to his patient.

"He was so pale. He hardly moved," said Rupert.

"The sudden pain would have put the system into shock."

Rupert was glad when suddenly Robert opened his eyes, stared at nothing, closed them again, opened them, stared and repeated this several times.

"Robert, what's the matter?"

"What happened? I feel so light-headed."

"You were shot."

"I have never been shot before," Robert mumbled drowsily, and closed his eyes.

Leaving him to sleep, Lord Rupert withdrew. Robert was his best friend, his closest confidant and to have him injured in his own home hurt him to the core. He was furious that someone had invaded his grounds and done this. "Have they caught the villain?" he demanded from Ellis.

"He was easily caught before he reached the boundary wall. He is being held in one of the stables, safely under lock and key."

"Good, I will question him later. I dare not lay eyes on him in this mood."

Robert had slept through the night and now sat wide awake propped up in bed, the bandage wrapped around his shoulder and with one of Rupert's hounds also lying on the bed. "Your dog snores," he commented when Rupert entered, followed discreetly by Ellis.

"As do you," Rupert smirked.

Robert patted the animal and tickled him behind his ears.

"He crept in last night to keep you company. He seems quite fond of you. But then you always make such a fuss of him."

The dog looked up at Robert, wiggled his way up the bed closer and began nudging him with his wet nose. His soft murmurings demanding to be rewarded, and a tickle under his chin was enough to have him roll over, stretch out and lay his head on Robert's lap.

"You scared me, Robert. I though the worst had happened," Rupert sighed.

Robert was also a little scared. With the light of day, it had not taken long for him to assess the situation. It had only taken a month for someone to find him. He had thought himself safe. So much for their assumption that he had not been at risk after all. Brimley had somehow found the funds to pay someone to take his revenge – or try.

"At least your colour has returned. How are you feeling?"

"I ache rather and I'm a little stiff. Otherwise I am fine. After a good breakfast I will be out of your way."

"Not so fast, Robert. There is no hurry."

"I have ruined your important reception party," Robert reflected.

"Not so. It will be the talk of the inner circle of power. It may yet do me a service. They may be reluctant to continue to make use of my home. I will have the place to myself and Anne, without any outside interference in our lives. That would be perfect."

They both smiled at the idea, pleased to find something good about the incident.

Lord Rupert walked to the window, stared out for a few minutes and turned back to face his friend. He shook his head, his concerned eyes focused on Robert, matching his now serious expression.

"I cannot believe you are still keeping things from me Robert."

Robert and Ellis quickly exchanged looks, worried what exactly he had found out.

"I am sad that your injury is all my fault. Dear Robert, you should have told me what you were doing. You have deliberately visited Stour Park. For my sake, I believe," Rupert challenged.

"I am not sure what you mean."

"Don't you dare feign ignorance with me! Your assailant has been most forthcoming. He has confessed he was hired in France by the Marquis Tree. Brimley was incensed you had broken into Stour Park, his country house and he paid this man to shoot you."

Robert masked his thoughts. No one knew he had been to Stour Park, not even Brimley. He might suspect it, but nothing more. Why had Brimley deliberately misled the assassin?

"I do not understand why Brimley considered your actions to be such an outrage that you needed to be punished," Rupert pondered.

"Neither do I," Robert put in quickly.

What else would this man know and be willing to tell? So far no mention had been made of the lodge on the coast. He therefore assumed that his assailant had not been furnished with the whole story, which in turn prevented Rupert from learning about the documents Robert had stolen. Robert and Ellis exchanged another questioning look. Lord Rupert frowned at each of them in turn.

"No more prevaricating, Robert. And do not look at Ellis for guidance. There are things here which do not make sense. There is more to this."

Lord Rupert did not understand how the man had been given a perfect description of Robert and the instruction to watch and wait for him at Hurl Place. How did he know what Robert looked like, and know of the connection between them?

"Maybe Brimley had seen me here in the past," Robert quickly offered, hoping his plausible response would satisfy his friend. It did not. Lord Rupert was as quick at thinking as Robert was at providing answers.

"I doubt it."

"Then he must have seen us together somewhere. How else can you explain it?"

Lord Rupert walked about the floor while he digested Robert's reply. Meanwhile Robert was trying to find his own answers. Had there been one of Brimley's acquaintances in the Treasury office, when he asked for the list of those involved in the scandal? Had they guessed the reason for his questions? Had they seen him comparing the list against Lord Rupert's guest list, and known or guessed of his connection with Rupert? But if that had been the case, Brimley would have recognised him at the lodge and he would have had no difficulty in finding him sooner. No, that did not fit. His visit to the Treasury had been long before his trip to Stour Park and the visit to the lodge on the coast. It would only be after the lodge and the removal of his papers that Brimley would have tried to find him. So how had he found out? Who would have mentioned he knew Lord Rupert and Hurl Place?

"I am immensely displeased with you Robert. You do not take your own advice. Let it go, you advised me, very firmly and persuasively, on several occasions, and yet there you were diligently pursuing such an irrational course of action."

"I was in the area. How could I resist the temptation? I had to know there was nothing hidden away even vaguely linking his plans to you. As it turned out there wasn't."

"There was no need to act so rashly for my sake. It was foolish."

Robert smiled and agreed. "Where is the man now?" he enquired.

"Packed off to languish in gaol, until I decide what charges to bring."

This was not exactly what Robert wanted. Since the incident would soon become public, it would not be long before his superiors at the Exchange eventually heard and asked their own questions. He had always hoped his employers would not find out.

"It is not right that one of the English nobility, already a felon, is responsible for such a scandalous act," said Rupert. "I will complain to His Majesty about this!" He was seething.

"Please do not. I am not badly hurt. Maybe that is the last of it. Besides, would you have me out of work, by broadcasting what I have illegally done?"

Rupert's mood softened; of course he would not. To have Robert punished for something he had done out of friendship? Never.

Later in the day when Robert made to leave and mounted his

horse, he noticed that two other riders at the end of the building copied his actions almost immediately. He looked at Lord Rupert, who smiled.

"They are for your protection. They will keep their distance or ride close as they see fit."

"I do not need your outriders."

"You have no choice in this, fair Robert. They will obey their orders from me, however you protest or barrack them," Lord Rupert continued very firmly.

Robert looked at Ellis for some support, but he merely shrugged, apparently in full agreement with his master's actions. Robert scowled at both of them. How on earth was he supposed to perform his duties with these two dogging his every move?

On returning to London Robert found his employers had soon become aware of the situation. They had learnt about the shooting and the reason for it. The assassin had been arrested and Robert's visit to Stour Park was now public knowledge. He was not sure what to expect from his immediate superiors or how much would be documented in official records. In fact their inquiry was quite brief and unremarkable in its content. They had no qualms about his visit to Stour Park, readily dismissing his illegal actions, since in their opinion, as an officer of the Crown he was expected to investigate anything he thought necessary. They were more concerned for his safety, for as a valued agent they were worried that he had put his life in danger. Although the fact that Lord Rupert was prepared to offer some degree of protection by supplying an escort came as a relief. His superiors willingly allowed such an arrangement because they wanted Robert as safe as Rupert did. Robert was simply too useful and too valuable a man to lose. Everyone accepted that if Brimley was determined enough, he would try again. While

Robert was not pleased at the decision, he was forced to accept the new procedure; his only request was that his family did not learn of the shooting.

No one made any further reference to the event and Robert resumed his assignments, although Henry and Edmund expressed their anger the next time they caught up with Robert.

"Why didn't you tell us you were in danger?" demanded Henry.

"What could you have done?"

"Something!"

"Such as what?"

They did not have an answer. They wished they had.

Robert thanked them for their concern and made light of the problem by mentioning that he would reluctantly have to adjust his whole programme to include the presence of two trailing riders on his long journeys across the south. This information made them feel a lot better, although Robert silently remained unconvinced by the whole idea.

There was one more thing he had to do before he left the city, and that was to visit the street market in Bermondsey. His escort stood at one end of the street watching everything that was taking place and waiting to see if Robert needed protecting. They were not about to shirk their responsibilities; Lord Rupert would not allow any failings on their part.

Shrugging off their presence, Robert strolled slowly to the spot where the children had stood before. He was pleased to see that they children did not look much different. Their clothes were shabby, but their faces were bright and alert. They might be under weight, but they were not skin and bone; someone was taking care of them. He bent down to study their new animals.

"Do you remember me?" he asked.

"Oh, yes. Are you going to buy any more?"

Robert chuckled.

"I am. But you would sell more if they were painted."

Their faces dropped, thinking he was having second thoughts about buying anything because they were unpainted. While they could find scraps of wood for free lying around, paint would have to be bought.

Robert stood up, plunged his hand into his deep pocket and withdrew some small pots of paint and a couple of brushes. He held them out to the children. Their eyes widened as they stood looking at the items, unsure if they should take them.

"Once you have sold the coloured animals at a better price, you will be able to buy more paint for the next ones you make," he pointed out.

"How many animals do you want for the paint?" they asked dejectedly.

"I do not want anything. The paint and brushes are a gift. They are to help you prosper." He put them into the tray alongside the animals while they were still thinking about this. "Meanwhile I will pay for a few more animals."

He picked out a couple and put the money in the tray. They were still staring at the paint as he walked away. It was a small thing to Robert, but it meant such a difference to them. He was please he had done it. Everyone deserved a little help.

His personal errand over and ignoring the escort, Robert was up in the saddle and off. He was not going to pander to their expectations of how he was supposed to behave. They could catch up when they could.

He rode through the familiar countryside to see Samuel, who as usual was to be found in his workshop. Samuel was delighted at the unexpected visit and more than pleased at the new commission offered. He made no reference to the two men left outside, assuming it was all connected to one of Robert's assignments. Robert promised to take him to Hurl Place and introduce him to Lord Rupert as soon as he returned from attending the forthcoming Hayward court hearing. They parted with a friendly wave.

Although Robert had been kept informed of the legal team's deliberations, now that the trial date was set, Robert could only wonder at how the family were coping. The latest speculation, that someone had stolen the deeds and was out to ruin them, was not a pleasant idea to accept. He had heard that Mr Hayward had wanted all his family to be there for support; typically, they would face the outcome together. Robert was eager to be there as well, impatient as ever to have matter settled. Accordingly, to preserve the familiar image the family recognised, he ordered the outriders to stay well away from the court buildings, for fear they would ruin everything. Although they did not like the idea, they knew better than to provoke a situation detrimental to Robert's occupation.

From his position in the gallery Robert could see the family sitting tense and desperately clutching each other's hands. He felt as nervous as they were, but the wide, confident smile on Lambert Hampton's face indicated that he had everything under control.

Like everyone else, Robert listened intensely as the eminent lawyer began his speech. He explained that while the actual deeds could not be produced, they could prove the sale of the property to the great grandfather, which together with the subsequent wills bequeathing it down the family to Mr Hayward, should be enough to legally prove his ownership of the farm.

Robert had been ignorant of this highly important factor, but then he had not picked up his last report from London, being delayed at Hurl Place. He listened intently as Sir Lambert explained how his team had found the vital evidence. Having worked out the time scale from the earliest will, it appeared unlikely to be recorded in any local archives, which had left them either to find the manorial records which covered the transactions of transfer and tenancy of property or the only other recognised authority in those days, the church. Indeed they had eventually found such a register, with the full details of the sale, locked away in one of the local church's dusty vaults.

Before anyone had time to question what had happened to the original deeds, Sir Lambert slammed his fist on the bench, startling everyone. He then broadcast his tirade against the apparent conspiracy they had uncovered against Mr Hayward, naming Ash and Hawk as the prime criminals involved. It was obvious from this evidence that the deeds had at some time been deliberately stolen in the hope that Mr Hayward would have to forfeit his property. Although a whole new investigation by the lawful authorities would be needed to hunt down the culprits, this dire development should not prevent the present case being concluded today.

The whole hall fell silent. Everyone was spellbound, their attention focused on this eminent man. He waited, looking around the room at each row of people. He held them for a few moments and then gave his concluding speech. In his opinion Mr Hayward was the victim in this, and he demanded that new documents should be drawn up to confirm the ownership of the property, to avoiding any further misunderstanding.

There was applause as he sat down. He looked back over his shoulder to the gallery of neighbours and friends who had come to support the Hayward family, and nodded. The decision was quick to be announced. The satisfied officials ordered the necessary documents to be drawn up as specified by Lambert Hampton. The case was finally over.

The Haywards had kept their home and they sat exhausted, drained by relief, before hugging each other and crying happily.

Robert had already slipped outside, feeling as happy and as relieved as those inside. He watched from a distance as the family crowded out into the courtyard, to thank the eminent lawyer again and again. With the assistance of clerks, accountants, auditors and investigators, a whole team all at his command, the most eminent man in the legal profession had made sure their home was safe from further threats.

"You are a man with a good heart. It was my pleasure to serve you," the lawyer repeated in an effort to extradite himself from the tangle of family members.

Joseph, who had been waiting with the family, was struck by the phrase and looked towards the figure across the square where Robert remained apart from the celebrations. Hadn't Robert used a similar phrase when he had left the Haywards' farmhouse, all that time ago?

Everyone was naturally noisy and joyful. Their happiness overflowed as the growing band of neighbours came to congratulate the family.

"Is that our soldier?" Mark asked Joseph.

"Yes it is."

Linking arms together, the boys ran back to their parents to tell them they had seen Robert.

"Father would have liked to see him," Martha volunteered.

"I expect he had other matters to attend to," explained Joseph, wondering why he was making excuses for him.

Joseph was waiting for Martha, who was chasing after a scarf a gust of breeze had snatched from her hand. Smiling, she leapt and snatched vainly in the air at the tantalizing game it played with her, until she finally stamped on a corner as it came to rest. Beaming back at him, she bent to pick up the fine material and then, standing with it in her hand, she stopped. In the street beyond, the lawyer and his team were standing by the row of crested carriages, obviously waiting for the final boxes to be secured. Fascinated by their grand manner, she saw the eminent man turn to speak to their soldier.

"Look Joseph," she whispered, dragging him beside her as he came to fetch her. And look he did, at the handshake and the smile between them, the acknowledged respect and friendly wave at the parting. Not only that, but the expression on Robert Sutton's face; his eyes shone, his smile radiant, for an immense satisfaction lit his whole being as he strode light-heartedly away.

Joseph considered the prospect. That Robert had made the effort to be here at this particular time was considerate, but was there more to it? Had a man with a good heart, his master, somehow been helped by an equally good man with an equally good heart? Although he could not understand, if he was correct, how Robert had achieved it.

The Hayward family still lingered, savouring the hour of triumph; not that Robert blamed them. He casually made his way back through the small crowd to his horse. Yet he could not leave until he had seen how Margaret was.

"Hello Joseph. What a relief. I am pleased everything has gone well," he commented casually as he passed by, leading the horse from the water trough.

"You were seen talking with the lawyer. You are at such ease with important people," Joseph commented, sensing there was more to Robert than any suspected.

"Oh Joseph, please. I had to congratulating them on the outcome, they deserved the recognition," Robert laughed.

"I believe you are acquainted with them."

"I am used to deal with all types of people every day. You are reading too much into it," Robert insisted.

Joseph realised that Robert had not really answered the question. He had become an enigma, a man of mystery who casually managed to keep so much to himself. He really wanted to ask Robert outright if he had played any part in these developments, but he hesitated and then there was no chance for further conversation because of the approach of the younger Hayward children, hurrying towards Robert.

Robert overheard the end of the two youngest boys' chatter as they reached him.

"Boys, boys. What did you just say?" he asked them.

"We were talking about our aunt and her secretary. They would have been nasty enough to have done this. For no good reason."

"Boys, that is a terrible thing to say. Your father would be furious if he heard you voicing such thoughts out loud," Joseph corrected them.

"Well it could have been," argued Matthew.

"That awful Cosmos was always poking about the place. He gave me the shivers."

"Who is this Cosmos?" Robert queried, beckoning them closer.

"Our old aunt's horrid secretary."

Their words rang in Robert's brain. Cosmos… an unusual name, but one he had heard before.

"And what does your aunt look like?" he continued, half-knowing the answer he was about to get.

"A witch, with her hair always pulled up on top of her head and feathers decorating it."

Robert smiled. There could not be another person in the whole of England who fitted the description more. The widow Jeskyns was their aunt! Robert had the answer. It was as plain as day. The children had hit the truth of the matter. Mrs Jeskyns could be behind all of this. He did not have proof, he did not need proof. He instinctively knew she was guilty. He had never been so sure of anything.

"I hope she doesn't come to stay again," complained Mark.

"Don't worry, I don't think she will," Robert reassured them. No, there was no way on earth would she be doing that, Robert silently promised. He shook his head, made his excuses to the children and Joseph and hurried off. He had to catch up with the lawyers.

Unfortunately he was halted in his tracks, as on turning a corner, he suddenly came face to face with Margaret. Despite being home only a short while, she had almost returned to the Margaret he first remembered. The colour in her face had returned, her hair was once more loose and her head no longer bowed. She faced the sun with a less strained expression. He did not want to be delayed, but Margaret obviously had something to say.

"It was kind of you to come today. Oh, Robert!" she sighed. "You knew that something was wrong at home, all the time, didn't you? Why didn't you tell me?"

"You were already unhappy. I didn't want to upset you even more."

Then taking her hand in his, he kissed it. She neither snatched her hand away nor drew back from him. He smiled, bowed politely and mounted his horse.

"I hope you will visit us again some time!" she shouted as he made to ride off.

Robert urged the animal faster out onto the road, forgetting all about his escort, who instantly followed at the same speed, because he had to catch up with the eminent lawyer again. This legal matter might be over, but the plot behind the case was definitely not. Their commission had not finished yet.

Lambert Hampton listened intently to what Robert had to say. Astounded by the complete lack of evidence or motive, he took a lot of convincing before he was persuaded to follow Robert's instinct.

For once Robert had the advantage. He already knew the names of Mrs Jeskyns' land agent and the solicitors handling the legal matters for the sale of her own property. Of course she would not have been foolish enough to use or implicate her own representatives, because she did not want any direct link to herself. But there were plenty of other lesser contacts who could have been involved. Robert needed Herbert to make some enquiries with the other senior members of their profession about her solicitors, as to any partnership they might have elsewhere or any connection to any less well-established associates. The answer had to be somewhere.

Whilst he left the legal profession to deal with their own, Robert felt incensed enough to want to find out more about the woman herself. He approached her land agent on the pretence of needing to know a little more about his client, before wishing to consider the property any further. The man was quite forthcoming. It was well known the woman had married well, which explained how she continued to run her home and large estate without any visible income. It also implied that she would be wealthy enough to surreptitiously fund these two illegal projects. Hers had always been was a fine home, although she cared less about the estate than she had done when her husband was alive. She had become eccentric, moody and unsociable of late.

During the meeting, Robert checked the name of her solicitors again. Robert was always thorough. He gave the excuse that he needed such details if his client proceeded with the purchase. What he had failed to mention was that the client, the junior minister, had already settled for and bought a beautiful period house at Sunninghill, with fine grounds and extensive gardens. His commission for finding him a home had finished months ago. Such was the discretion of the transaction that few were aware of this.

Robert needed the pretence to last a little longer, in order to have the excuse to call on Mrs Jeskyns without warning her of the true nature of his meeting. Once he had been home for a rest and to remind the family he still existed, he would be visiting the woman.

He had not been home two days when his sister dashed into the stables, excited and wide-eyed. "Henry has come!" she shouted. She grabbed his arm and tugged at him, pulling him from the stalls. Blowing the straw dust off, Robert followed his impatient sister outside.

Sure enough, there was Henry in the yard, still mounted and patting his horse. He did not look unduly concerned and even casually turned his horse ready to continue his journey.

"I am on my way to Maidstone and then Tunbridge Wells," he explained. "Sir Francis Caslon left a message for you at the Exchange requesting you visit him when convenient, but preferably soon."

"Any idea why?"

Henry shrugged and cast a glance at Elizabeth. It was obviously nothing to do with their normal work, otherwise he would have said more. How intriguing.

A day later and without an escort, because they had not known of his plans, Robert arrived at the home of Sir Francis. He was welcomed, shown into the study and bade to make himself comfortable. The door was then closed behind them, indicating the privacy of this meeting. Robert still had no idea what this was about.

The man looked a little uneasy as to how to proceed. "Mr Sutton. I hope you are recovered. I was alarmed to hear you had been shot while at Hurl Place."

Robert thanked him for his enquiry and assured him he was fine.

"I don't know to put this. I had been very pleased with the home intended for my daughter, but I would hate to learn that such unpleasant incidents were commonplace at Hurl Place. Lord Rupert and Ellis are inclined to make light of it, so as not to frighten myself or Anne. But I would rather have the liaison between them ended than have my daughter put in danger."

So that was it. The man was justly worried for his pretty Anne.

"She will not go there if I think it is unsafe," continued Sir Francis.

Robert had never expected such a declaration. Lord Rupert would be devastated. He could not let the repercussions of the shooting jeopardise Rupert's happiness.

"Please tell me why such a thing happened there?" Sir Francis asked. "I have to know the truth."

Robert considered his reply.

"It is unfortunate that there are occasions when my occupation and my decisions create enemies. I made a series of mistakes which turned someone with a grudge into someone who hated me. It had nothing to do with Lord Rupert or his home. That I was shot there was purely because that was where he found me. It could have happened anywhere."

"You are Lord Rupert's close friend. You are often at the house. It could happen again."

"No. The assailant has been caught and arrested."

Robert's attempt to ease the problem did not seem to be working. The man still frowned. There was only one thing he could offer to prevent the drastic measures Anne's father was prepared to take.

"Lord Rupert would never forgive me if I was the reason that Anne was removed from his company," said Robert. "He is so fond of her. If it would make any difference to your decision, I will promise to curtail my visits to Hurl Place permanently, thus removing any possible repetition of the incident."

"You would do that?"

"For his happiness and Anne's, yes."

"That will not be necessary," her softer voice interrupted.

"Anne!"

She had entered the room without either of them knowing.

Robert stood up sharply. "Miss Caslon."

"Mr Sutton," she replied, offering her hand.

"Robert," he corrected, bowing over her gloved hand in his.

There was that becoming genuine smile which had won his friend's heart and the bright sparkling eyes which looked directly into his.

"Rupert would never ask such a sacrifice, and neither would I," she said. "You are his valued friend. What would he do without your advice and guidance?"

"He will have you and Ellis. You are his future," was his soft reply.

Leaving her father to mull over Robert's desperate offer and her argument against it, Anne took Robert's arm to walk with him about the garden. She explained that Rupert had been very open about Robert's involvement in his life. She knew he been involved in protecting Rupert on many occasions, not just against the advances of other women, but concerning other more serious matters. Rupert had told her details of their earlier differences over the horses and the wine which had begun their friendship, and Robert's warning concerning the incident at the dinner, later connected to Phillip Brimley. He had even admitted to Robert's ride to prevent him from challenging Lady Arabella.

"Although Rupert has confided much, I can understand he wishes to prevent me worrying unnecessarily," she said. "I know I am young, but I have to share the bad as well as the good."

Anne wanted Robert to explain the cause of the shooting to her, because she knew from what everyone had told her, that Robert was a fair man and would not lie. He might refuse, but that was his choice.

Robert could not believe the astuteness of this lovely girl. The thoughtfulness of her astounded him. Yes, he would tell her of his recent mistake in breaking into Stour Park. He would also tell her that the shooting had been the result of the grudge Brimley had against him for daring to do so. But nothing more than that. Even Lord Rupert did not know the rest, and that was the way Robert wanted it to stay. Only Ellis and he kept that secret.

"I let suspicion overrule my actions. I had to make sure there were no false papers trying to implicate Rupert's dinner that night to Brimley's later financial scheme," he said.

"Thank you Robert. Tell me, would you have kept your word never to go to Hurl Place again?"

"Yes. But Rupert is not restricted to living the whole of his life at Hurl Place, is he? He does venture elsewhere."

Anne smiled. The promise would not have been such a hardship as she had expected. She would have to learn to listen to his very precise choice of words in future and not assume they meant more than they did.

"The promise will not be necessary," she said. "I know my father worries for my safety, but I have every faith in Rupert. And I am determined to do my best to make him happy."

"He is a lucky man," Robert acknowledged.

Anne loved Rupert, and that alone would be the deciding factor in winning any argument with her father. Robert could see that Anne would be a good influence on his friend. Rupert would gradually mellow under her guidance. She would be the one to protect him and care for him in the future. Yes, women constantly proved themselves to have more depth than he thought.

Robert was impatient to go to Tadworth and tackle Mrs Jeskyns, but Lambert Hampton insisted he waited until they had the rest of the evidence they needed. They had to find out for certain who else was involved in the scheme.

Hampton and Williams had been confounded by many connections to the prime solicitors, Peldon, Amble and Clarke. They were associated to Ashfields and Stephens of Epsom, who had two other offices, one in Redhill run by Oliver and Finch and the other by Mr Cross in Leatherhead. They were all equidistant to the Jeskyns house at Tadworth, although none of these other firms had an obvious legal connection the widow. It was proving to be very difficult to uncover which ones, if any, had acted as Ash and Hawks.

There appeared to be only one answer: to have two closed carriages set up near to the offices of each of them in turn, where the occupants could discreetly view the several suspects. Redick and his partner, having been released temporarily into Hampton's jurisdiction, were in the first carriage with one of the legal team. The other contained the former mayor, with another legal representative. These were the only ones who could definitely identify the men who had posed as Hawks and Ash. Of course Hampton needed two independent sightings, to verify they were both right. He did not want one influencing the other.

And so the plan proceeded. Systematically the coaches positioned themselves outside each office in turn for several days, but despite having a clear view of the suspects for a considerable time, none of the supposed guilty men were picked out. Everyone was disappointed.

The main principal suspects had already left for the day at Redhill when the witnesses inside the carriages were suddenly staring at the men they had been looking for. The clerks were closing the offices. They bustled out of the door, turned the key and walked off along the street. Redick and his partner and the former mayor were positive these men had posed as Hawks and Ash. What seemed incredible was that they were back in their normal employment as if nothing had taken place, which left Sir Hampton wondering if their employers were involved. Were Oliver and Finch in league with Mrs Jeskyns? There was only one way to find out. A little later Sir Hampton had these two men taken off the street quietly, without any fuss. For the moment Oliver and Finch would remained ignorant of what was happening. It was a Sunday, which prevented any other interested parties learning the clerks were in custody.

Lambert Hampton meant to have the truth from them, but they were both reluctant to say much. Their initial denials delayed the proceedings until they were confronted by both sets of witnesses and shown the written signed statements they had already made. Then there were so many questions to answer; how they had become involved, who had approached them and who had paid them for their trouble. Had the same person employed them for both schemes? Had they ever met Mrs Jeskyns? Slowly the whole story began to unravel.

Robert was sent the information by special courier, and he could at last set out to confront Mrs Jeskyns. He did not understand why she was so determined to have the Haywards lose their home. She had nothing to gain by its possession. There was no indication that she had any intention of living there herself, for it was meagre in comparison to her own home. For whatever reason she had done this, it could never be justified and Robert intended to make very sure the witch would regret her hand in this.

CHAPTER EIGHT

Robert had read the written statements and had most of the answers, but not all. He still did not know why Mrs Jeskyns had done what she did. For the moment he desperately wanted to start interrogating the culprit herself, before she heard of the impending proceedings against the clerks. Another reason for acting quickly was to prevent Mrs Jeskyns from destroying the incriminating stolen deeds, which he was certain she had, before he arrived.

Robert needed no excuse for calling at Tadworth. He was happy to let the widow simply assume it was in connection with the house sale. Whatever other business could he have here?

She greeted him cordially and settled down in her comfortable chair for what she hoped would be a satisfactory and productive meeting. Robert put his leather folder on the table and took out a few papers, indicating his intention to check a few details.

"Tell me madam, is it correct that Peldon, Amble and Clarke are handling the sale of this property for you?"

She nodded, completely oblivious where the direction of this conference would lead.

"I believe they are associated with the branch of Ashfields and Stephens, who also have other partners?"

She looked a little confused.

"I am not sure. I do not understand your questions. What has that to do with the business in hand?"

"These other colleagues of Ashfield and Stephens, Oliver and Finch, have unfortunately had their clerks arrested."

He deliberately paused to let his words sink in. The expression on her face indicated that she had not heard that piece of news yet. Good.

"The whole firm is presently under investigation, which leaves me wondering if your representatives are to be trusted. Any dealing they are involved with may be in jeopardy, including the sale of this property," Robert stated, deliberately keeping the topic centred on his concern for their proposed transaction. He did not want her to guess where this interview was leading.

"What? No! You cannot blame my solicitors for the mistakes of others. They are beyond reproach. They have always served me well," she gulped, more than a little flustered.

"Indeed. Who do you mean, Peldon, Amble and Clarke? Ashfield and Stephens? Or Oliver and Finch?"

"Peldon, Amble and Clarke, of course. I do not need to deal with anyone else."

Robert smirked as he laid some of the papers on top of the folder.

"Have you ever met the clerks of Oliver and Finch?"

"I would have no reason to." She was clearly on the defensive.

Robert knew the opposite; he had read their statement several times.

"You would never have involved yourself in proposing they assist you in something dishonest? Something amounting to a criminal act?"

He let his words hang in the air. The room was silent. His host seemed more nervous.

"Mr Sutton, what kind of a person do you think I am?"

He was amused that the woman actually managed to sound astounded at the impudence of this official. He picked up the top papers, held them towards her and tapped them.

"How strange then that these clerks have mentioned a scheme to ruin a relation of yours, one Mr Hayward. They claim they acted on your instruction. Is that true?" His tone was severe. His accusation had come so quickly that the woman froze where she stood. The stance, harsh tone and stern expression of her visitor together with his unexpected words, made her incapable of answering at all.

"Your dubious activities are known to the proper authorities. These signed and witnessed statements indicate you are responsible for trying to deprive Mr Hayward of his livelihood and his home. I really do not understand why, when he is one of your own relations."

Robert had encountered quite a few selfish and inconsiderate people in his life, but he could not believe how this woman had managed to create such a drastic effect on the family. He paused as the woman desperately looked at him, her instinct for self-preservation telling her to keep silent.

As well it might. In Robert's opinion Mrs Jeskyns must have spent a long time planning her subtle campaign, because of the devious nature of her schemes. He was annoyed how underhand she had been right from the start. She had always intended to steal the deeds. Once she had them in her hands, she needed to make sure that there were no other records available. It was for this purpose that she had instructed the clerks to surreptitiously ask the then local mayor if he knew of any such documents. Assuming Mr Hayward would have his own deeds, they had been curious about her request, but they were getting paid well for their time and had thought little of it.

She had then tasked the clerks to make some discreet private enquiries about the corn trade and prices for her, because they were an important part of the survival of the farm. There had been nothing illegal in either of these first requests and the men had again been well paid for their trouble. The clerks had stated that they had been most reluctant to get involved with the next part of her complicated and unlawful agenda. They regretfully admitted that they had been persuaded and had soon found a suitable and struggling corn merchant willing to help. The said corn merchants had then cheated the Hayward family and others in the same area, unaware of her aim to hurt Mr Hayward's finances in particular. Everyone had been kept ignorant that the widow had hoped it would be enough to force Mr Hayward to ask the bank for a loan, for which he would have needed the deeds as collateral.

Robert tapped the papers thoughtfully. She must have believed she would soon achieve the success she wanted. Unfortunately for her, this man, this government agent facing her, had ruined her scheme and prevented the initial disaster. But Mrs Jeskyns had been prepared to bide her time and eventually this year the dire consequences she had originally hoped for had unexpectedly come to fruition. Mr Hayward, through no influence of hers, had approached the bank for a simple loan and the whole scenario had escalated beyond imagination. Thank goodness Lord Rupert and Lambert Hampton had saved the day.

"No doubt you were disappointed with the outcome of the recent court hearing," he said. If he had not learnt to master self-control in his occupation, he would gladly have shaken the woman until her bones rattled. As it was her body crumbled as she sank further into her chair, where she sat clutching her hands together, her eyes cast to the floor. There she remained for some considerable time, unwilling to move.

"Why did you set out to ruin Mr Hayward? What was the purpose of it? Why would you do such a thing? What is so special about the farm that you would have it taken away from him?"

Robert did not expect her to answer. He had some clue as to her reason, but he found it hard to accept, because it was so petty. The clerks had inadvertently overheard her ranting and raving about the farm to her secretary. They had stood silent, embarrassed by her bad mood, especially as it showed no sign of abating, despite their presence in the room. She had cursed her own father for signing away his right to inherit the farm, declaring the farm should have passed to her side of the family instead of Mr Hayward's grandfather. Although she had no legal claim on the farm, it was clear it peeved her that the present Mr Hayward had a comfortable living there.

Robert waited for some gesture of remorse, but it never came. So he moved on to main reason for his visit. He walked towards her and stood imposingly closer to her to make sure she heard his next words.

"Now for the second part of my business here. I know you stole Mr Hayward's deeds. The documents do not belong to you. Will you please give them to me so they can be returned to the correct owner?"

Mrs Jeskyns did not blink, nor did she speak. The instinct to ask how he knew such a thing or to deny she had stolen them was never voiced. For a moment Robert wondered if she was about to try to pretend she did not have them, even at this stage of the interview. So he raised his voice into that loud official tone used by those in authority.

"Madam, I do not have all day. You will notice I did not come alone. I have men at my disposal waiting outside. It will give me great pleasure to have the whole house torn apart, if you do not hand them over immediately."

He sat and waited while she looked about the room, thinking about it. To produce them would conclusively prove her guilt, but then she must know they would be found in any case. Would she save the house from being wrecked as he threatened?

Slowly she stood up to walk to the bureau against the far wall, where she turned the small key and opened the top drawer. She lifted the documents out and came to place them on the table next to Robert. Then she sat down again, all without saying a word to him.

Robert carefully checked them over, reading every line deliberately slowly for impact, before folding them into the leather satchel he had with him and turning to her.

"How can you be such a vindictive, evil, nasty woman? Mr Hayward is a good man. I cannot imagine he has ever done anything to warrant such wicked behaviour on your part. It will give me great pleasure to assist in any criminal charges brought against you. You have my word on that as an officer of the Crown. I bid you good day, madam."

The interview, such as it was, was over.

As Robert left the room he found Cosmos on his knees in the hallway, where he had been knocked to the floor as Robert opened the door. He must have been listening at the keyhole. Robert frowned briefly at the man, wanting to put one of his stiff black boots into his face, but Cosmos scrambled up and rushed away, embarrassed at being caught. Other members of the household hardly gave Cosmos a glance and Robert strode away from the house to ride off with the broadest of smiles. For once his escort had proved their usefulness just by being there.

The firm of Hampton and Williams suggested that Robert should have the pleasure of delivering the deeds back to Mr Hayward, himself, since he had been the one to force the guilty party to hand them back. All the findings had been passed onto the correct authorities and the legal firm had completed their task. They had even arranged for Redick and Partner to be released from prison, since their story was now collaborated by these latest events. Their only extra paperwork consisted of tying up the loose ends, by informing Mr Hayward of their recent alarming discovery. His own aunt had surrendered the documents she had stolen for them to return to him. Prudently they had decided not to mentioned her other plans to ruin him, and Robert would remain unconnected with the whole incident.

Robert was not sure about returning to the farm, wondering if he could he keep his escort far enough away from the house to remain unnoticed. They had become his ever-present shadow, and he had even grown used to their annoying presence in his daily life, but he wondered at the impression this gave to others.

It was still mild for the end of October when Robert rode alone into the yard, where everyone rushed to greet him, pleased and excited at his unexpected arrival. The boys were soon making a fuss of the horse, the dogs jumping up and down around everyone. Mr Hayward began shaking his arm and guiding him into the house, whilst the girls rushed to help their mother find refreshment for him. Before he could give any explanation for his visit they were soon all seated in the small parlour, with the youngsters firing questions, eager to hear any news from the rest of the county.

Once they were more settled and he had managed to draw

breath himself, he bent down to the saddlebags and withdrew a large leather folder, which he handed to Mr Hayward. He told them he was delivering a package from the lawyers who had recently represented them.

"I hope it is not a bill for their services," his wife sighed anxiously.

Robert smiled to himself as Mr Hayward undid the cord and several sealed envelopes and the deeds fell out on to the table. Everyone stared at the deeds, not sure this was real. Slowly Mr Hayward picked them up, turned them over and then clutched them to his chest. The delight on the man's face was wonderful to see.

"But how? Where have they come from?" Mr Hayward asked.

Robert shrugged. He was only the courier charged with delivering this, he protested. He casually stood up ready to depart. Insisting that any private contents were not for his eyes and begging to take his leave.

Mr Hayward nodded absently, still holding the precious deeds, as if he was frightened to let them out of his hands ever again. The rest of the envelopes on the table held little interest for the moment, because everyone was still fussing over the important parchments.

Robert strode quickly out of the building to his horse, eager to be away from the place. He could not imagine the effect on them when they found that their own relation had been responsible for stealing the deeds.

A few minutes later Robert turned to find Margaret had chased after him.

"Robert, wait! Do not rush away. I want to speak to you. A courier who needs an escort, however discreet, is not common. They were on your heels the moment you left to chase after the lawyers who represented us. Am I right in thinking they are close by even now?"

"Their company is not at my request. They were imposed on me."

He stopped, and she stood smiling at him, expecting more. Sadly, he was not about to enlighten her. Margaret could sense his reluctance, but whatever the reason for it, he was still her friend and she would have the truth.

"You say so little about your employment."

"My work involves keeping my clients' confidentiality. It would be morally wrong to betray the trust they have in me," he said. He made no attempt at further clarification, except a kind grin as he patted his horse.

"Evasive as ever," she said, hitting him, but not hard. She shook her head, almost forgivingly, and smiled.

"Sir Eustace regards you with great respect, as do others I believe. I can only wonder what you have done to deserve such praise."

"Nothing except my job, to the best of my ability."

She looked at him curiously, her head tilted to one side. Margaret's shrewd brain had not finished sifting all the facts.

"Yet I believe you are much more than you pretend. From what I observe. From what is not said. From the occasional glance Sir Hampton discreetly gave you. You are not the usual poor itinerant worker."

Yet he was an itinerant worker, just not in the sense she thought. He was an itinerant worker for the Crown, with all its vast and different requirements.

"What can I tell you? I am here today because the lawyers thought you would appreciate a familiar face delivering them back to you, rather than a stranger. Can't you be satisfied with that?"

Margaret screwed her face up. It looked as if she had no

choice.

"You had better go back in, I am sure your father will need you," he added. Margaret looked at his face. His expression was enough to make her run back to the house.

The engagement celebration for Anne and Rupert at her home involved a mixture of the country gentry and some selected elite friends. The house was full of people happily milling about with refreshments and a grand selection of food set out for them to taste. The elaborate clock stood centre stage in the lounge and other touches of exuberant decoration added to the congenial atmosphere. Even at the beginning of November Lord Rupert had been thoughtful enough to obtain an abundance of sweet-smelling flowers, the displays of which filled the main rooms. It had been a most congenial day and everyone expected the same of tomorrow.

The assembly regathered the following evening at Sholdon Hall for the ball Whinney had arranged in their honour. The carriages filled the forecourt, drive and stable yard. Everyone was excited and enthusiastic, the music played as the ballroom filled with more and more people.

Robert had danced with many of the young ladies and had enjoyed the comfortable company, the affable atmosphere being reminiscent of Rupert's grand events.

"Robert, this is my cousin Isabella," Anne trilled at his side, during one of the intervals.

The sound of that name gave him a brief moment of panic, sending an ice-cold sensation through his veins. He had never expected to hear it again. It did not exist in his world any more. He had shut it out decades ago. His heart missed a beat and he took a deep breath as he prepared to smile at the Isabella he was being introduced to. He took in the appearance of this elegant young woman. She was slim, dark and tall; thankfully her features and colouring were nothing like the girl he remembered so well who had once shared her name.

"What is it about my cousin you seem to dislike?" Anne asked him, after they had exchanged the briefest of conversation and Isabella had moved on.

"I am sorry I gave that impression. I hope I was not impolite. She is a charming young girl."

Anne was not about to let him get away with that. She knew him well enough by now.

"Then what caused you to dismiss her company so quickly?"

Robert closed his eyes. He would not answer. When he opened them again, he did not look at hers. He took both her hands in his, lifted them to his lips, bowed politely over them and turned away, to leave her company. The memory was buried again.

Anne was still staring after him when Ellis, having seen the manner of his retreat, enquired what was wrong with him.

"I think I have hurt him, although I don't know how," she said.

Ellis had wondered about Robert of late, more than normal. This was not the same man who had frequented Hurl Place in the early years of his friendship with Lord Rupert. He was burdened by a continual shadow hanging over him and Ellis wished he could magically turn back the clock, to make it all right.

Back on the road, Robert called on Thomas the blacksmith. They exchanged their normal chat and he headed off towards his next destination. Margaret had seen him ride through the market square at West Dean, although he had not seen her. She rode after him, straight past the escorts without even a glance, making Robert pulled his horse to a stop.

"Margaret! What's wrong?"

"Nothing. Please don't ride by without coming to the house. Do you have time to visit? Father would like to see you."

It did not seem too much to ask and they rode on slowly together in the direction of the farm.

"Has your father come to terms with his aunt's behaviour yet?"

"Father was upset at finding out that she stole the deeds. But he was more put out by the idea of a conspiracy which was bandied about in the courtroom. It hurt him to think that someone had been so wicked as to plan all this, but faced with the revelations he had to accept the facts. None of us can understand who would be so wicked."

It was good that no one had made the connection, as it was better for them not to know the truth yet. And yet, here was this girl he admired for her tenacity; Margaret, whose recent sacrifice to duty for her family had proved her inner strength and loyalty. This young woman had believed his reasons for being at Stour Park, because in her world there was no reason to lie. She had trusted him, but hadn't he always lied to her with half-truths to protect his job? Didn't he owe her something? Didn't she deserve that? She was certainly brave enough to handle the truth if he told her.

He stopped his horse and waited for her to do the same. He wasn't going to lie to her this time. He would put it as simply as he could. She did not ask why he had stopped, because she could tell by his expression that he was about to say something really serious.

He slid from the horse and suggested they should walk for a while. She matched his steps, waiting for him to unburden his thoughts.

"How would your father react to knowing his own aunt had

deliberately plotted the whole scenario from the start? That she had been responsible for all the terrible anxiety he has suffered over the past two years?"

Margaret gulped. "Why would she do that?"

"Because she was aggrieved that her father had signed away his claim to the farm when he was young. She felt it should have been passed on to her, even though she had no intention of living there. It is nothing more than that."

Margaret listened to the rest of the story in silence, accepting every word he said. He explained how once their aunt had the deeds, she had sent people to search the local offices to make sure there were no other copies available. He told her their aunt had been behind the corn merchants' attempt to cheat him and his neighbours and that she had men using false names to bribe them into acting as they did, hoping her father would need a loan from the bank and knowing he would be unable to supply the deeds as collateral.

Margaret shook her head; this was hard to believe. But Robert had told her the truth, she could see it in his face. She did not ask how he knew all this.

"There, you know it all. It is a lot to digest." He paused. "I'm sure you have the ability to keep the worst from your father. I am relying on your judgement."

Margaret was deep in thought, obviously churning it all over in her head. She sighed a few times and kicked the ground with her foot. Then she stopped and looked at him.

"I believe you were the one who visited our aunt. You made her give the deeds back."

"I had no authority to do so," he admitted.

"Robert! You never cease to surprise me. You never hinted at what you intended to do."

"How could I? I did not want to raise your hopes. You might have expected me to do more than I was able to do. I did not want to disappoint you."

Margaret looked at the face she had studied for so long during his recuperation, the scar now faded but still visible. He had hardly changed. There was always more to this man, but no matter how hard she had tried she could never quite fathom him out. He had kept his personal interventions with the corn merchants, and now with their aunt, so secret. Dare she think he had been responsible for finding the lawyers, that he had asked someone else to help them? Someone who had paid for the expense for no other reason than Robert had asked it? That someone had done that said a lot about this man. She wished she knew him better, although she knew she never would. Here they were comfortable friends who linked their arms together.

"You are the best of friends Robert. You have helped us keep our home. Thank you," she sighed.

He gave her a little hug. He was fond of Margaret and luckily they were both too set in their ways for it ever to be any different between them. They walked on a little further before he told her he would not come to the farm today. He considered she had enough to contend with. She nodded and parted with a promise.

"I will not forget all your kindness."

Robert had hardly been home a couple of days when a courier from London arrived unexpectedly. He looked flustered and embarrassed.

"Whatever is wrong? I am not scheduled for any journeys until next week," he asked.

"There is a problem. The shipment you arranged from Lewes never arrived."

Robert was astonished at the statement. He knew the carrier well. He had never failed to deliver any goods on time before. He did not understand what had happened.

"He sent no word? No explanation for the delay?"

The man shook his head. The firm clearly wanted Robert to investigate and report back. Immediately. So as the courier left to return to London, Robert made his plans to depart.

He arrived at Lewes late the next day, a little dusty and tired from the hasty journey. The carrier looked relaxed and smiled at his approach, offering his hand.

"How good to see you, Mr Sutton. Have you come to tell me when you now want this shipment sent?"

"I thought we had finalised the arrangements the last time I was here?"

"But you sent word by another of your colleagues to delay until I heard from you again."

Robert frowned. He had sent no such message. And neither Edmund nor Henry would have counteracted any arrangement without instructions from London and notifying him they had done so. He was keen for the courier to describe this other colleague, but the description fitted neither Edmund nor Henry, who shared responsibility for this section of the south. Someone was deliberately interfering with their work, but the delay had harmed no one, although the carrier was quite concerned at the mistake. Robert patted the man on the shoulder and gave him a friendly smile.

"There's nothing to worry about. It is not your fault. There must have been a mix up in communications."

Robert waited in Lewes for a couple of days to see the goods on their way personally before heading back home. While he had made light of the matter to the courier, he did not like the incident. What had the imposter hoped to achieve? The fact that he had come and gone without his usual escort in attendance was the only difference he could find. There had been nothing to gain except to have himself riding out to chase up the problem. Had that been the point? To see if he could be drawn away from his normal schedule and therefore his escort? The small port of Newhaven was not far from Lewes. Had Brimley or another agent resurfaced? Was he testing what could be done? Was he about to try something else?

With no other theories to occupy his mind, Robert concluded he was probably right. Much as he wanted to convince himself he could be imagining too much. Robert knew the truth when he saw it. Somehow Brimley had learnt his name, that he worked for Exchange, and his schedule.

Robert accompanied Samuel to Ham House, met the present owner and waited as Samuel made numerous sketches and took measurements. They had returned to his workshop to examine the various types of wood Samuel had in stock and make a list of what else he would need. This would be a difficult piece of furniture to make, but Samuel was sure he could match the delicate inlay and design. Robert could see from his face that he was excited about getting started and have it take shape.

Robert left him happily humming a tune as he engrossed himself in his plans and made his way back up the lane to call in briefly to see Rebecca. She had just come in from the vegetable plot and was washing the dirt from her hands.

"You do not seem in the best of spirits of late," she said. "What is wrong?"

Becky dried her hands on her apron and came to sit, ready to listen. She tilted her head and waited for him to tell her. She would be just the right sensible person to confide his concerns to, over the problem at Lewes. But he would not say too much.

"I am tired," he said. "I encountered a few problems with one of my schedules. It sorted itself out, it has not happened again, but you know I don't like things going wrong."

Robert pulled a glum face and Becky smiled forgivingly.

"You always expect things to go exactly your way. Life isn't like that. You must learn to be more philosophical."

He was doing his best to be philosophical about his life, but it was not easy. None of the others had had any difficulties or had their work interrupted of late.

From here he was going straight on to Tunbridge Wells to collect some paperwork and pick up his escort. His outriders changed every month and Robert was getting bored with the whole business.

After a few hours' ride, he stopped at a small village to rest the horses and himself.

Here there were a few cottages cut out of the declining woodland on the edge of the heathland. Their little vegetable plots were positioned close to the buildings, with a few chicken coops, but the pigsties were empty, since the tenants let their animals forage the open heathland to supplement their meagre living.

He took a leisurely amble out across the heath, intending to stretch his legs for a change, while the escort sat by the water trough. He had not walked far when the twisting path narrowed and he had to pick his way carefully through the thick tufts of grasses, overgrown brambles, gorse and bracken to keep to the track. The land dipped and rose into ridges across the open space; it was peaceful and quiet.

He had stopped to take in the surrounding, wondering when to turn back, when a shot hit the dirt track a few feet in front of him. It sent up a small divot of dust, causing him to stare at the mark it made. The fact that the bullet was so wide of its mark surprised him. Had it been meant as a warning? Robert ducked low to the level of the bracken as a precaution, wondering about its direction.

As he turned to retrace his steps the way he had come

another shot flew past his head, another warning, except this time a piercing scream further up the slope followed. Instantly Robert sprinted towards the sound and found a sight he had never expected. A small child lay still, crumpled on the ground, blood covering his chest. There was nothing he could do. The child was dead. Another ragged child knelt frozen, staring at his companion.

Robert stood up, a clear target, but he did not care; he was too angry.

"You have killed a boy!" he yelled.

There was no response, no other shots, no other sounds. The assailant, wherever he was, had gone.

Robert bent over the child again. This poor boy who only a moment ago had been alive and playing happily with his friend lay dead. He took his hand; it was still warm and he held it tight, wanting to transfer his own energy to somehow bring the child back to life. Just as he had done all those years ago with Isabella, wanting her to come back to life. He shook his head. Isabella! The memory seemed to suck all the energy from him.

Suddenly the other child was now in floods of tears, and Robert had to turn his attention back to the present. He soothed the boy and asked his friend's name.

"We must take him home. We cannot leave him here," he whispered.

Carefully Robert lifted the dead boy, his limp body surprisingly heavy, and bade the other child lead them back towards the scattering of cottages on the edge of the heath.

Robert did not remember much of the short journey back. His heart was pounding and his body trembled with the sensation of holding this limp child against him, still warm in his arms but slowly growing cold. As he walked he could not shake off that other long-buried unwanted memory fighting for recognition. If only he could.

His escort were the first to see the returning group and were alarmed at the blood on Robert's shirt, not realising it was not his. The other inhabitants were soon clustering around as the other child was now gabbling the story of what had happened to everyone. Then the horrified parents appeared at their door, summoned by the shouts from the neighbours. Silently he carried the child into their home and laid him down on his simple bed by the window. The wailing and tears made it almost impossible for Robert to grasp their name or explain the circumstances.

Outside, he asked the direction of the nearest church and sent someone to find the local vicar, who would see to their distress and comfort. His heart was still beating fast and while he waited to have words with the church representative, he enquired as to the location of the nearest magistrate. He sent one of his outriders off to warn the magistrate of the situation and inform him that he would be there shortly to give his account of the accident. When the vicar came rushing along the track, Robert saw he was a capable man, used to helping his parishioners. The shocked and distraught family would need his support. Before he entered the cottage Robert spoke to him briefly and then left to follow his own man to town.

After he had informed the magistrate of the tragedy and signed a written statement, Robert sat in the office, his mind still churning. They needed to set a day for the formal inquiry, prompting the magistrate to ask when Robert could be back. He still had to complete his current assignment. His journey would take him through Ashdown Forest to Burgess Hill, before returning via Haywards Heath. It would take a couple of days, was his reply. The magistrate agreed that this would be convenient, then wrote it in his ledger and marked the date for the attention of the clerks, to make sure all would be attendance.

With that Robert got up and left, promising to attend as required.

Robert returned for the official enquiry before the local magistrate, held in the small village hall with very few people in attendance. The procedure was simple, to establish the reason for the death and for it to be recorded in the records.

"Does anyone know why this child was shot?" the magistrate asked.

Glances exchanged about the room, with no one having an explanation to offer. Robert stood up and took a deep breath. Everyone was looking at him.

"Sir, forgive me, but I believe it was an accident. The assailant was shooting at me," he said. He might as well tell it as it was. The truth could only help the family, and besides the other child was bound to confirm the terrible tale, if he was ever asked.

"I was on the heath when one shot hit the ground in front of me. Then the second shot passed me, hitting the child by mistake."

The magistrate had never encountered such a statement before, but he was fully aware of Robert's occupation and knew that as an officer of the Crown, his word was to be accepted. He had no reason not to tell the truth.

"Do you know why or who would want to shoot you, Mr Sutton?"

"I assume I have upset someone, although I have no idea who the assassin was." Robert was being careful about what and how much he said.

This was correct. He had not known who the assassin was. Robert might well know who had sent him, but that was not the question he had been asked.

He looked at the gaunt faces of the tormented parents. Their expressions were so like Isabella's parents had been. They sat stunned, silent and still unable to comprehend the tragedy. Their distress was hard to bear. To inflict this on a family who struggled to exist was not fair. As he stood there he wished he had died instead, rather than let his happen. He felt awful. This was all his fault.

While the magistrate concluded it had been an accidental shooting by a person unknown and the inquiry was closed, Robert was trying to deal with his own demons. That awful illogical, all-consuming memory of Isabella's death took hold of his mind and would not shift, because this time it was bound together with the death of an innocent child. No one knew why the boy's death had touched Robert so deeply; no one knew the similarity of events, and he had no reason to explain. If only he had not been reminded of Isabella. Isabella dead at his feet on the floor. Isabella, Isabella... the name rippled silently through him. Now it had resurfaced, it took control, despite his resolve not to allow it.

For the first time in his life, Robert now abandoned his schedule. He sent a message to Thomas to pass on to London and dismissed his escort. He was going home. It was the only place where he wanted to be. He held the awful emotion in check as he rode on, desperate to be home, desperate to be alone. He could let it go once he was home, not before.

Elizabeth realised the instant her brother came home early that something was wrong. She saw the state he was in, and she knew from his blank face, downcast eyes and quietness that it was serious. She also instinctively knew that he wanted to be alone to sort himself out. It was his custom to sit in a quiet spot and switch off from everything to collect and organise his thoughts. He dealt with such things in his own way; he always had. Robert rarely shared private worries and she knew by past experience when to keep her distance.

Robert slumped into the hollow of the old tree in the orchard and sat staring at the stream, allowing the dark, swirling hypnotic ripples to obliterate the world around him. All that emotion he had locked away and refused to acknowledge was pounding his head, desperate to be released. He had been ten years old when it happened and he was now a few years from thirty. After all this time he could finally let himself grieve for Isabella. He had so loved his childhood friend, her chubby round face, her little button nose, her thick straight chestnut hair and her uncontrollable giggle.

The full pain and sorrow of that day leapt back into his vision. One minute she had been dancing about on the landing calling for Robert, then seconds later while dodging out of her brother's grasp in their game of chase, she had slipped on the solid stone stairs. She never made another sound before she landed on the floor of the hallway below. His precious Isabella, the girl he had promised to keep safe, lay dead.

He remembered being that boy who had sat crying, the tears rolling down his face as he had said her name over and over again. Isabella, Isabella! He had spoken her name again and again until it choked him.

But that had not been the end to the tragedy he had seen and been a part of. Poor Andrew, her brother, had blamed himself for the accident and committed suicide days later. Unable to end his overwhelming misery, he had thrown himself off a cliff top into a quarry.

Robert had watched the others dealing unsuccessfully with their sorrow, determined not to let the same insanity which had taken Andrew touch him. After their parents had moved away to Suffolk, with no reminder, he had finally been able to bury the dreadful memory completely. He had never spoken of Isabella to anyone; Elizabeth had been a newborn baby and his parents and other sister had passed away the next year. There was no one to remember the incident once they came to live with his aunt and uncle. Now he sat in the orchard, crying for Isabella, for Andrew and for himself.

Several times Elizabeth had started to walk down through the orchard, but she had always turned back upon seeing he was still in the same position. She had never seen him take so long before to pull himself together.

A hollow misery echoed through his mind, resounding back and forth, absorbing every corner of reason. He was lost in a vacuum and growing cold. That long-buried grief from his childhood resurfaced with a vengeance. His body shuddered with great gulps of air, snatched amongst the great outpouring of his tears. He would never have imagined he could have wept like this for so long. His sleeves were damp from where he had laid his head on his arms. Why could he not stop the tears? He did not know how much later he finally exhausted their flow.

Elizabeth returned to the top of the orchard, pleased to note that at least he had regained his composure. She had never seen him cry before and she ached to comfort him. But as she carefully made her way nearer she saw his expression was still drawn, tired and unhappy. His eyes were red and puffy. It stopped her where she stood. She did not want to intrude. She crept away again.

Robert did not want anyone to see him in that state and he bent down by the stream to splash cold water into his face. Again and again he repeated the action, until his hands and face were bitterly cold. He shivered and stood up. Then he brushed himself down, pushed his hands through his hair and adjusted his clothing to make himself more tidy.

He gathered all his senses together to walk back to the house, only to find he had to stop, catch his breath, clench his jaw, suck in his cheeks and close his eyes. That tearful, remorseful outburst had not finished with him yet.

No one asked why he had suddenly come home. Neither did they ask why he stayed isolated in the orchard or avoided their company for days. Robert was his own man, a grown man who faced the world in his own resolute way.

CHAPTER NINE

The news of the shooting and the inquest quickly spread through the Exchange and Robert's fellow officers. Once again his employers made very little of the incident, because they were thankful he had not been the one killed. They were quite prepared to forget the whole matter and tactfully ignored the sudden moments of melancholy about the boy's death which hit him. They made allowances for his jaded face and withdrawn periods, although they were alarmed that the supposed escort had failed to protect him.

The news had even reached Thomas the blacksmith, who on their next encounter, whilst understanding Robert's regret over the tragedy, was puzzled by the whole affair.

"There must be someone who knew your exact routine, to have attempted this, but who?" he asked. "No one could watch you that long, to know where you would have been this month. Only those in the same office would be aware of your schedule."

Yet they both knew that no one in the Exchange would give

out information like that. While their routes were not officially secret, their work required discretion and sensitivity, which made it unlikely it would be discussed casually or freely. It was worrying. They both reluctantly acknowledged the awful truth that once anyone knew Robert's routine and schedules, it would be easy enough to try again.

"What do I do?" Robert asked, not expecting an answer.

"Changing your job would be the obvious solution," Thomas suggested. Robert had never considered such a radical idea.

At Hurl Place, Robert was tired of Lord Rupert's furious ranting and raving against the escort which had allowed Robert to come under attack again. Robert himself had been quite philosophical. How were they to supposed to warn him of someone no one had seen? He would not have them blamed for something they could not prevent.

When Rupert suggested increasing the number of men around Robert, effectively providing an armed guard, Robert turned on his friend with unusual severity, attacking the stupidity of such a ridiculous over-reaction. How was he expected to continue his occupation under such intrusive conditions? It would be impossible to conduct any of his assignments. He refused to listen to any more and stormed out, leaving Lord Rupert to stare after him.

Ellis caught him on the way out, expressing his concern over the recent incident.

"My only worry is that someone else may get hurt when they try again. It could be family or friends next time," Robert admitted.

"I thought you would be safe now," Ellis commented sadly.

"So did I. How long can Brimley afford to pay these

assassins?"

"Who knows? He will not dare return himself. He could not risk being identified."

Robert shook his head. He was tired of thinking about it.

"Maybe you should retire from this hectic chasing about the country," said Ellis. "A change would not hurt and for practical reasons, it might be safer."

How strange that Ellis had offered the same advice as Thomas.

Weeks later Robert, Edmund and Henry met up again, as they did when their assignments allowed, and were spending an hour together in the coffee house. Then Christopher, his previous replacement, who had since been assigned to cover the Essex area, appeared and rushed up to Robert, beaming proudly. None of them could imagine why he looked so pleased with himself. His reputation for being too eager to ingratiate himself with the other colleagues had not been appreciated.

"Hello Robert. I had the pleasure of meeting your cousin recently at Bury St Edmunds. Did he mention it?"

Robert felt himself tense up, because he had no idea what Christopher was talking about.

"I do not have a cousin in Bury St Edmunds," Robert replied slowly.

"No, he said he was passing through on his way towards Kent. He said he knew we worked for the same organisation. So I presume you must have mentioned me to him at some point."

Christopher paused, pleased that he was apparently at last being accepted amongst his fellow operatives. Robert remained stony-faced and the others glared at Christopher, anticipating his next damning words.

"Did he catch up with you? He thought he would if you

were still engaged on the same routes."

"And you told him?" Edmund asked grimly.

Robert let out a long sigh, his shoulders sagged and he shook his head. Here was the answer. Bloody Christopher had been the one to leak the information to Brimley's agent. Christopher who would know his routes precisely, since he had been his temporary replacement last year.

"Wait. Did this cousin ask for me specifically by name?"

"Oh yes, and he asked if that mark of grey hair still showed."

"You fool. What have you done?" Henry snarled through clenched teeth.

"But..."

"But nothing! How dare you jeopardize your colleagues? Genuine relations aware of the delicate nature of our work would certainly not be asking such questions," Edmund growled.

Their brief conversation in the coffee house ended with Henry and Edmund standing up and grabbing Christopher by each arm to firmly escort the culprit back to the main office to report his stupidity. Robert was left on his own with his own thoughts while Christopher sheepishly endured the wrath of his superiors, and his friends collected their new orders and set off to their next appointments.

Robert was still trying to work this all out. Somehow Brimley must already have had some idea that Robert worked for the Exchange before trying to find out his routes. But how did they know Christopher was another operative? He was young, over eager and not as discreet as the rest of them, but even so, how had they found him? Had he been flattered by someone and made to feel he was important? Had someone wheedled it out of him? There were too many questions filling his brain. This was ridiculous. Would he ever have the answers, and in the end, did it matter? It had happened, he could not change it. He was learning to be philosophical.

Elizabeth had been waiting for her brother to come home, and ever since he had returned she had been close by, waiting her chance to be alone with him. She had been deliberately patient through the meal, glancing now and again at her aunt and uncle and sighing softly as they beamed at her. Robert had not noticed the unspoken expectation of collusion, and even when the aunt and uncle deliberately made themselves scarce, nothing had registered.

When she followed him into the next room to sit quietly on the window seat while Robert spread some papers from his saddlebags onto the table, he raised an eyebrow quizzically. He put the papers aside and looked at her, wondering what she was up to. Then she smiled that wonderful relaxed, bright smile and came to him.

"Robert," she began softly.

"Elizabeth?"

"Michael wants to marry me."

"Do you want to marry him?" he teased.

"Oh, of course. We love each other."

Well - that was no surprise.

"He has spoken to his parents, who have no objection. And he wants to ask for my hand formally, properly."

"And so he should. It is a credit to him that he does things correctly. It bodes well for your future."

"He wants to ask you for your permission for us to marry."

"Me? What is that to do with me? I would have thought our uncle would be the one to ask. He would be delighted at the honour."

"No Robert, I have mentioned it to our aunt and uncle and they both agree, it is for you to give permission."

Elizabeth was holding his hand. She looked radiant. He had

meant to tease her by pretending he needed to consider it before giving his consent, but he did not have the heart to dampen her happiness today.

"I await his visit then. Michael may call on me whenever he wants."

His sister threw her arms around his neck and kissed him. Now she sat meekly at his side, gently snuggling up to him as they had done as children when they had wanted to confide something special.

"I don't want a long engagement," she said, blushing.

"Elizabeth, I am shocked at your forwardness!" He grinned. Then he cuddled her and kissed the top of her head. His lovely young sister, with those sparkling blue eyes. He was pleased for her. She would be cherished and loved and be deeply happy.

"Love is a gift, Elizabeth. Treasure it," he whispered wistfully.

He had never been that lucky, but then he had never sought that kind of love. He had never thought himself good enough to share the whole of himself with anyone.

"What of you, Robert? You never mention your hopes and dreams."

"I don't have any," he admitted.

"That is sad. You are not being fair to yourself, you push yourself too hard. You never let anyone get close to you."

His sister was becoming too wise. It was time to end this conversation.

The interview with Michael passed easily, which left him with one outstanding secret pilgrimage to make before he returned to London. Robert knew he really ought to find the courage to go to that special place where Isabella and Andrew were buried. He could not put it off any longer. It would be an emotional experience, but it had to be done. He owed it to them. So one afternoon after he had finished his few chores, he set off as usual over the hill towards Luddesdown Church, down into the valley and through the wooded lanes.

He found the gap in the overgrown hedge where the gate had once been and pushed his way through. The path had disappeared and even the tiny abandoned chapel after all these years was half-hidden by saplings, brambles and ivy. The roof had half-fallen in and the windows were broken. It felt a sad place with the rustling leaves, and the birds made the only sounds.

He walked to the spot between the two trees where the children had been laid side by side. Like everything else around it, their resting place was overgrown with brambles and ivy. He had dreaded this journey.

The moment he tore the ivy away and stamped the brambles down, the sight of the headstone with her name on it hit home. He sucked his cheeks in and swallowed hard. He thought he had stopped breathing. He lowered his gaze and his vision blurred. His head bowed, he felt a tear slowly trickle down the side of his cheek before he forced himself to look at her name again. The memory of her dear face was too precious to abandon again. He must learn to hold it and treasure it for as long as he could. "Isabella," he whispered, the soft sound trembling in his throat.

Robert stood there remembering what he had missed; that he had never held her as a woman, felt the warmth of her body or danced with her in his arms. He had longed to feel her touch on his face, kiss that button nose and bury his face in her wild chestnut hair. She would have made him happy.

He returned slowly along the narrow lane, shaking his head with the realisation that no one would come again to brush the moss away from their names or break the branches back to let the sun shine briefly on them. No one knew they were here. They would be left untended and alone for ever. He sighed. Life was never fair.

"When are you taking this dog home with you?" Lord Rupert joked as the animal made its usual fuss of Robert.

Much as Robert liked the young dog, he could not expect it to keep pace with his journeys. It would be footsore and worn out after the first day. Instead he promised to take it for a long a walk to the village with him. He intended to take lunch at the inn, to fill in time until his friends Samuel and Becky arrived that afternoon with Anne's present.

He sat outside at one of the many tables overlooking the green. Trade was busy, but he did not mind waiting. He patted the nuzzling head at his knee. Then, having eaten and downed a cool beer, he began their walk back up the lane. It was a shame the hound would have to stay at Hurl Place when he left tomorrow.

He did not understand why he felt so cold on such a warm day. He felt shivery and put it down to the start of a chill. He felt so tired. He flopped down against a tree for a rest, leaning against the trunk, suddenly exhausted. In quick succession he felt every muscle in turn go limp, from his hands to his toes, as if his body was closing down. His mouth and lips were numb. His eyes stared at nothing, unable to focus. Even his hearing was muffled. It was a most peculiar feeling. Nothing hurt, he was in no pain; he was just drifting away. It made him wonder if this was dying, and if it was, why did he feel no fear? Instead a vague acceptance drifted about his senses. In a way he did not mind if he lived or not. It would end everything. It would stop his family becoming the next targets on Brimley's list. That would be reason enough.

Robert tried to smile as dear Becky bent down to him, in this distant mist of reality. That she was here was a comfort; at least he would not be alone in his final moments. This was quite a pleasant end, he decided.

Samuel and Becky had arranged to meet Robert at Hurl Place. Robert had wanted to see the finished cabinet as much as Lord Rupert did. The cabinet had been well wrapped and secured in the wagon, which rode carefully along the track to its destination. The pair of them were enjoying the day and looking forward to seeing the delight on everyone's face when the cabinet was revealed. It had been a work of love. Samuel had excelled himself and Becky was proud of his achievement.

Becky tugged on her husband's sleeve and pointed ahead, curious to see Robert asleep by the side of the road. She leapt from the wagon and quietly crept up on him, picking a long length of grass on the way. She tickled his ear, waited and tickled him again. He was looking at her, but he did not blink or speak. She looked anxiously back at Samuel and waved for him to join her.

"Robert, what are you doing here?" asked Rebecca. "Robert! Can you hear me?"

Robert was clearly in need of urgent medical help. There was no telling what was wrong with him. It would take too long to take him to Hurl Place on the wagon; he would be better left there while Samuel unhitched the horse and rode on for assistance. The wagon and cabinet were temporarily abandoned while Samuel set off on his mission and Becky sat talking to Robert, frantic for some response.

Becky's words became softer and softer, until she gave up talking and simply held his hand. The frantic sound of riders and a light carriage being driven at speed were not long in arriving. Lord Rupert, Ellis, Samuel and the physician raced towards them. In the distance Samuel's own horse was being brought back for the wagon by another groom.

Becky was looking quite pale as her husband helped her up. She shook her head. She knew it did not look good.

"What is it? I have never seen him like this," she said.

The physician was meticulous in his examination. He looked at Robert's eyes, moved his head slowly from side to side, checked his breathing, felt his skin, listened to his heart and noticed the limpness of his responses and limbs.

"The symptoms indicate some kind of poison," he said finally.

Lord Rupert gasped. All were horrified at this diagnosis.

"We must act quickly if we are to save him. It will not be an easy or a pleasant remedy."

"Where is the puppy?" Ellis asked out of curiosity.

Lord Rupert looked perplexed. He had forgotten that his friend had set off with that young, attentive hound. He quickly set about looking for it, knowing the dog would not have abandoned Robert.

Then Becky screamed. She had found the puppy lying a little way off. It was dead, without a mark on it. They assumed it had shared Robert's lunch, since Robert would have normally treated it to scraps from his plate. Sadly it had shared the same poison. Samuel picked it up and put it in the wagon to bury it later, then he rehitched their horse into the wagon's shafts to follow after the others.

Anne and her mother were staying at Hurl Place to help her become acclimatised to her future home and discuss what changes she might like to make. Lord Rupert had deliberately arranged for her to be there at this time, because he wanted to see the delight on her face when the cabinet arrived. Now that plan was thrown into disarray.

Robert had been taken back to Hurl Place in the carriage

and a complete set of rooms were swiftly allocated for his care. Naturally they were well away from the main function rooms, since the treatment would be particularly unpleasant and severe. The physician instructed that Robert should be made to empty his stomach by making him sick with salt water. They were to continue to force him to vomit until there was nothing left to bring up. After that they were to continue for two more days, or stop at the first sign of blood in his saliva. Then he would be starved for days before being allowed any broth. He would be weak, very weak. It would take time to restore his strength. He would need full-time nursing for quite a while.

Robert became everyone's concern, and none of Lord Rupert's loyal staff baulked at the tasks involved. Samuel and Becky, who had been invited to stay, were more than willing to take it in turns to sit with their friend. Thus the house settled into its unusual duties.

A void of blissful obscurity had beckoned Robert, the greyness drawing him closer, becoming part of him, but complete oblivion never materialised. He had not succumbed to the blissful, uncomplicated release and peace he expected. Instead noises leapt at him through the mist, stabbing his brain. His frame shook, his whole body convulsed repeatedly. His wretchedness was unbearable; he wanted a rest and an end to this suffering. He had nothing left in him. He was utterly exhausted, but even so he found he was not free of more punishment. Further obnoxious liquid was forced down his throat. Why were they doing this? Why couldn't they just let him alone?

Lord Rupert and Ellis were constantly in and out of the room for reports on his condition. Either that or they were joining Samuel in his frequent pacing of the hallways. No one could settle to their normal routine and a strange hush settled about Hurl Place as the days passed.

The Exchange had naturally been informed of Robert's plight, but that still left the problem of whether to fetch his family or not, considering the seriousness of the situation.

"I would hate them to see him like this," Samuel sighed.

"They should not be worried unnecessarily," Becky agreed. She could imagine his aunt storming about the place, his uncle's pacing and sweet Elizabeth - well, she dared not think how upset she would be. But Becky had every faith in Robert's resilience. This was the boy she had known like a brother, her friend whom everyone wanted to recover. She prayed he would soon be restored to the Robert they knew.

"We should have told his family," Anne insisted later.

"I do not want any more sorrowful faces prowling these corridors. What could they do except sit and wait anxiously in a silent hush like us? I would be the first one to send for them if I thought he would not pull through," said Rupert.

Anne leaned against her dear Rupert, squeezed his hand and smiled sympathetically at his tired eyes, knowing how concerned he really was for his friend. Indeed she had quickly become as fond of Robert as her future husband was.

"How am I to keep him safe?" asked Lord Rupert. "First the shooting in my own grounds and then this poisoning. I fear it will put Robert off coming here again."

"What shooting?" Samuel and Becky demanded in unison.

Rupert had forgotten that his family and friends had remained ignorant of the matter.

"It was a minor accident. He was not hurt badly," Ellis said quickly.

Becky and Samuel exchanged sceptical glances. That Robert himself had not thought it worth mentioning seemed to confirm the lack of importance that Ellis's comments suggested. Robert's occupation was not dangerous, but Rupert's few words had implied that the poisoning had been deliberate.

"Why should he need to be kept safe? Is that why he had extra riders with him?" Samuel asked sharply, suddenly seeing a connection.

Only when Samuel and Becky could see Robert was getting better did they at last allow themselves to return home. Samuel had to catch up on his other work, as there were clients waiting for completion of their orders. Lord Rupert thanked both of them for staying on and for Samuel's wonderful work. He paid him handsomely and added a large bonus, despite Samuel's protest. Rupert knew when to be generous.

The cabinet had been unloaded and set in its place in the small private sitting room for Anne. It truly was a beautiful piece of furniture and Anne loved it, but everyone's enthusiasm had been tempered by the concern for their guest.

Robert had finished heaving out his innards. He was drained of every ounce of energy and lay exhausted and weak, wondering if this remedy had been worth all the effort. As he lay day after day in the now quiet house, he found he was quite unperturbed by what had happened. He had survived. No doubt Brimley would try again, but it did not seem to matter, for the moment.

Isabella's memory had crept into his long hours. He found these days he could think of her without pain. He smiled to himself as he remembered a happy child, full of life. He recalled her dancing across the cornfields, pausing in the middle and smiling back at him. They had sat in the sun and splashed each other in the stream. They had shared dreams, made a children's bond and promised to be brave. They had created castles and they were the hero and heroine of every story they knew.

He tried to imagine her as a grown woman with that same

cute button nose. He liked to think she would have had the mixture of youthful innocence and enjoyment of Elizabeth and Anne, together with the kindness of Rebecca and the composure of Margaret. Yes, he had loved Isabella. She would always be pretty to him, and he could only wonder if his own life would have been different if she had lived.

The hours came and went unnoticed as he reviewed the story of his past. What had he done with his life? Nothing special. He had made some serious mistakes. He had suffered injuries. He was getting older. His father had told him to make the best of his life and instead he had settled for what he found easy. He had never had any ambition, or set himself a goal.

Robert was at last well on the road to recovery and was becoming aware of the hours Rupert was spending with him.

"You do not need to spend so much time keeping me company," he told his friend. "I'm sure I am keeping you from more important matters."

"I have little else to do with my days at the moment," replied Rupert. "Even my ambassador duties are at a lull. I am kicking my heels for something to do."

Robert was puzzled by his lack of reference to the most important person in the house.

"Anne will not appreciate your long absences from her side, surely?" he asked.

"Anne has returned to her parents until you are recovered."

"I don't understand?"

"It was, my dear Robert, the manner of your recovery which affected her. I would not allow her in the sick room, for you were a wretched sight to behold. She was most concerned for you, as she listened in the corridor to the sound of your continual heaving racking the room. Your groaning and moaning seemed endless and her distress was hard to watch. She was in tears all the time. I should have sent her away earlier."

"You were kind to take me in. I have been a burden to everyone. I would not have Anne so upset."

"My dear Robert, where else could you have gone? I have the resources and the dedicated staff to take care of you. Besides I am the cause of all your recent misfortune. I cannot forgive myself."

"Please Rupert, not again. You know my own stupidity brought all this upon me."

Naturally the conversation turned to debate about the poisoning. Robert had obviously been followed. His employers, distressed at another attempt on his life, had sent constables from the city to question the owner of the tavern, but he could supply no evidence. The kitchen had been busy with people passing through all day. How it had been done was a mystery. Who was responsible for its undertaking was not; it had to be Brimley.

"I must admit I never want to endure another remedy like that one," said Robert. "How could you put me through it? It was like medieval torture. I would have preferred to die."

"I dared not let that happen. Anne would never have forgiven me. I am a coward, Robert. Besides, we would all miss you too much."

As soon as he was fit enough, Robert went straight back to work as if nothing had happened. Assignment after assignment, his superiors kept him busy, which was exactly what he wanted. He had his own agenda these days. Robert intended that no one else would be injured because of him. There would be no more mistakes. He wanted to be out there, in the field, to be seen at every opportunity. He wanted it over with, one way or another.

He was waiting for any unusual communication which would divert him away from where he should have been. That would be the signal for the next attempt. In between times he was back in the saddle and chasing the deadlines his employers had set for him.

There were moments when he managed to completely forget. Then once more he leaned into the wind, his mind free to be at one with the animal he rode. The rhythmic movements of the galloping horse filled him with satisfaction as he raced for sheer pleasure over the vast green landscape. He eventually slowed to a halt and looked back to wait for his struggling escorts to catch up. Then, smiling, he was off again in exhilaration. He was determined to make the most of his days and enjoy his freedom while he could.

Robert had been sent to the horse sales near Goodwood House to pick out a few more good, sturdy horses for the relay stations, one of his more enjoyable tasks. It was inevitable that he would encounter Sir Henry Wake at the auction, and Robert made a point of talking to him. He did not have any problem with exchanging a congenial conversation with a man who also liked horses. It was only his wife he wanted to avoid, and she was not there. They happily discussed the choice of animals available and with the successful bidding concluded, they left the auction shed together.

Sir Henry seemed a little anxious, and carefully pulled him aside from the others.

"I am glad I met you today, Mr Sutton. I was not sure how to contact you quickly." He looked around to make sure no one else nearby could hear. "I have heard of this latest awful incident at Hurl Place. I cannot believe Phillip Brimley has a personal grudge against you."

"That I broke into Stour Park to look for evidence appears to be the reason."

"A great number of officials have searched his property for evidence. It seems a very poor excuse to take it out on you." He paused, looking around again. "I do not like to alarm you, but Phillip Brimley has recently been seen here in Sussex. Our steward informed me that he had been seen at a midnight cockfight the day before yesterday. I do not know how long he has been back in the country."

The man was genuinely concerned, and Robert could only thank him for the information.

So Brimley was in England. The moment was close for that meeting with Phillip Brimley again, face to face. It was the obvious conclusion, and Robert now intended to make it as easy as possible for the man to find him.

Robert had waited; he was becoming used to that, these days. Then it came, at last. The landlord of the inn where he was staying had been approached by a prospective buyer of a property nearby. Apparently the man had called in last week for a meal and during the evening had asked if the landlord if he knew of anyone who would give him a truthful and unbiased opinion of the land and its potential, if any. The inn owner had recommended Robert because of his farming knowledge. Having mentioned that Robert used this hostelry regularly for an overnight stop, the landlord had suggested he might be there to provide some guidance in a few days' time. The man seemed pleased at the suggestion and had called in the previous day to say he would be at a local farm, the Batim farm, today, if Robert was in the area and felt like joining him.

It all sounded very casual and polite. Nothing too suspicious in its performance. Robert asked for a description of the man he was intended to meet. It did not fit Brimley, but why should it? Although not indicating his decision as to whether he would go or not to the innkeeper, Robert meant to play along. If

Brimley was in the area and wanted him on his own, then Robert meant to oblige his enemy.

In order to prevent any of the others knowing what he was up to, Robert set out to subtly persuade the escort to take the day off. He ate his breakfast slowly, yawning and stretching, his head nodding occasionally as he sat there. Then with one extra-large yawn, he muttered that he was still tired, had a headache and was going back to bed for a few more hours. Once in his room he checked from his window to note that the escort had strolled out towards the pond on the small green opposite. This allowed Robert to slip down the stairs and out the back way to collect his horse from the stables.

Robert knew his way to the tenant farm mentioned. It had been vacant for a while. The poor soil had contributed to its demise; the buildings stood empty and the fields were overgrown with weeds. No farmer would take it on. The track to the homestead took a meandering route, twisting and turning up and down, past stone walls and various copses. Yes, Brimley had chosen the ideal spot for their encounter. The isolated location would have no witnesses.

Robert led his horse quietly down the lane and out of sight of the inn. Soon he was mounted and ready and on his way, but as he turned the next corner, he was confronted by a solitary rider waiting for him. It was the last person in the world he expected to see there. He could not help being surprised. It was Lady Arabella who sat on horseback in the middle of the track, blocking his route. She must have ridden hard to get there, judging by the state of her horse and her clothing.

"Lady Arabella! How did you find me?"

"After the horse sales, it seemed a logical place for your routine stopover."

He did not quite believe her. She had obviously been asking questions somewhere. No matter, it made no difference.

"I came to stop you from doing something stupid, Mr Sutton," she went on. "You are the talk of Goodwood House. They say Phillip is responsible for the attempted poisoning. And you think Phillip is in the area."

"What makes you think that?"

"Because my husband spoke to you two days ago warning you that he had returned to England. Because you are out here alone without your escorts."

Robert laughed. "I am often without my escorts. It is a game I play these days, to see how soon they can find me."

"Stop being so flippant."

"Don't you think it is rather foolish for you to be out here alone?" he asked, moving the conversation on.

"No more foolish than you deliberately sneaking away from your escort just now. I saw the manner of your departure from the top of the road," she told him plainly.

Touché! This was an Arabella he had never seen before, outspoken and completely serious, devoid of the normal society airs and graces she was famous for.

She studied him sceptically, but he gave nothing away. Then she realised.

"You are going to meet him!" she declared.

"Don't interfere. Please, go back home. This has nothing to do with you."

"Nothing to do with me? Phillip ruined my life socially. I am an outcast from society because of him."

"For my sake, please go home."

Arabella shook her head. She would not leave unless he went back with her. They sat staring each other out for a while, both refusing to give in. Eventually Arabella reluctantly gave up and slowly turned her horse away. He watched her until she was out of sight.

Robert was perfectly calm as he rode on. The confirmation that Brimley had been seen only clarified the certainty of what was ahead. Ever since the poisoning, he had tried to prepare himself for this encounter. Now he put everyone out of his mind; it was the only way he could cope with the possibility of his own death.

He rode past the little clumps of trees and dismounted once he was in sight of the farm buildings. Tethering his horse, he intended to walk the last part of the road, yet he had not taken more than a few steps when he heard the noise of the hammer clicking back on a pistol. He did not even bother to turn around.

"I am pleased to see you," said Brimley's voice.

"It was an invitation I would not miss," Robert replied, sounding braver than he felt. In fact all his energy had been spent dealing with anticipation of this moment.

"Phillip, Phillip!" a voice screamed in the distance. The unexpected interruption had them both turn as Arabella galloped into view towards them. Robert stared, utterly taken aback. She had ridden safely away before he had continued his journey. He could not believe she had followed him. Brimley was equally astonished, and cursed.

"The authorities already know you are in the country," she yelled angrily at her cousin as she came closer. "Do you think you were not seen? They will find you as easily as I have!"

"Damn you, Arabella!" roared Brimley.

Then Robert could hear the sound of other horses; no doubt his escorts, having been summoned by Arabella, were rushing towards him. He could see them now galloping towards them at full stretch, their hooves thundering on the track. They look quite resolute in their determination to resume their responsibility for his safety, and Robert could only shake his head in disappointment.

The two outriders galloped down the hill to arrive in a cloud of dust, swinging their mounts close to him. As the dust cleared they found that Brimley had vanished like a puff of smoke. Suddenly confronted by reinforcements, he had done the only sensible thing and vanished.

They were all equally surprised that he had disappeared so easily. Was there any point in looking for him? Robert was convinced Brimley had fled the scene. He kicked the dirt and the broken stonework, pacing across the open ground, his slow steps indicating his disappointment that after all this effort, nothing was settled.

"Arabella, I wanted this over," he growled softly.

He turned, heading off to collect his horse. There was little point in staying. It had all gone wrong, it was not over and Brimley was out there somewhere planning his next move. Robert was fed up with being a victim and a target, but he was aware that he would have to go through all this again whenever Brimley decided. He had long since come to terms with the inevitable, and had already prepared for the worst. Unknown to all, he had put his finances in order months before, making bequests to friends and family. He had set aside money for his sister's wedding and a little extra. He had also made an allowance for a boy to at least have a proper headstone. Everything was in place.

He was back in London a few days later, having put everything back into perspective. After discussing various amendments to regulations all afternoon with one of the local officials and countersigning the necessary documents, he had been invited to dine at his house afterwards. It had been a fine meal and the man had proved to be a jovial host, leaving Robert to feel gratified as he strolled back to his usual lodgings near the Exchange. His eyes crinkled in a grin. He was even humming one of Edmund's tunes. It had proved to be a very pleasant day for a change.

A watchman he knew by sight had been waiting for him at his lodgings. The man explained that he had been expecting a boat to dock the following day at Rotherhithe jetty instead of at the wharf and would appreciate a second pair of eyes to check the cargo list as it unloaded. Robert was in such a benevolent mood that he readily agreed, quickly dismissing the idea that Brimley would risk being in London. It would be too dangerous for him.

A church clock struck four as the boat tied up and by the time it struck five the cargo had been unloaded and cleared off the jetty into the wagons. The task had been completed, the boat had cast off and the wagons had moved off. The watchman thanked him and wandered back to his normal post by the entrance to the docks further around the corner.

Robert wandered off to the far end of the jetty to watch the boat go down the river and stood for a while looking at the murky river and its dark swirling currents and twisting spiralling patterns. The rubbish of the city passed around the metal feet of the jetty, catching and clogging on the supporting stays. He pulled a face at it and turned to go back, only to see a huddle of men arguing at the jetty entrance. He was at a disadvantage being there on his own. If only he had not stayed so long. He desperately wanted to avoid any confrontation with these men, since he did not know who they were. With his exit blocked and no way past them, he was not sure what to do.

Even as he watched, the men began to move along the jetty towards him, threatening and pushing each other. Trapped and outnumbered, he did not want to be seen, let alone dragged into a brawl where he would come off worst. Where the hell could he hide?

He hurried down the hinged metal slope onto the pontoon below, which rose and fell with the tide. There was nowhere else he could go. Once there he stood back under the overhang, out of sight as the men above continued their fight.

At the edge of the pontoon a small rowing boat bobbed at the end of a long rope. He tugged it to him. It was in poor condition, but it would have to do, he decided. He undid the rope and stepped in. He stopped to check he was still unnoticed, then, holding onto the stays, he moved hand over hand to pull himself and the boat under the centre of the jetty. After that he pulled himself further and further away until he had reached the furthest end of the jetty. Here he looped the rope around the upright and one of the stays to keep the boat safe. There was half a dirty old tarpaulin in the bottom, ideal for covering himself to give further concealment, which he did. Then, wriggling about until he was as comfortable as he could manage, he settled down to wait while the noise above continued. Unfortunately the shouts, the heavy thumping footsteps and the running did not appear to be about to stop.

He must have nodded off, because the next thing he aware of was waking up with a jerk. He shivered. It was quiet; it seemed he was still safe. He became aware that the gentle rocking of the boat against the jetty had changed, and the boat was rocking more than before. The sounds of the water lapping around him also seemed to be different.

He peeked out from the tarpaulin, and was horrified to find that the boat was adrift. He grabbed at the rope trailing in the water behind; it had obviously frayed and snapped. He was floating downriver on the changed tide.

The light was fading, and despite frantically peering at the river bank he could not make out where he was. The timber shuttering shoring up the river front with its usual collection of buildings were gone. Not a pier, wharf or warehouse could be seen. Where in hell where was he? Any sign of habitation had given way to a long undulating earth bank on the right side, where the river began to bend. He must be passing the long curve around Redriff Marsh.

He flung the tarpaulin aside, looking for the oars, and the boat jarred and thumped against something solid in the water, making it rock unsteadily. Grabbing the sides of the boat with his hands, he waited for it to settle before bending forward again for the precious oars. But on picking them up he discovered that they were not as solid as he would have wished, and when he slipped them into the rowlocks, they rattle as if they were going to fall out of their mountings.

He swore aloud. This would make it difficult to get a decent stroke as he rowed. Then, to make matters worse, he noticed a puddle in the bottom of the boat which had not been there before. He would have to keep an eye on that.

Desperate to land as soon as possible, he coaxed the craft towards a gap in the bank, hoping he could beach it on the mud and scramble ashore. In fact even that short journey was hindered as more rubbish in the river hit the boat or caught on the oars. It seemed to take ages before the boat finally thumped into the mud and held firm. As he looked down to the bottom of the boat he saw that he had only just made it in time, for the water had risen considerably.

Standing up, he made a leap for the bank and grabbing a few tufts of grass, he managed to scramble to the top. He looked for a pathway across the emptiness in front of him, but could see none. He needed somehow to find his way across the marsh towards Rotherhithe. He would have to keep roughly parallel to the bending river.

The rough terrain was overgrown and scattered with unseen ditches and dykes, as he discovered when despite his careful steps, he stumbled heavily into a ditch. As he struggled on, he fell full length into a wet, muddy dyke. He pushed himself up from the squelching quagmire, covered in stinking mud. He struggled to crawl out, slipping back several times before he succeeded.

Once on the top again, he tried to shake off the clods of mud from his coat. His sodden clothes felt heavy, even his good boots had taken in water over the top and his feet were squelching in them as he set off once more. He shivered and sneezed, which did not bode well. But what else should he expect after landing himself in such a situation?

CHAPTER TEN

At last Robert was among the buildings and sheltered from the onshore wind. Although it was dark there were still people about, and they would surely notice his wild and dishevelled condition. He would be noticed and remarked on, something he had hoped to avoid.

He paused and leaned against a wall. His legs were beginning to ache and his feet had cramp. Then there was a tug at his sleeve.

"Mister, mister!" A boy was smiling at him, a boy with his brother. The boys from Bermondsey market!

"You're dirty. Are you hungry?" asked the elder boy.

The next thing he knew, the boys had taken his hands, one on each side, and were cheerfully guiding him through the narrow streets. Their footsteps skipped, while his feet were slow to keep up. They pushed aside some wooden fencing and urged him to follow them across a small empty cobbled backyard. They burst excitedly through the door, calling out, "Granma, Granma! We found the man who gave us the paints."

Inside the room a startled old lady stared at Robert and took in the state of him. He stood in the doorway, refusing to come any further, until she smiled and came to usher him inside. Meanwhile the children had huddled around the warm, welcoming stove and were sipping hot, steaming broth from their bowls.

"You will eat with us, however little we have," she said. She drew him to the table, brushing the bench for him to sit. "A kindness for a kindness. My lads have not forgotten you."

She fetched him some broth, and once he had taken the first spoonful he devoured it swiftly. He would have been glad of more, but he was sure the old woman had already made sacrifices to share their food in the first place.

The two boys had finished their food and were sitting by her chair, eager to be taken into her arms for the night. It was obvious they doted on their older relation, while she in return did her best for them. Although it was not the best of situations, it seemed they managed to survive. They got by - what more did he expect? He might secretly want more for them, but they were a family bound together by circumstances. It was not for him to interfere.

A moment later he stirred himself. He had sat too long, he was getting stiff. Now a little drier, he dusted off some of the dirt and finally set off again.

When Robert reached his lodgings in the early hours, the innkeeper hurried out of his booth in the lobby to catch him before he disappeared upstairs. The watchman had left a note for him, hoping he had managed to avoid the rabble who had appeared on the jetty soon after he had left. Apparently the fighting had become a riot and the militia had been called to break it up.

Robert put the note in his pocket and hauled himself up to his room. He was not feeling kindly towards the militia. If they had turned up earlier, he would not have been trapped on the jetty and had to take evasive action and cross the marsh, ruining a good set of clothes. Damn the militia! He sneezed again.

Robert's sneezes and snuffles were cured by some good doses of country air as he travelled through Kent on his next assignment, his escorts in tow. Having been to Canterbury, he naturally took the opportunity to call in to visit Becky and Samuel on the way back, leaving his escort to wait in the village. As usual his friends were pleased to see him, but now they had him on his own, they took the chance to badger him with questions. After all they had heard at Hurl Place, they wanted to know the truth behind these supposed 'accidents' and the attempt on his life.

Robert grimaced; he hated having to tell them anything. Reverting to his usual explanation of the incident at Stour House being the cause of the problem, he was forced to sound light-hearted and unconcerned, and to persuade them it was not that serious. Becky was quick to question why he still needed outriders if that was the case; she had seen them as they left him in the lane.

"That is merely Lord Rupert being unnecessarily cautious," Robert joked, attempting to dismiss their doubts.

Samuel frowned and pulled a face at him, indicating that he was not getting away with that, while Robert gave an innocent smile back and then tried to change the subject.

"Do I get some of that pie I can smell, or is it just to torment me?" he asked. Becky took the hint, and soon they had settled down to eat. "Don't think you are let off the hook that easy," she told him as she served him a second helping.

They were put out that Robert stubbornly refused to say any more on the subject. The conversation returned to the casual manner of old, and once more they enjoyed his company as the time passed.

Robert had just enjoyed a pleasant ride back to London and with his escorts having returned to Hurl Place, he sauntered into the coffee house expecting to see his friends.

"Where is Henry?" Robert enquired as he joined Edmund.

"Doing you a favour."

Robert was mystified, awaiting clarification.

"A watchman from Rotherhithe left a message for you. For some reason he thought the contents of an abandoned warehouse would interest you. Since we did not know how long you would be, Henry decided to deal with it, in case it was important."

Robert instantly tensed up. Every instinct told him this had not been a genuine communication. His eyes widened with concern. Someone had seen him in Rotherhithe with the watchman. Someone was watching him and using that information to draw him elsewhere. Robert did not want this to be Brimley, yet he knew in his heart it had to be. Brimley was in London.

"Where has Henry gone?" he asked.

"Somewhere in the docks around Bermondsey, he did not say exactly. He put the letter in his pocket and just sauntered off. He shouldn't be long."

Damn, damn! Robert swore in his head. Henry had inadvertently put himself in danger in his eagerness to help a friend. He stood up. He would have to go after him.

"I have to find him. He will be in trouble."

Edmund was alarmed at Robert's reaction. He obviously considered something was seriously wrong. He never doubted Robert's knack of being right, even without proof.

"I'll come with you," he said.

"Sorry Edmund, you will slow me down."

With that Robert was gone, almost running through the streets.

He paused in the market, sure that Henry must have come this way, and soon spotted the boys he knew. They had keen eyes; with any luck they had noticed Henry.

"Have you seen a young man dressed in a dark coat and boots like mine? It should not have been too long ago," he asked. The boots and coat were the uniform they all wore. "Do you know which way he went?" he asked.

They nodded, beaming at their friend. They thought Henry had been heading towards the riverside at St Saviour's dock. He thanked the boys, flipped them a coin and rushed on. That gave him somewhere to start his search.

Slowing his pace, he walked along the dock front. An abandoned warehouse was the only clue, so the busy ones with too many people were of no interest. At the far end some older buildings were tucked around the side of the creek near the watergate. This had to be the location. The large front cargo doors facing the waterway were closed and barred, leaving him to explore the back alleys for some way of entry. He listened for any sound as he carefully entered through the rear door of each of them in turn before moving on to the next.

The adrenaline was making his heart thump as he quietly opened and closed the door of the next building. He thought he heard muffled sounds, but then there was silence. He paused in case this turned out to be the right place and quickly scanned his surroundings to get his bearings. The dilapidated warehouse had the usual trappings; the metal gantries, a collection of pulleys and hoists and wooden partitions along the side to store the various cargoes. The emptiness felt odd; there were a few items casually scattered around and left looking forlorn. Daylight filtered through the broken roof and gaps in the timber walls.

A draught from the river rattled the large doors as Robert crept into the middle of the dusty warehouse. He instantly saw Brimley's back. He was bending over Henry, who lay in a heap on the floor.

"Everyone interferes with my plans. Why did you come!" Brimley bellowed.

Henry did not answer. He was not moving.

The sight was enough to halt Robert for a moment, but he took a deep breath and stepped out to present himself for Brimley's full attention. He had to prevent Henry from further harm.

"You can leave him alone now, Brimley. I am here. I'm the one you wanted, not him."

Brimley straightened and turned. He was smirking as he abandoned Henry and walked towards Robert. He came to a halt within inches of him.

"Mr Sutton. I am pleased to see you."

No doubt you are, thought Robert, facing the man who glowered at him and tilted his head sceptically, whilst never taking his eyes from his. If Brimley hoped to assess Robert so easily or find his weakness, it would take more than that.

"After all this time, you could not wait a little longer for me to arrive?" Robert said casually, to provoke him.

"After all my other attempts on you I am surprised you risked coming alone. You clearly realised I would be here. You knew I wanted you dead," came the response.

The pistol in his opponent's hand was slowly raised until it pointed at Robert's head. He stared at the barrel, expressionless, his breathing calm and his body relaxed, offering little sign of a man who should be shaking in his boots at this confrontation.

"Surely you must have wondered how easily I found you after our meeting at the lodge," Brimley went on. Robert refused to give him the satisfaction of admitting his curiosity.

"I had my own spies within the Treasury, to alert me to any danger during the developing Pavilion venture," said Brimley. "I had been told someone was looking at the list of investors some considerable time after the event went wrong, but your curiosity was no threat to us. We had disappeared from the public eye. We were safely hidden and planning our escape. How did you find out about the lodge?"

"By luck," Robert shrugged nonchalantly. He was not going to betray his source.

Brimley was not particularly bothered, preferring to continue to boast of his own investigations.

"It was only after your audacious removal of my papers at the lodge that I needed more enquiries made," he went on. "My agents confirmed that the earlier enquiry had been made by someone employed by the Exchange, a man with a distinctive mark in his hair. That was the major clue to who you were. Yet the discreet nature of the Exchange operatives made it hard to find out anything about individuals. Despite numerous subtle attempts we could not even find out which area you were assigned to. Yours is a close-knit unit, and cautious. I could get no information. Then we had a lucky break."

Somehow they had found Christopher, to flatter and coerce. Robert didn't listen to the details.

"Once we had that, it was merely a matter of testing your schedules and routine. Yes, it took time, but I am not one to give up that easily as you know, after what you had done to me."

At least Robert had the complete answer, although it might

not do him much good, if he did not survive to warn the Treasury of Brimley's close acquaintances with in their ranks.

"You displeased me greatly," Brimley went on. "I had to sell some of my valuables to fund this vendetta. Valuables I intended to grace my new home. A new home in the West Indies, which I am also deprived of because of you. You have cost me a great deal."

"It was my pleasure," Robert smirked, with a flourish of the hand, knowing it would annoy him.

"You stole from me!" Brimley growled.

"You stole from hundreds of investors," Robert snapped back.

Brimley looked astonished, and frowned at this unexpected accusation. This war of words would not do. He was supposed to be dictating the situation, not his adversary. How did this man have the nerve to challenge his control, despite the fact that Brimley was the one holding the loaded pistol? He would have to remind Robert Sutton that he had the upper hand here, and he knew exactly how to make his point.

"If you think I am going to let your friend live after I have killed you, Mr Sutton, you are a fool. Indeed the whole idea is most appealing, especially since you will never know the method of his slow and painful death."

A snarling grin accompanied this statement, and Brimley's eyes were wide and glinting with hate. He knew how to torment Robert, and he enjoyed it. Robert knew Brimley would indeed have no qualms about killing Henry. Whereas he had been mentally prepared for the likelihood of his own demise, he had never allowed for Henry to become involved, even by default. It was always meant to be just Brimley and himself. Henry was not supposed to be here; his presence confused the issue.

Robert was angry. The threat to Henry changed everything. He lowered his head, his mind racing. He realised he needed a whole different strategy. He would have to fight Brimley to save Henry.

Robert was not a natural fighter; he lacked the willingness to physically hurt anyone. His experiences were limited to the childish brawls he had had at school and the light-hearted rough and tumble with neighbours on the farm.

"Although there may be a better way to take my revenge," Brimley pondered wickedly, taking a few steps up and down in front of him, still waving the gun at him. "Making you a cripple first would give me much pleasure Mr Sutton. A bullet in the kneecap will do nicely. I would relish your squirming in agony as you watch your friend die."

Robert felt inwardly sick at the thought of it, although he was trying not to think about it. Brimley's threats were winning the psychological war of nerves. Robert wished he would stop talking. He must stop listening. He must pull himself together.

Robert stood there, his arms down, offering no resistance as Brimley lowered the pistol slightly, obviously satisfied that his threats had had the desired effect. Robert felt beaten and tired. All his nervous energy remained silent and controlled, for the moment. The gun was lowered further and no longer aimed directly at him, giving him the opportunity he needed. He had no option except to attack.

He charged at Brimley, throwing himself at his chest in the hope that he could wrestle or knock the gun out of his hand. It was a ridiculous idea, but it was preferable to having his knee blown off and watching Henry die.

They fell to the ground and rolled apart, the gun sliding away out of sight across the dirt floor. The gun no longer seemed important, as Brimley then leapt to his feet, balanced and poised in the stance of an experienced boxer. Trained at the sport, as were most gentry, he intended to punish Robert with a burst of blows as soon as he was back on his feet.

The first two blows landed in quick succession to Robert's face, crunching his jaw and jerking his head from side to side. His lip was cut, a few teeth felt out of place and blood was filling his mouth from inside. As he bent to spit it out, he was hit again, this time in the body and then back to the side of the face. He head was ringing. The accuracy and speed of the blows allowed Robert little chance of defence. Robert was suffering, and Brimley was delighted.

"This is too easy, Sutton," he snarled.

Brimley landed another forceful punch to Robert's body and jaw, which sent him sprawling to the ground. Brimley stood poised, ready to swing at the rising figure, but Robert was reluctant to push himself up. He had felt his damaged elbow give way, and a pain shot up and down his arm. It was almost without strength. He had to find another way to compensate.

Robert kicked out at his opponent's feet, as hard as he could, making Brimley lurch sideways and lose his balance. It brought Brimley down in the dirt beside him, the wind knocked out of him, which briefly gave Robert the advantage. He threw himself on him and pressed his good arm across his throat with all the force he could muster. Gurgling and spluttering, Brimley fought back, his arms and feet flailing in the air, his body wriggling and squirming, until his superior strength managed to throw Robert off.

They were now on their knees, both breathless, Brimley glaring at him, ready to pounce. Robert waited, glad of the brief pause. Soon they were exchanging blows again as they progressed across the uneven ground. Robert had nothing to use against him. Exhausted, he could only try to defend himself, blocking blows and staggering away dazed when another punch landed. He was on the ground again and in trouble. He knew he could not go on much longer. Sooner or later Brimley would overpower him. There must be another way. Henry was depending on him.

Then a resounding bang echoed in the still air. The dazed and beaten Henry had somehow crawled his way towards the pistol and fired it at Brimley. He now lay back collapsed into a heap by the effort, the gun dropping from his hand.

While Brimley scrambled and lunged towards the gun, Robert struggled to his feet and grabbed the nearest thing he could find, a lump of broken timber, and swung it with full force to hit Brimley on the head. Brimley crumpled without a sound. Robert waited to strike again, but Brimley did not move. He was unconscious and bleeding from the wound.

Not that Robert gave a damn about Brimley; his only concern was for Henry. His swollen and bruised face was as white as a sheet. His eyes were closed. But at least he was still breathing, and the steady slow pants and the regular rise and fall of his chest gave Robert some relief. Poor Henry had been severely beaten about the head and body, but although his wounds were still bleeding and needing attention, no bones seemed to be broken. He felt quite cold, and Robert took off his long top coat to tuck round him.

He took a quick glance to check that Brimley remained unconscious, then carefully pulled the crumpled Henry into a sitting position, propping him against some remaining grain sacks to make him more comfortable and hoping as he did so that there were no internal injuries. He did not dare move him anymore. He would have to go for help, although he did not like the idea of leaving him. Even an unconscious Brimley was a threat. He would have to tie him up.

"Henry," he whispered, hoping for some response, but there was none. He wanted him to know his plan. He did not want him waking up alone and wondering why he had been deserted.

Robert realised he would have to tie Brimley up before he

came round. He frantically set about searching the practically empty warehouse for rope or other bindings. He turned over bales and opened boxes, searched under sacking, kicked the sawdust and ran his hands along the shelves. Even the wooden hooks on the partitions normally storing quantities of rope for tying up the cargo bales held nothing. A few bits of string which were nowhere near strong enough and some odd pieces of rope were all he could find.

He turned to check that Brimley was still on the floor – too late. Before he knew it his assailant was upon him again, knocking him to his knees. His bloodied head, piercing eyes and snarling mouth were an awful sight.

"I underestimate you every time," Brimley gurgled. He had drawn a knife from his boot and charged towards Robert, who looked about for something to defend himself with, but Brimley did not allow him the opportunity. The knife slashed wildly across the space in front of him, forcing him to step back and back again. Then it cut into Robert's arm. Robert winced and grasped his arm. He felt dizzy and leaned back against one of the wooden partitions, expecting a final attack. But Brimley began to torment him, waving the knife threateningly and jabbing at him, making him jerk back.

Then as Brimley aimed at Robert's body, Robert, leaning on the wooden upright for support, kicked out full force with both legs, the heels of his stiff boots finding contact with the man's groin. Doubled up, Brimley dropped the knife, it bounced on the ground towards Robert, who grabbed it.

They were soon grappling together, their arms wrapped around each other, as Brimley struggled to hold and twist Robert's wrist. They bounced off the wooden partitions, the solid wall and the uneven stacks of abandoned goods until they were rolling on the floor again.

Now at last Robert found hate and anger fuelling his

strength to fight; it even obliterated his awareness of his own wounds. He hated Brimley for all the pain and torment the man had put him through over the recent year. He was angry for the innocent boy who had died on the heath, and angry for what he had done to Henry. He might be fighting for his life, but that no longer registered. He wanted this man dead, no matter what it took.

A red mist had descended, and when Robert found his arm suddenly free, he did not hesitate to drive the blade forward hard and into Brimley's chest. He had inflicted a serious wound. Brimley looked incredulously at him, his eyes wide in disbelief as his body went limp. His rib cage had stopped the blade going in further, but Robert quickly withdrew it and placing both hands on the handle, this time using all his force, he plunged it in again. This time the knife went in up to the hilt and Robert held it there as the blood welled up over his hands.

Brimley's mouth twitched and a deathly warble sounded in his throat. If his enemy had assumed that Robert had no stomach for killing, he had been wrong. Robert remained with his full weight on the knife in his chest until Brimley lay still and there was no breath or life left in him.

Robert looked at the dead body, still hating his adversary. At last he sat back, leaving the knife where it was, firmly planted in Brimley's chest. It was done.

A cough caught Robert's attention, and he found Henry looking directly at him. They exchanged a weak smile, and then the rear door swung open and Edmund, several constables and one of their own superiors burst into the interior. They stopped at the sight of the dead body, alarmed by Henry's condition and at the blood on Robert. The blood was mostly Brimley's, although his own arm was still bleeding freely. One of the men used his ragged shirt to bind it tight, while another was sent to find for a physician for Henry and another for a magistrate. A death also had to be reported, and arrangements made for the body to be removed.

"Why can't we just throw him into the river?" complained Edmund as he walked around the corpse.

Robert shook his head. Even now he was keeping to the rules, although neither their superior nor Edmund would have blamed him for acting differently.

Edmund explained that he had returned to the office to inform his superiors, who in turn had sent for as many constables as could be found to embark on their own search. There had been no doubt in their minds that both Henry and Robert were in danger. The boys in the market had played their part, and it was the report by a member of the public of a shot being fired which had eventually led them here.

"It is time we had a proper organized police force here in London, like the Edinburgh Town Guard, to deal with the growing unsavoury population," his superior complained to the magistrate. "Without one we are prey to any villain, and with only the local lock-up to house these people it is no wonder the criminal underworld has the upper hand."

The physician soon arrived, and after some expert bandaging Henry was able to give his account of the proceedings. This left the magistrate satisfied enough to have the body removed. With matters taken over by those in higher authority, Henry was helped into a carriage with Edmund for company and Robert was sent off to his lodgings to rest.

But Robert was too agitated and angry to rest, or sleep. Everything was turning over in his mind and churning his stomach. Now there would be an official enquiry and a court case, and all those secrets he had carefully kept would no doubt become public.

He made the journey home knowing that he would have to explain his actions to his family. He gathered them together around the table, their puzzled faces looking at him, not knowing what to expect. This was awkward, for he was about to ruin their perception of his blameless character. He chewed his lip and fidgeted about.

"I have killed a man," he told them.

No one said a word. They waited for the complete explanation, because this was Robert with his reputation for fairness and doing the right thing, and they all knew it must have been an accident.

How to begin? There was much to tell them about the attempts on his life and why they had happened. About a mistake which had caused so much chaos.

"All your worries, your private silences," Elizabeth told him, with the clarity and wisdom of someone much older. "Too stubborn, too proud to burden us. Always determined to handle everything yourself. You don't have to be so brave."

When Robert had finished his story, they seemed to accept what had happened without any sign of criticism or judgement. The only thing on their mind was the danger he had been in.

"You saved Henry's life," gasped his aunt.

"You killed Brimley in self-defence," added his sister.

His uncle stood up and came to pat him reassuringly on the shoulder.

"Oh Robert, I despair of you sometimes. You hate to admit you are as vulnerable as everyone else. All this time! You should have shared these fears with us. We are your family. No one expects you to be perfect, Robert. Didn't you trust us to understand? You must know we would never think less of you for being human."

Robert was humbled by the man's frank expression; there was a warmth and kindness in his acceptance of Robert's failings. Did he deserve it?

Elizabeth was the next to reassure him as she snuggled up close to hug him, her eyes looking attentively in his and smiling.

"We all love you," she told him, as if he ever doubted it.

Robert appeared in front of his superiors braced to answer their questions about Brimley's death, although there was always the possibility that his private journeys and his personal involvement with Lord Rupert would come out. But the internal inquiry was brief and to the point; because Henry had been witness to the final confrontation, they saw no reason to delve further.

Within days, as if prompted by the importance of the Exchange, the judge had instructed a private hearing of the court case, restricting attendance to a select few who were connected to the case.

"So we are here again Mr Sutton, with further attempts on your life," he began. "Another shooting and a near-fatal poisoning. Mr Brimley seems to have been quite determined to have you killed. Your first assassin is still behind bars. His statement would have us assume that you were shot at Hurl Place because you broke into Stour Park, Brimley's home."

Robert nodded.

"No doubt looking for clues concerning the whereabouts of the known felon?"

"I had no orders or instructions to do so," said Robert. This ambiguous answer did not verify their incorrect assumptions or betray the real reason. Although he had risked his career by admitting his actions, they had nothing to do with his employment. His choice of words had been very precise. He had no intention of mentioning Lord Rupert.

"Although you found nothing, your actions were quite within your remit as an officer of the Crown," continued the judge. "You are expected to use your initiative, be it connected to your present assignment or not. You cannot ignore your duty to assist and protect the law of this country."

There was a pause in the proceedings. The men sitting on the bench shuffled some papers around and passed them from one to the other, to read and re-read, before facing the court room and Robert again.

"You have stated here in your signed statement, that you later repeated your investigation at another property on the Dorset coast," said the judge.

"I had heard rumours that Brimley had a lodge on the coast in the Purbeck hills area. I did not know exactly where. I did not know what I would find."

"Which is where you came into direct contact with Phillip Brimley."

"Yes."

Lord Rupert's mouth dropped open slightly. This was the first he had known of any of this. He looked daggers at Robert. Then he looked at Ellis, who showed no sign of surprise at the revelation. How much else had they kept to themselves?

"It was only after he caught you there that he began to want you dead. Why?"

No one asked where he had heard about the rumours which had led him there. No one asked what else happened at the lodge. They were being careful with their questions. Similarly he had been very selective in his statements.

"Because I stole some papers from him at the lodge, without realising how very important they were."

"A credit note and several other vital financial papers, I believe? If you did not know what these papers were, why did you remove them?"

"Brimley was about to flee the country. I wanted to make it difficult for him any way I could," Robert lied.

Lord Rupert felt himself go cold, knowing Robert had in

truth been looking for anything to connect Hurl Place with the financial scandal. He was disappointed that Ellis had conspired with him to keep another secret from him. All this time Robert had carried this burden without trusting his best friend with the truth of the real reason for Brimley's attacks on him. He studied Robert's composed face, the set of his jaw and his eyes fixed firmly on the man in charge. Robert was not the same, and it hurt Rupert to think he did not know his friend as well as he thought he did.

"No matter how you achieved the restoration of the illegal funds, the government is grateful for their recovery. You are to be commended for your actions," said the judge.

There was another pause in the proceedings as the men conferred together, and Robert was allowed to stand down from the witness box. Then Henry was required to take the stand and give his account of that evening. Whilst the judiciary might have challenged his evidence as being biased, Henry was another respected officer of the Crown and as such would be expected to tell the truth. Besides which, he too was an unfortunate victim. He related how he had gone to the docks and been attacked and beaten by Phillip Brimley. He told them how angry the man had been because the wrong person had come there. Phillip Brimley had seemed a man possessed by pure hate, in his opinion.

"I was in a bad way when Robert arrived and I was sure he was going to kill me for the sheer satisfaction of seeing Robert suffer," he said. He concluded by relating what he could remember about the fight between Brimley and Robert, which was not much except for the end.

Robert was getting tired, and his arm was aching for no reason. He wanted it over with quickly. His head hurt remembering it all.

"Mr Sutton." The stern voice made him look up. "In our

opinion you have served the government well and at risk to your own person. You have done nothing wrong, except become the unfortunate target for Brimley's hate campaign."

No mention had been made of Lady Arabella's interference at the proposed meeting at the Batim holding. In fact much had been omitted from the lengthy statement he had given to the authorities, including the fact that Phillip Brimley had close acquaintances inside the Treasury's ranks.

The men on the bench conferred again, nodding in agreement over their findings.

"The panel has considered all the relevant evidence and the written statements provided," said the judge. "You acted in self-defence after Phillip Brimley instigated the attack. The felon intended to murder you and possibly your associate, while you had not planned to murder him. We have ruled that no criminal charges will be made against you. You are lucky to have survived and you should not blame yourself for his death."

Blame himself! If only they knew how he really felt. They had misunderstood his reluctance to talk about it. He had kept quiet because it was expected of him. He was expected to be an upright officer of the Crown. It was a part he had played to perfection, always concealing his true viewpoint and controlling his emotions.

He remembered looking at the dead body after the fight. It had meant nothing to him. In truth the sensation of that knife cutting into Brimley's flesh had given him great satisfaction. He did not expect they would like him to admit in public that he had taken pleasure in killing this man.

The hearing had been brief and Robert left the tribunal, fully aware that the whole procedure had been a fiasco. Far from being disciplined, receiving a severe reprimand or worse, he had been commended for his enterprise. From the limited questions and the direction of the short answers he was allowed to give, it had been obvious from the outset that the findings would exonerate his actions. He suspected the law had been influenced and guided by his own superiors, which caused him to wonder if even Lord Rupert would have used his royal connections to persuade the law to be lenient.

That he had killed a man had obviously meant little to them, although even his own deep sense of right and wrong had not once troubled his conscience about killing Phillip Brimley. Justice was a strange thing, depending totally upon who was handing it out, Robert concluded. And whether he deserved their leniency or not, the whole matter was finally over with.

Lord Rupert was waiting outside by his carriage, anxious to speak with him. "I will hear more of this," he told Robert bluntly.

Robert knew he was referring to his visit to the lodge and the papers he took, but this was not the place for a discussion. He would face that later, once Lord Rupert had finished sulking, by which time he would have seen the sense of Robert's behaviour.

"Another time," he told Rupert. He thanked him for his concern and appearance at the courthouse. It was kind of him to travel this far, he remarked. Then, their pleasantries over, they parted with the usual reference to seeing each other soon, although Robert knew deep down it would be far from soon. He doubted he would return to Hurl Place much after all this. Anne had made an immense change in their relationship. They would no longer ride together or race each other across the estate for the pure thrill of it. Those days were gone.

Robert patted his horse's neck, pulled his ear and looked into his wonderful big eyes.

"What do you think, Toby? Have I done enough here?"

The horse snorted and nudged him in the shoulder, understanding his mood and indicating that it was time to go home.

CHAPTER ELEVEN

Back home everyone was pleased to see Robert back and relieved that the inquiry was over. They all expected everything to settle down again into the normal routine. Indeed Robert now spent his time working in the orchard hard and long, cutting and pruning the trees with his uncle, sharing the work and each other's company as they had always done. The family ate and talked as usual, with gentle affectionate teasing and laughter. Nothing had changed between them, but the usual satisfaction he should have felt at being there did not come.

His rest period over, he went back to his duties for the Exchange. He was as busy as ever, chasing deadlines and no longer needing an escort. Yet as the days passed, he found he had ceased to notice the landscape he knew so well; it flitted by without recognition. He visited home, attended the village fair and exchanged the usual pleasantries with his uncle, aunt and neighbours. He had talked with Thomas the blacksmith and visited Samuel and Becky as usual, but having left them, he found he could not recall any of their conversation.

He had been analysing his situation for some time. Over the years he had proved himself to his employers. He worked for the sake of working, and it no longer seemed important. He was fed up with dragging himself around the country. He was fed up with being fair, fed up with his life. He desperately wanted something different.

Robert stood on Henley Down, looking out at the familiar landscape he had known most of his life, wondering if he could actually turn his back on everything he knew. He wanted to change his life for the better, but what exactly did that mean?

Elizabeth was slightly out of breath, having rushed after him when she had seen the direction he was heading in. She wanted to speak to him.

"Robert! Don't shut me out any more. Talk to me!" said Elizabeth, giving him a punch on the arm.

"Ouch! There was no need for that."

She grimaced at him, her bright eyes narrowed, demanding a proper answer.

"I am just trying to sort things out in my own mind first."

He paused before delivering what he had decided. "I am going away, Elizabeth. I am leaving everything."

She did not even blink at this statement. He had every right to feel the way he did, after his recent tribulations.

"You do not have to leave because of happened with Brimley," she said.

"No, I have been stuck in a rut too long. It has been too easy to follow the career I had. I never made the best of my life. I never challenged myself, and it is time I did. I should have made this decision ages ago Elizabeth, before this all happened."

The tone of resignation was evident to Elizabeth; she knew he meant it. But when he talked of going away, she sensed that he meant far away, far from his home and friends.

"You are too independent, Robert. You should have married Becky when you had the chance," she told him quite plainly.

Robert decided his little sister was getting much too shrewd these days.

"I never stood a chance. Besides Samuel was right for her, not me."

Elizabeth took his shoulders between her hands and turned him to face her, about to scold him for never believing in himself. Then she suddenly saw something she had never seen before, a secret inner quality in his eyes she could not really identify.

"You have always loved another," she said. She did not know why she said it or where the notion had come from. It surprised even her.

Robert let the gentlest of soft smiles drift across his face, and his eyes crinkled affectionately. "I had not realised how much until recently," he admitted quietly.

Elizabeth put her hands on his heart. It did not falter; it was beating its steady, strong rhythm. He put his hands over hers and held them there. She looked at his face, and it was mellow and kind. Would he tell her or not?

He nodded, sensing the question in her head. It had never been the right time before, but today, he did not mind sharing dear Isabella's memory with his dear sister, because it did not hurt any more. He began to talk.

When he had finished, she let out a deep breath. She had never seen the depth of his feelings expressed before, never known him to mention her name to anyone. Now she knew who the tears had been for in the orchard. She had seen his pain. She understood the hurt he had carried. But because he had kept it to himself, she had been unable to hold him and comfort him, as he deserved and needed. That made her sad. Then her dear Robert offered to show her where Isabella and her brother were buried, if she was up for a long walk. Yes, she wanted that, she insisted. She wanted to be part of that special precious bond he had with Isabella. She wanted to be included.

Robert took her hand in his and swung back and forth as they walked along together to the abandoned chapel site. It was like they had done when she was small and it felt wonderful to skip along together with the dappled sun dancing through the trees overhead.

Once there he stood silent for a while, taking it all in, accepting that this would probably be the last time he would come here and see her name spelt out in large letters. These graves would be there in perpetuity. The satisfaction of knowing they would always be there somehow gave him an inner satisfaction.

Elizabeth stood back, appreciating his need for these precious private moments, and made her own private promise. She would come back one day long after he had left them and scatter some wild flower seeds around the graves, to brighten this spot with colour. She might even bring Michael with her.

"No one else knows about my decision. You are the first," he told her on the way back.

"You are really giving up your occupation?"

"Yes. Although I cannot imagine my employers will be too pleased when I tell them."

She took his hand in hers and held it softly as they continued to walk back up the hill, over Henley Down towards the farm. Elizabeth could see he looked more content than he had done for a long while. She was not going to argue or attempt to change his mind. After all that had happened to him she understood that he deserved to find his own way somewhere new. Although she hoped this brother she loved would not leave them too soon.

Whilst she might keep his secret until he was ready to tell everyone, she did not envy his conversation with their aunt. Her reaction would be fearsome in the extreme. So many people would be shocked. Robert hoped she would forgive him, but he could not be sure. In fact she seemed to accept his decision without too much fuss. Slowly he had pushed her from him, reminding her that she had her own life to lead with Michael. He wished them well and told her they would have a wonderful life together.

She closed her eyes briefly before giving him a radiant grin, then she kissed him and threw her arms around his neck, at which he put his own arms about her back and swung her around and around on the spot, as he had often done before.

"Go on, off you go. No doubt Michael is waiting for you," he said kindly when he had finished, pushing her toward the house. He watched her dance across the grass, turning at every few paces to look back at him and wave. This image of his sister, with her springy bouncing steps and her smile as bright as the sun, was something he hoped he would remember for a long time.

When Robert returned to London and handed in his resignation, his superiors were astonished. Despite the recent difficulties, they had never expected this decision. They tried to change his mind, but no amount of praise and persuasion made any difference. Robert no longer wanted the responsibility. He wanted a new life, a new start. It was as simple as that.

Now he had told Elizabeth and his employers, he set off to visit Becky and Samuel with the news. They could see immediately that he was happier and altogether more at peace with himself. Thomas the blacksmith also soon heard of his resignation, as had his other contacts and friends throughout the organisation. Everyone was surprised.

Lord Rupert was so horrified at the Robert's decision that he forgot to chastise Robert about his previous deceit concerning the lodge and the papers. They were unimportant compared to this latest development. To have his best friend abandon his occupation and just wander off, without prospects or secure promises of employment, was sheer madness.

"Robert, you cannot go!" Rupert declared. "There are times when I could shake you. Always the sensible one, Robert. Until now."

"Robert, you will miss the wedding. I want you to be here," Anne pleaded.

"Anne is fond of you. All the ladies are fond of you. Even Whinney's sister was taken with your charming manner," Rupert argued.

Robert smiled weakly. What a shame he had not been fond enough of them. He was not averse to female company; women had delighted him and pleased him on occasions. Their light touch had been warm and affectionate, but he had never fallen in love. He accepted that his ongoing reluctance to sacrifice his unpredictable lifestyle to pursue any romantic relationship had been a poor excuse. He had let chances just pass him by. He had unwittingly been affected by a subconscious refusal to believe he could make anyone happy.

"I wish you well Robert. It is time you put yourself first," Ellis told him.

"I never expected to want change, but now it is all I can think of."

"Changes are normally for the better," Ellis agreed quietly, as he accompanied him to the door, where they shook hands. Henry and Edmund were all smiles, and secretly envious. Their responsibilities and duties influenced their lives, just as they had done Robert's. But their friend had shaken off the shackles to do anything he wanted. It did not seem fair.

"I want to go with you," Edmund demanded.

"So do I," added Henry, who had only taken a few weeks to recover his old familiar grin and return to his normal perky self.

"We can't all suddenly desert the Exchange. Besides how would the country cope with three of us on the loose? It would be mayhem," Robert joked.

At which they all laughed. They did not want to be sensible, and it was fun to imagine for a moment or two the fun they would have together. They reminisced about their time together and drank to his future, the pair of them admitting that it would not be the same without him.

"Just as long as we don't get Christopher as your replacement again," Edmund sulked, screwing up his face as they parted.

Robert had one more errand. With a bulky parcel under his arm and a smaller one in his hand, he slowly made his way through Bermondsey and eventually found the small shack he was looking for. He had planned his visit to coincide with the children being out selling their wooden toys, because it gave him the chance to talk to their grandmother properly and sensibly.

He tapped gently on the door and called out, hoping they were still living there. It was very quiet, with no sign of movement inside. He peered into the window and could just make out the old woman sat huddled in her chair. That was good enough. He opened the door and stood there so she could see clearly who it was.

"Good afternoon, madam. Do you remember me?" he said.

She nodded and beckoned him in, commenting that it was

good to have a visitor. Her days were quite lonely most of the time.

Robert put his parcels just inside the door on the floor as he entered and walked forward to take her outstretched hand of welcome. The room was exactly as he remembered it, except that the fire was out and the ashes cold, although she sat by it as if it still gave warmth. Like many others they lived in one room, with little furniture. The one bed sat in the corner, its straw mattress covered with a few inadequate blankets, and there was a stool for each boy, a table and a bench and the old armchair where she sat. With the shawl draped around the woman's shoulders, it was easy to imagine her sitting there of an evening watching over her young charges. He noted the wooden shavings littering the floor near the table, where the unfinished carvings and the jars of paint and brushes sat on top.

The old woman had watched his slow appraisal of her home and the silence worried her. She shuffled her feet, preparing to rise.

"Please do not be alarmed," he said. "There is no need to get up. Although I do have something difficult to talk to you about."

He explained that ever since he had been to their home the boys had mattered to him. What would happen to them when the old lady was not there to look after them? At the moment they lived on the edge of a notorious slum area, an impoverished place where the dwellings were all crammed together amidst narrow alleyways. He wanted more for them.

He could see the panic in her face and no wonder, he was still a stranger. He quickly drew up one of the stools and took her wrinkled hand in his as he sat down beside her to reassure her.

"When the time comes that they are alone, I would like them to have a better future. If you would let me," he said.

The old lady shivered as she heard his words. Had she understood? He waited. Why should she trust him? He could sell them into slavery and she would never know. Somehow he had to convince her. It was time for some very, very gentle persuasion.

"I know a lovely couple in the country who would give them a home and take good care of them," he said. He had already sounded Samuel out about taking on an apprentice and when he had seen the carved animals Robert had brought with him, Samuel had grinned and nodded. After hearing the story, he had promised to take him and his brother in when it became necessary. Becky had also been delighted with the suggestion, having always wanted children. She had considered it a blessing for them both and had thanked him with a smothering hug. The boys would be getting plenty of that in their new home.

"I promise they will be loved, cherished and well looked after and go to school," he added. The old lady did not answer. She was trembling and crying and rocking back and forth in her chair in an agitated state. Had he been wrong to suggest taking them away from everything they were used to? The city might not be an entirely healthy place, but maybe she knew they would not be happy living elsewhere. Maybe his good intentions were misplaced.

"I did not mean to upset you," he said. "If you think it is a bad idea I will not interfere. I will let it be as you wish."

She instantly grabbed his hand, wrapping both of hers around his very hard, holding them to her.

"You would do this?" she pleaded.

"Only if you think they would be happy. Would the open countryside frighten them?"

She closed her eyes briefly and gave a deep sigh before looking at him again. This was more than she had ever hoped for them, she confessed. She could not believe what he had said, asking him to repeated it all a second time very slowly.

When he had finished, he took a letter from his pocket and placed it on the table in front of her. She looked sadly at it and him, shaking her head.

"I do not read, sir."

Robert smiled. "You do not have to. I wanted you to keep this letter safe for the boys. There is an address on the front of the envelope. All they have to do is ask the way and present it at the lawyer's house. Everything has already been arranged for them. There is money put aside with the lawyer for their journey and to pay for some kind motherly soul to accompany them. I would not want them getting lost."

"Bless you," she muttered, pulling the thin shawl around her and just staring at him.

Robert had not quite finished being the Good Samaritan yet. He returned to the larger parcel inside the door and ripped the paper wrapping off, leaving it to be used later to light the fire. He placed two thick woollen blankets on the bed and laid a large warm wool shawl around her shoulders. Then Robert unwrapped his smaller gift, producing a portion of meat he had brought in a tin, covering it with a cloth and leaving it for her to cook when the boys came home. As he left the old lady was lost in a daze of wonderment as she sat there happily rocking herself, clutching the new shawl tightly around her.

Robert had been pleased to find a letter from Mr Hayward waiting for him on his last visit to Chichester. It had been there a while, but it did not need an answer. The man had thanked him again and wish him the best for the future. He went on to let him know that they were all well and that there were improvements planned for the farm. Apparently his aunt had sold up and moved north. They were unlikely to see or hear from her again. Instead of being arrested for the theft of the deeds, the authorities had allowed her to make reparation by settling most of the excess proceeds from the sale into their farm. He was delighted to announce that their own future looked secure for generations.

There had been no mention of the aunt's other activities, and Robert assumed that Margaret had managed to keep the bad news from them. She would keep that secret, bless her. Robert might never pass that way again, but he easily pictured them altogether, a happy family blessed with the noise and chatter of the boys and two girls who could be themselves again. Robert smiled to himself. Rural life could be difficult and unpredictable, but this was one family who would survive.

The news of his resignation from the Exchange had soon spread and Robert unexpectedly found himself swamped with offers of employment. Letters were arriving in London every week. Previous clients, including Sir Eustace, all wanted his services. Even Lord Rupert had been instrumental in bending ears and using his influence, to encourage his aristocratic connections to consider Robert's knowledge and experience with horses. Some important and influential owners intended to develop a racing stable and national stud at Newmarket in Suffolk, and Robert seemed the ideal person to improve and develop the bloodstock.

Everyone seemed to be in a hurry to benefit from his reputation and talents, but Robert did not know what he wanted or what he would do. He could turn his hand to most things, as a jack of all trades and master of none. And for once he welcomed the idea of a simpler freedom, of drifting along from one thing to another. It would make a pleasant change.

Naturally his aunt and uncle would be concerned by his decision - he did not expect any different - but while his uncle would be more sympathetic, he could not imagine his aunt would be so understanding. It was time to face her. He had put it off for days, and he could not make it wait any longer. Robert tactfully waited until she had had her afternoon nap and was sitting in her favourite place by the window before mentioning the topic.

"I gave in my resignation last month, Aunt. I intend to go away," he said.

She heard what he said, but she did not believe a word of it. "Tish, Robert, you can't throw away a worthwhile career just because you are feeling a little low in spirits. How can you waste all that experience and knowledge? This is just a whim. You can't have thought it through."

"My priorities have changed. I need a new start."

"Very few people have the ability to deal with everything you do. All those transactions, commodities, contracts, reports and even assisting visiting dignitaries."

"You mean I am kept busy racing from one task to another, carrying out whatever is required of me."

"You cannot deny you love your work and chasing around the countryside."

"Yes I did, but no more."

His aunt was in full flow and Robert buried his head in his hands. He could not argue with her in this agitated state. He escaped from his aunt to walk through the fields. He needed some space to shake off her tirade. He leaned on top of the gate, his chin resting on his folded arms, for once not wondering about his future. He did not have to prove his worth to anyone any more and he had already abandoned that desperate sense of purpose which had dominated his life before. His devotion to his office had made him trusted and respected by his masters. He had acquired a reputation for fairness in all things. But had he ever been as diligent or as fair as they all assumed?

People trusted his open face, while he trusted few in return.

He was too good at pretending, misleading and lying when necessary, characteristics which had become part of his trade. He had been manipulative, secretive, sharp and harsh when dealing with miscreants or anyone who flouted the rules. He had seen the best and the least savoury side of society, too many faces, too many places, the harsh and the beautiful. He had enjoyed fraternizing with London's social elite. He smiled to himself. He was glad that Arabella and her husband had been taken back into society, at Lord Rupert's instigation. He lifted his face to feel the breeze. Like the wind, he was at last free from the strict controls he had let dominate his life.

The country was undergoing economic changes, commerce was improving and there was public debate. So where did he fit in all this? He was just an ordinary man, nothing special. In fact less than ordinary; he was not in great shape with his duff elbow and his bad back playing up now and again.

He laughed. The accident and Margaret's blow had a lot to answer for. He was approaching thirty, yet he felt like forty some days. He laughed again. So what would he do? He would probably take the offer at Newmarket as an interim measure, and then perhaps try to find something else after that. Who knows? It did not matter. He had stopped planning his days.

His aunt had come to talk to him again, refusing to believe she could not make a difference.

"Robert, you belonged amongst your family and friends. I will not hear any different. How dare you think of leaving? I will not have it. I will not let you go!"

Robert understood the anguish he caused and stood silent under her barrage. Surely she knew she could not physically stop him? Surely she would accept the inevitable soon?

Not so. She constantly made attempts to make him change his mind. She tackled him umpteen times, first quietly, then urgently and then angrily. She continued to rant and rave. She had never been so belligerent; it was upsetting the whole household.

It was his uncle who surprised him the most. He made no demands for him to stay, nor badgered him with questions. His practical acceptance of the situation came easily. He had walked into the stables where Robert was grooming his horse, and settled to watch him.

"You don't have to worry about us, Robert. Everything will be fine, despite what your aunt says. She is only upset because it is hard for her to let go. We both relied on you too much over the years. You have never disappointed us. I know your main concern was for your sister's welfare, probably to make up for your parents not being here, in some way. Am I right?"

Robert gave a slight nod. Nothing had mattered except ensuring Elizabeth was safe and well. Even though his uncle and aunt had taken them in, Robert had felt it his duty to be more than just the brother she played with.

His uncle's eyes crinkled, his benevolent smile indicating that he had always understood.

"We were used to you always coming home, however infrequently. It will be strange without you, but you have your own life to lead. You go with my blessing, Robert."

Robert stopped what he was doing and came to sit with him.

"I don't know what I want any more, uncle. Nothing seems important, no one really needs me to make a difference these days. Elizabeth has Michael to take care of her in future."

His uncle patted his hand. "Oh Robert, you have already done more than was necessary. And not just for us, I hear."

Robert was not sure what he knew. He had never told the family about his other activities in assisting the Haywards or Rupert, but maybe Henry might have mentioned something now and again, when he had seen them.

"I believe you are a good man, Robert," said his uncle. Robert got up to avoid hearing any further embarrassing remarks, heading back to his horse, which made his uncle laugh out loud. "You are not used to compliments Robert, or praise," he said. "You are not used to a lot of things."

Robert was not quite sure what he was hinting at and he was not going to ask, although he sensed that this conversation could turn very personal if it continued. He began brushing Toby again, stroking his fine coat with his hand in between each brush stroke.

"You will find there is a lot more to life. This is your crossroads, Robert," his uncle concluded, before making his way out of the stable block. He paused at the door to look back at the figure he had known since he was a child.

"Your aunt will never accept that you are going until you have actually gone. Make it soon, Robert. All I ask is that I may wake up one morning and find you have left quietly and without any fuss. I don't think I could stand the scene of your actual leave taking. Although Elizabeth seems to have come to terms with the idea, I doubt that will stop the floods of tears. And as for your aunt, I really cannot imagine the drama which will unfold there."

Robert patted his horse, bent his ear affectionately and looked him in the eye. His horse snorted as if he knew what had been said. Then he butted his shoulder, blew straw into his face and turned to roll in the hay, undoing all the grooming Robert had spent ages on.

So one morning Robert rose very early, before it was fully light. He picked up the small wooden carvings from his window sill, the rabbit, the mouse, the duck and the owl. He wrapped them in a handkerchief and put them in his coat pocket. Then he folded the blue ribbon belonging to Elizabeth in with his clothes and neatly stored everything in the saddle bags. The house was quiet and no one was about as he made his way through the house, and even the hounds did not stir as he passed them. He took some bread and cold meat from the kitchen, wrapped them in a cloth, added that to the saddle bags and headed to the stables.

"Come on Toby, let's go," he whispered as he swung into the saddle. He knew better than to look back as he trotted out of the yard, for he had to treat it as if it were a normal day, although inside he knew differently. Chin up and facing the world, he gently urged his horse forward. They had a fair journey ahead of them. He patted Toby's fine mane. He would come back one day. Or maybe he would not.

Racing had not really flourished until Charles II had organised the first ever race under written rules on the Heath, known as the Newmarket Town Plate. That race and regular meetings had been run ever since and the area had flourished. Robert's job in Newmarket was to assist in organizing a new centre for the owners to house their finest thoroughbreds.

However, when he arrived he discovered that his contract involved a great deal more than Lord Rupert had mentioned. He swore at Rupert for misleading him. Trust Rupert to make sure he had a decent living! But since it involved horses, how could he really mind?

The stable yard and inner paddocks did not need much alteration, just some improvement. The suggested area and length for the training gallops were discussed and prepared. The horses were scrutinized and the training routine adjusted to suit their temperament, their diet modified and a regular supply of feed, proteins and supplements organised. Robert then found it was his responsibility to select the right grooms and stable lads to take care of these expensive animals. He was also expected to share his assessment of the proposed race jockeys with the owners.

The position he had acquired at Newmarket was almost a full-time job, but at least it allowed Toby to be housed on site, with paddocks to roam in. And in between his tasks, Robert made time to groom and exercise Toby himself. He believed in taking care of his own animal and it allowed him the opportunity to explore further afield. So much for it being an interim measure. So much for drifting from one employment to another!

The contract lasted longer than he had intended. It took much commitment and hard work, but he was soon free to move on to a less demanding position as estate manager at Milden Hall, although it was agreed he would remain on a retainer for the stables, for they were loath to lose his expertise. Which was why one day found him in Bury St Edmunds on an errand for one of the owners, to look at a new horse.

Afterwards Robert was walking down the main street when a voice hailed him from behind. "I say, Sutton!"

Robert turned to see the cheerful face of Catchwick, his old colleague from the Exchange, rushing to join him.

"I'm surprised you are still here in England," said his friend. "I expected you would have flown your wings completely and set off for foreign shores by now. I am told there are a wealth of opportunities."

Opportunities - or dangerous, life-threatening ventures? Robert remembered all the rumours he had heard from Captain Ben. Immigrants had flooded to the various new states in America and colonies. A series of forts had recently been built along the New England border. India and the Caribbean were being developed. The English had set up trading posts in the East. All parts of the empire were being exploited, and there was potential for trouble everywhere.

"I don't think I could manage the months at sea for any of those destinations," he said. Robert had never once considered the idea of leaving England. He loved his country for all its faults; and besides, there were people here he cherished.

"So what are your plans?" Catchwick asked.

"I do not have any," Robert declared proudly. "Anyway, enough of this idle debate about me. Dare I ask about Christopher these days?"

Catchwick's eyes widened and he gave Robert a mischievous grin. "He is long gone. The Exchange got rid of him. Having made several bad judgements, he compounded his blunders by boasting of his occupation and mentioning his exploits in public. It was unforgivable."

"I see. So how are you? Still enjoying the Suffolk allocation?"

Catchwick was as enthusiastic as he had been originally, and there was so much variety the in landscape. The meandering coast and the fishing villages, the abundant farmland and agriculture. There was a host of occupations, including jobs in the flour milling industry. He liked being out on the road and out and about in all seasons, the same as the rest of them.

It had been pleasant to see Catchwick again, but it was his reference to the flour mills which prompted Robert to make another journey. He turned his horse towards Stowmarket; why, he was not sure. Except that was where Isabella's parents had gone soon after losing their children. It might not be the best of ideas, but he suddenly felt the need to see them after all this time, if he could find them.

Isabella's father watched the man who rode slowly through the copse to alight and settle himself overlooking their little cluster of buildings. It was not an uncommon occurrence, for many travellers found it was a pleasant place to stop and rest on their journey. Yet there was something about this man, something which made him keep looking at him. A stranger who had travelled without any bidding, as if under a spell, he now began to walk towards their house.

Suddenly, Mr Fairland knew exactly who it was. Robert was so like his father. The intuition sent a slight shiver down his back, but he stood up and rushed out of the door towards him.

"Robert my boy, it is you! How truly wonderful to see you."

"Mr Fairland."

Robert had never expected such a welcome. The next instant he was being held and hugged. Affection overflowed as the man then held him at arm's length by the shoulders to look at him properly, nodding the whole time and grinning from ear to ear, before giving him another hug, even stronger than the one before, and then merrily rocking himself on the spot. The man's reaction quite overwhelmed Robert. He should have come before.

"What a day," Mr Fairland went on. "Agnes will be over the moon." He slipped his arm about Robert's and led him, chattering and chuckling the whole time, towards the open door. "There is so much to catch up on. I haven't let you get a word in. You must stay for a couple of days."

He stopped for a second and pointed across to the other cottages, the outbuildings and the windmill with its great sails standing prominent against the sky.

"I work the flour mill with my brother and his family," said Mr Fairland. "They will be pleased to meet you."

Robert smiled, convinced he could think of nothing better.

Soon Robert had been away for two years. He had never returned to Kent, although he had often thought about his family and friends and Rupert and Hurl Place. He did not regret his decision to leave them all. If he had never left, he would never have arrived at this destination, and never have found where his heart belonged.

It was Isabella's cousin, Ellen, who had set him free and filled him with hope. From the moment he first saw her standing there with flour on her hands and face, he knew.

"Thank you," she whispered to him one day.

"For what?" he queried.

"For being you."

His hands gently reached out to reassure her, to take hold of both of her hands in his, to take in every detail of her features once more. Her wonderful shining light chestnut hair which stirred in the afternoon breeze, the delicate wisps dancing about her cheeks, the freckles on her nose, her merry eyes reflecting the brightness of the sun, her inquisitive glance and the unspoken words on her lips. Her twinkling smile and her cute button nose.

At the same time, Ellen absorbed every characteristic of Robert's charm. The dark unkempt hair, the rugged good looks and the tormenting curl of his mouth as he smiled and the flicker of movement about his dark eyes. She loved this man, in every respect.

"Tell me - what is in this man's heart?" she asked softly, as if she did not know.

"No words can describe it," he murmured.

Robert stood outside their cottage door in the early evening light, as was his habit of late, filled with utter contentment. Inside, Ellen was singing softly. This special woman who smiled at him every day and lifted her eyes to his whenever he gazed in her direction. Often he would pull her to him with a quiet growl, to enjoy her whole being in his arms, and her sigh would indicate her delight at being softly wrapped in his embrace. How he would murmur her name, until the merest touch of her hand to his lips stopped him.

Yes, there were a lot of things he had not been used to before, most of all the intensity of these feelings and the subtlety of making her happy. Who would have imagined that he had the capacity to attain that immense happiness which everyone else seemed to find so easy? Ellen had become his very existence.

The aroma from the stove beckoned him back indoors, but he paused for a few moments more to treasure the new precious bundle which snuggled in his arms. Every time he held her it filled him with such a powerful sense of wonder. This, his bonny daughter with her button nose and mass of curly chestnut hair, was part of him.

"Isabella, I will keep you safe," he whispered softly, not wanting to wake her. He was content and complete, the warmth of the baby filling every fibre of his soul. Now he knew that this was what his father had meant when he had told him to make the best of his life.